T0244794

Readers Love A[illegible]

The Mastermind

"Delicious fun."

—*Booklist*

Familiar Angel

"Lane (Selfie) infuses a sizzling paranormal erotic romance with humor and suspense, then doubles down by finishing the work with a veneer of sweet innocence. …Both striking and sensual, the thought-provoking novel pays equal attention to love, sacrifice, the divine, and family."

—*Publisher's Weekly*

Shades of Henry

"*Shades of Henry* is a beautiful character study and I can't wait to read more in this series."

—Rainbow Book Reviews

All the Rules of Heaven

"*All the Rules of Heaven* is an intriguing, whimsical, and sometimes dark story. I particularly enjoyed the development of the primary and secondary characters."

—Love Bytes Reviews

Shortbread and Shadows

"Lane deftly builds a world where magic feels both plausible and inevitable, and inserts this magical world seamlessly into our own. This cosmic comedy of errors/romance had it all: a gripping plot, tender and funny moments, and some very steamy scenes."

—Roger's Reads

Fish Out of Water

"Fish Out of Water delivers an intense plot as well as a sizzling relationship between Ellery and Jackson."

—Gay Book Reviews

By Amy Lane

An Amy Lane Christmas
Behind the Curtain
Bewitched by Bella's Brother
Bolt-hole
Christmas Kitsch
Christmas with Danny Fit
Clear Water
Do-over
Food for Thought
Freckles
Gambling Men
Going Up
Hammer & Air
Homebird
If I Must
Immortal
It's Not Shakespeare
Late for Christmas
Left on St. Truth-be-Well
The Locker Room
Mourning Heaven
Phonebook
Puppy, Car, and Snow
Racing for the Sun
Hiding the Moon
Raising the Stakes
Regret Me Not
Shiny!
Shirt
Sidecar
Slow Pitch
String Boys
A Solid Core of Alpha
Three Fates
Truth in the Dark
Turkey in the Snow
Under the Rushes
Weirdos
Wishing on a Blue Star

BENEATH THE STAIN
Beneath the Stain • Paint It Black

BONFIRES
Bonfires • Crocus

CANDY MAN
Candy Man • Bitter Taffy
Lollipop • Tart and Sweet

DREAMSPUN BEYOND
HEDGE WITCHES
LONELY HEARTS CLUB
Shortbread and Shadows
Portals and Puppy Dogs
Pentacles and Pelting Plants
Heartbeats in a Haunted House

DREAMSPUN DESIRES
THE MANNIES
The Virgin Manny
Manny Get Your Guy
Stand by Your Manny
A Fool and His Manny
SEARCH AND RESCUE
Warm Heart • Silent Heart
Safe Heart • Hidden Heart

FAMILIAR LOVE
Familiar Angel • Familiar Demon

FISH OUT OF WATER
Fish Out of Water
Red Fish, Dead Fish
A Few Good Fish
Hiding the Moon
Fish on a Bicycle
School of Fish
Fish in a Barrel

Published by Dreamspinner Press
www.dreamspinnerpress.com

By Amy Lane (cont'd)

FLOPHOUSE
Shades of Henry
Constantly Cotton

GRANBY KNITTING
The Winter Courtship Rituals of Fur-Bearing Critters
How to Raise an Honest Rabbit
Knitter in His Natural Habitat
Blackbird Knitting in a Bunny's Lair
The Granby Knitting Menagerie Anthology

JOHNNIES
Chase in Shadow • Dex in Blue
Ethan in Gold • Black John
Bobby Green • Super Sock Man

KEEPING PROMISE ROCK
Keeping Promise Rock
Making Promises
Living Promises
Forever Promised

LONG CON ADVENTURES
The Mastermind • The Muscle
The Driver •The Suit

LUCK MECHANICS
The Rising Tide

TALKER
Talker • Talker's Redemption
Talker's Graduation
The Talker Collection Anthology

WINTER BALL
Winter Ball • Summer Lessons
Fall Through Spring

Published by DSP Publications

ALL THAT HEAVEN WILL ALLOW
All the Rules of Heaven

GREEN'S HILL
The Green's Hill Novellas

LITTLE GODDESS
Vulnerable
Wounded, Vol. 1
Wounded, Vol. 2
Bound, Vol. 1 • Bound, Vol. 2
Rampant, Vol. 1
Rampant, Vol. 2
Quickening, Vol. 1
Quickening, Vol. 2
Green's Hill Werewolves, Vol. 1
Green's Hill Werewolves, Vol. 2

Published by Harmony Ink Press

BITTER MOON SAGA
Triane's Son Rising
Triane's Son Learning
Triane's Son Fighting
Triane's Son Reigning

Published by Dreamspinner Press
www.dreamspinnerpress.com

THE RISING TIDE

AMY LANE

Published by
DREAMSPINNER PRESS

5032 Capital Circle SW, Suite 2, PMB# 279, Tallahassee, FL 32305-7886 USA
www.dreamspinnerpress.com

Trade Paperback ISBN: 978-1-64108-450-5
Digital ISBN: 978-1-64108-449-9
Trade Paperback published October 2022
v. 1.0

Printed in the United States of America
∞
This paper meets the requirements of
ANSI/NISO Z39.48-1992 (Permanence of Paper).

Mate. Always Mate.

Author's Note

Bad things happened while I was writing this, and my own personal world almost came to an end. But when I got back to a place where I could write again, my characters were waiting for me. I just want to say thank you all for reading—having a place for these characters to be seen is really a wonderful thing.

Prologue

HELEN HAD waited a long time to do this—maybe too long.

As she buzzed along the suburban streets of Folsom, California, on her beloved Ducati, she had to admit that the neighborhood had changed in the last thirty years since she bought her cottage. She'd seen it happening in increments, but it hadn't really hit her until some damned fool had put up three prefab houses on her once empty cul-de-sac and those damned college kids had moved in.

She felt her shoulders hunch, which she couldn't let happen because once you hit a certain age, hunching over a motorcycle could be considered an actual injury.

Okay, okay, breathe out. Remember, resentment trapped the bad feelings in. The bad feelings created the shackles that held you down.

Sounded like new age crap, but after a long talk with her mentor, she'd come to realize that it was something more. It was the reason her life had *gone* to crap over the last ten years. Held grudges, a refusal to move, to motivate herself to break the chains that had bound her. She was a powerful witch. Age made those powers stronger, not weaker, and her metaphorical chains had become magical, physical manifestations very quickly.

She'd needed to break them before they consumed her, but in her panic, she'd done the unthinkable.

She'd shoved the keys to her *very* magical witch's cottage into the hands of the most responsible of the young people who'd moved into her cul-de-sac and had run.

That poor kid. God knows what had happened to him once he'd taken her keys and her hurried admonition not to touch any of the distilled oils. The kid had been smart as a whip. Friendly, kind. Offered to help her with her groceries once a week, was gentle to the nine feral cats she fed. She'd been desperate, but holy Hecate and blessed Brigid, what had she done?

As she rounded the corner of the perfectly normal little suburb, the chill wind of February settled more firmly into her bones. This wasn't snow country, but the wind still had a bite on top of a motorcycle, and for a moment she was concentrating on a small spell to warm herself.

And then she realized where she was and almost laid out the damned bike.

"The actual hell…," she murmured.

The cul-de-sac was deserted.

The three prefab houses had signs on the front proclaiming new developments to come from Asa Bryne, but judging by the dust on the windows, they'd been vacant for months. Helen's eyes sharpened—she'd been out in the world. She knew that vacant houses often attracted squatters, drug addicts, indigents. But in spite of the likelihood of that happening, all she saw were a couple of turkeys wandering desultorily across the cul-de-sac and some owls perching on the gutters of the house in the middle. The house on the end appeared to have more than its fair share of squirrels, and there were starlings everywhere.

What in the everloving hell?

And then she saw her own cottage—or what had once been her own cottage—and for a moment, she had to fight hard to breathe.

It was… it had been….

It had… *imploded.*

That was the only word for it. The little shake roof, the neat wooden walls, the rickety front porch—all of it had been demolished in a way that implied a giant vacuum from the inside had sucked all the walls inward and the house had collapsed, the roof falling mostly intact on top of it.

Her feral cats, all of them more or less enchanted, had left.

She felt a pull toward the middle of the cul-de-sac and turned to see three stars, marked in faded tape and with the power of what had once been much use.

The first star was three-pointed and close to the center of the four houses. The next star had five points, and it was set a little farther back from the three-pointed one. Enough space stretched between them for a circle of people to form around each star, with nobody bumping elbows. The next star—seven-pointed—was set farther back from that, and Helen stared at the lot of them, stunned.

She could sense their power from the sidewalk. Those college kids had done this. Or rather those *post*-college kids had done it. Every iota of energy emanating from those circles had gone into keeping this neighborhood safe from the forces Helen herself had unleashed.

Her eyes burned.

Oh, those brave damned kids.

They'd taken her cottage, her library, her years of accumulated knowledge and run with it. And when the presence of ennui, of abnegation, had gotten too large, started taking over the neighborhood, they'd used those powers to fight it.

They weren't here slaving away, growing old and hopeless, locked in the dance that the presence had locked Helen in for so many years. In fact, she felt… nothing. Nothing but the faint buzz of their protection and the residue of one holy hell of a spell. And the lingering scent of patchouli and rosewater and the myriad other oils she'd accumulated during the years, which had probably been released when her house had been destroyed.

They'd done it. What she'd failed to do for years. They'd broken those chains, and now she was well and truly free.

And so in debt to the universe she could hardly breathe.

She reached into her saddlebag and pulled out her satellite phone to call the one number she had.

"Marcus?"

"Helen," he said warmly. "Have you visited your neighborhood? Have you made it right?"

She swallowed. "I found it, and the presence has been vanquished. But Marcus, those kids did it themselves. They… they took all my knowledge and, you know, fixed it. Fixed the world. I…." Her voice broke. "I owe such a debt. I should find them and—"

"No," Marcus said softly. "They've started on their own path and apparently taught themselves. Do they have your library? Your familiars?"

She smiled sadly, thinking of her nine furry companions. "Yes. The nine are gone, and the library…." She looked toward the destroyed house and could spot nary a page. "I think they took the library with them." She let out a sad laugh. It had taken thirty years to build that library, rare book by rare book, estate sale by lucky find. "They earned it if they could free this area from the presence that took it over."

"Yes," Marcus agreed. "They did. But we need you back here, honey. You'll make amends. Maybe not with those people specifically, but I think there will be ways you can pay the universe back." His voice took on a sad, thready quality she could never remember it having, not after thirty years of friendship, some of those years more than friendly. "Spinner's Drift needs you, Helen. We need you back here. I feel it. All your karma… you can pay it back here."

"Of course," she said softly. Marcus had taken her in two years ago, listened to her barely coherent tale of the witch's cottage that had begun to dominate her life. Of the presence that had sucked all her animation away, all her personality, all the energy she'd once offered the world.

He'd listened, and he'd kissed her, and he'd healed her. She'd left to sec if she was needed and to sell the property outright and clear up some of her finances so she could start again.

"Are you sure I shouldn't…?" Those kids. All of them right out of college, starting their lives. They'd been so fresh-faced and optimistic. So ready to find their places in the world. What a terrible burden she'd placed on their shoulders.

"Your paths will cross again," he said softly. "I feel it, Helen. It's written in the starlight. But Spinner's Drift needs you." His voice lowered humbly, as it wouldn't have done thirty years ago when she'd left the first time. "I need you."

And that decided her. It was true that hedge witches and wizards tended to live astoundingly long lives, but sixty was sixty, and she was too old to take another minute for granted.

"Let me clear up my finances," she promised. "I should be back in two weeks or so."

"What are you going to do?" he asked.

She thought about it, about her personal library, now out in the world to do what she sensed had been so much good. "I'm going to buy a bookstore," she said, "that also sells coffee and pastries. And has cats." The thought of it gave her a pleasant magical buzz. Oh yes. The karma gods liked this idea.

"What will you call it?" he asked.

"I don't know yet." She smiled, that buzz pulsing along her skin, making her graying ponytail lift from the back of her neck with static. "But it's going to be extraordinary."

The Wide World

ALISTAIR QUINTERO'S voice thundered in Scout's ears. There was a terrific whooshing wind, a clap of thunder and white light, and *shazam*!

Scout was exiled from the only home he'd ever known and alone in the woods that surrounded the wizard compound, the family home he'd grown up in and had never managed to escape, even to see the surrounding area.

Until now, when he wasn't allowed back in.

Holy Goddess, Alistair was a dick.

He suppressed a whine—he was twenty-four, godsdammit, and whining was *not* attractive—and looked around, trying to discern east from west to figure out in which direction the road was. They'd been allowed to look at maps; he wasn't *completely* in the dark about modern geography. But the compound was really several buildings surrounding the family mansion, with acres of land, developed and wilderness, inside the perimeter. He didn't know any of the landmarks outside the compound, and his head ached fiercely from the portal his father had banished him out of as well.

Scout tried not to fume. He understood that most of the time, portals made a person tired anyway, but that *Alistair's* portals tended to be a lot louder and more violent than the usual.

Again. Holy Goddess, what a dick.

He took a deep breath and fought off another childish impulse—this one to cry. As he did so, he felt a thump against his ribs, coming from a pocket in his ceremonial robes, and he stiffened.

His brother, Josue, had dropped the robes off by his quarters and helped him dress, giving him emergency instructions as he did so. Scout had been too nervous to pay attention—Josue was a mother hen most days, telling the younger boys (men now!) to remember fennel in their spells to deceive deceivers or oak for strength. Telling them to remember their blue shirts to show fealty to Alistair or their red socks to show care for their mothers. But this time he'd been practically whispering, muttering things that, Scout now realized, had been instructions and warnings.

"He's going to banish you no matter what, Scout. Be ready for it. I've put things in your robes that will help. Don't forget to check the pockets. Remember—I love you, your brother Macklin loves you, and you're not the only one to get out of this hellhole and thrive."

Scout reached into the robes, which he realized were Josue's. He must have given Scout his so he'd have time to put things in the pockets. In one pocket Scout found a wallet with a forged driver's license with Scout's picture on it and his official name: Scotland Damaris Quintero. Oh heavens, Josue had known. He'd said it. *He's going to banish you no matter what.* He must have had this ready for months. There were two cards, both of them with bank account numbers and passwords taped to them, and Scout had to swallow against tears, moved by love and gratitude as he hadn't been by fear and anger.

Five thousand dollars each. Josue, who held a job out of the compound to manage the compound's investments, had squirreled away ten thousand dollars for Scout because he'd known. He'd known Scout wasn't going to make it. He'd known Alistair would banish him. He'd known, and he'd silently prepared for it, and….

Scout wiped under his eyes with his palm and felt the thing in his other robe pocket buzz. He reached inside and found a cell phone, a thing he knew from books that most children knew how to use at ten but that the kids in the compound were not given. Computers they could use for their studies, but the use was closely monitored. Phones? Not necessary. Books were to be read in paper format so any adult could read it. Allowance could only be spent on approved books or magic supplies.

But Josue had bought him a phone and had written the passcode on another Post-it swacked to the back.

Scout tapped the passcode in and smiled through the burning behind his eyes.

His brother had sent him a text.

Sorry, brother. He found your stash of forbidden books. It didn't matter if you made a portal or not, he was going to send you away.

Scout grimaced. "Forbidden" in this case meant "romance." The kind with two male romantic leads. He'd been refusing to choose a wife for years now, making vague excuses, but obviously Alistair had not been fooled.

Our brother Macklin has been waiting for your call. Here's his number. Call immediately, and he'll be there.

Scout stared at this. Macklin? Macklin had left when Scout was a kid—off to sow his wild oats, Alistair had sneered often enough. Not quite a year ago, though, something had changed. Alistair had shown up for breakfast one morning looking as though he'd been pecked to death by ducks, and after that the first person to ask about Macklin's long-anticipated return had been blown through a wall.

Scout's younger sister, Kayleigh, had woken up after a week, unable to remember what had happened, and nobody had dared to mention Macklin Quintero again.

Apparently, whatever had happened, Macklin had come out on top, and Alistair was not happy about it.

That decided Scout. Anything that pissed Alistair off was enough to make him a fan.

He looked around the woods again, thinking he may have heard cars to the southeast, and cursed the fact that wearing his ceremonial robes when he'd been banished meant he was barefoot.

Seriously. Alistair Quintero. Fuck that guy.

With a bit of fiddling—these little devices were really very self-explanatory—he thought he had it.

Macklin? This is Scout. Josue told me you could help me?

He stared at the screen, thinking, *Wait? Don't these things need internet or something?* But whatever Josue had done to charge and power this thing—and Scout felt a small soft-sided box in his pocket that he assumed held power cords—it apparently was ready to work.

Scout? Where are you?

I, uhm, don't know. Out in the woods by the compound, maybe? I was just banished.

There was a pause, and Scout noticed little bubbles by where Macklin's reply would appear. Very comforting, those bubbles, he thought.

And he just left you there? What. A. Dick!

And that, right there, was when Scout realized Macklin might be the family member he loved the most.

Right?

He sent it almost without thinking. He was going to ask questions then, but Macklin beat him to it.

Do you need anything? Money? Transportation? A map?

Shoes? Scout typed in, angry all over again.

We'll be there in ten minutes.

Scout frowned. Be there? They'd be there? Who would be there? But… but Macklin was presumably banished too. Granted, he was supposedly the pride of the Quintero wizard family before he'd been banished, but didn't that mean he wasn't allowed to do magic anymore?

Could *Scout* still do magic?

Ooh… interesting question.

The *stated* reason for Scout being banished had been that he didn't have enough magical power to be more than a (disdainful sniff) *hedge witch*. That was how Alistair said it too, like being a hedge witch was too small to even worry about. Certainly not talented enough to ever be *real* family.

But Scout *had* possessed power. Sometimes it was wonky, and sometimes it listened to his heart instead of his head, but it was there. Once, he'd been asked to conjure a crossbow. Why, he had no idea. They didn't hunt their own food. They had it shipped in, in giant quantities. Were they hunters now? Because that didn't really work for Scout, who was much happier with some toast and jam than raw bleeding deer meat on the hoof. But a crossbow he'd been asked to conjure.

He'd gotten toast and jam instead. *He'd* been delighted, but Alistair had thrown it away dismissively and told him to do some *real* conjuring.

This time, Scout got an entire loaf of bread, a brick of butter, and a *jar* of jam. His favorite.

He hadn't let Alistair throw *that* away, insisting that it must have come from the kitchen and he'd return it. The fact that he'd taken it to the kitchen, toasted himself a snack, and disappeared for the rest of the day had never been mentioned again.

And he'd never learned to conjure weapons either.

So Scout wasn't really a brilliant wizard, but he *did* have power, and he rather enjoyed the feeling it gave him. Not that he could lord it over people or conjure a crossbow to lay waste to his enemies or anything. That never occurred to him. It was the feeling of oneness it gave him with the rest of the world. The wizard compound was stifling, and all the boys were housed in the same quarters, and Scout wondered if it was possible to have a thought not permeated with stinky gym socks and the midnight sounds of the teenaged and twentysomething boys masturbating in the dark.

Meals were family affairs, everybody seated at the table looking suitably grateful and chastened that the women—who were never given a word of thanks from Alistair or the elders—had slaved away for the meals before them.

All of this togetherness, and the only time Scout *didn't* feel alone was when he snuck some toast and jam and wandered off into the wooded part of the compound. He'd bring his sketch book and write poems or sketch badly, or bring Kayleigh, his favorite sister, and they'd find pictures in the clouds or talk about the things they'd snuck into their reading or away from their studies that Alistair hadn't seen.

If they missed lunchtime, they conjured food. If they needed a book from their study, they conjured that. If they wanted to try their hand at levitation or talking to the animals, they did so, and failed and tried again and failed and sometimes succeeded.

Those moments of peace, of playing with Kayleigh, throwing words or ideas or potions back and forth, those had made him feel more connected than anything. And not to Kayleigh, but to, well, the world. Even without Kayleigh, those moments in the woods, alone with his thoughts, had made him less lonely.

But still, Kayleigh had helped, and he thought about her now, mourning one of the two people in the compound who had given a damn where he was. Would he be able to see her again? She was pretty powerful, but she was also twenty-one, and Alistair was trying to marry her off to "strengthen the bloodline." Scout had managed to evade Alistair's machinations for three years, but Kayleigh was supposedly betrothed to someone from the south already. Oh Goddess. Kayleigh, with her sparkling brown eyes and apple cheeks. The thought of her married to a hovering despot like Alistair made him physically ill.

He started to pace, looking at his phone, wondering if he could ask Macklin to help him get her out. Could they mount a rescue? Alistair had *thrown her through a wall* for simply asking about Macklin. What would he do to her for protesting Scout's banishment?

His worry for her grew, and that power, that oneness he'd always felt when alone in the woods, grew too. He found himself reaching out for her, wanting to grab her hand and just *yank* her out of the now-invisible compound. He closed his eyes and conjured her image behind them—brown eyes, sleek brown hair in a ponytail, apple cheeks, and all, and thought, *Kayleigh!*

"What?"

Her voice was so real and so honest that his eyes popped open, and then he screamed and she did too, because she was *right there*. Or rather *he* was right there in their spot in the compound, and *she* was sitting under a tree crying.

"*Scout*?"

"*Kayleigh*?"

"Did you just rescue me?"

He stared. "We're still in the compound, so I'm going to say no!"

She stared back. "But the portal is right behind you."

"I can't conjure porta—"

She didn't give him time to finish. She launched herself at him and hugged him so tight his eyes almost popped out of his head, sobbing, "I'm free! I'm free! I'm free!" and he stumbled back, through the gateway of space and time he'd apparently opened up. In a heartbeat, they were back in the spot Scout had recently left, the portal had closed, and he was freezing his ass off in his ceremonial robes in the New England woods in the brisk early days of September.

And that's where they were when a guy in his late thirties—not too tall but not short, with the Quintero black hair, square jaw, and Scout's cobalt eyes—appeared in the forest through another portal about twenty feet from them.

"Scout?"

"Macklin?" His eyes strayed to the objects dangling from Macklin's fingers. "Oh my Goddess, are those *shoes*?"

Those eyes—so much like their father's that Scout quailed a little when he first saw them—had crinkles at the corners that one only associated with kindness.

Macklin smiled and his eyes crinkled, and the family reunion was complete.

MACKLIN APPARENTLY had been kicked out of the compound for being the cool older brother every kid needed and Alistair didn't want them to have.

But the resemblance to Alistair was still a little spooky—and never more apparent than when he was chivvying Scout and Kayleigh through the woods.

"Look," he said as they made their way carefully along what appeared to be a deer path. "I hate to hurry you both, but my boyfriend—erm, *fiancé*—is renting a car from the nearby town, and I want to be near the road by the time he drives by." He gave Scout an apologetic glance over his shoulder. "We're going to take you to buy some clothes, and there's apparently a cheap hotel in the town. It's one of those places right off a major freeway where you can stop for food, gas, and lodging. We can regroup there and see what your next move is."

Scout opened his mouth to argue, because he always argued. He always had a better plan or wanted to know the why of things. But Macklin had just *given* him the why of things, and the guy had come in from… wait. Where *did* he portal in from to save Scout and Kayleigh's bacon?

"Where were you?" he asked, wondering at the sort of power that could portal two people simultaneously from a distance of hundreds of miles.

"California," Macklin said easily. "It's a good thing Jordan's so frickin' powerful. If I'd done this myself, it would have knocked me on my ass."

Scout stumbled. "Calif—isn't that three thousand miles away?"

Macklin gave him a wry nod over his shoulder. "It is indeed."

"But… but that's *Alistair* level power."

Macklin snorted. "That is the power of one very determined hedge witch," he said. "With some training up."

"And he's your… your fiancé?" So Scout's cool older brother was not *just* cool, he was also *queer*, and Scout had never been so happy to be a Quintero.

"Yup. For a year now. Getting married at Beltane, along with four other couples who make up our coven." He practically hummed with joy. "There's going to be flowers, and sunshine, and the baby's going to be toddling around by then—"

"Wait," Kayleigh said. "Baby?"

"Yes. One of the couples, Josh and Kate, they have a baby. Kid's spoiled rotten—the apple of the coven's eye—and she's barely a potato."

"This doesn't sound like… like what hedge witches are," Scout said doubtfully. It had been drilled into them. If they couldn't portal by twenty-five, they'd be as useless as a hedge witch, confined to small spells of no consequence, miserable and bitter and making potions to poison the neighbor's dog. It did *not* sound like a big joyous group wedding with a spoiled infant in the midst of people who could teleport themselves across a continent.

Macklin paused, looking around and obviously getting his bearings before turning to Scout. "My boy, you've spent your entire life locked in that compound, am I right?"

Scout nodded, suddenly lost and out of his depth.

"How would either of you know what hedge witches—or even regular people—are like? You both have so much to learn."

Next to him, Kayleigh gave a wicked little cackle. "I can't wait."

And with that they broke through the woodland to a shoulder on the side of a busy road. No sooner had Macklin started to look around to see what to do next than a dark sedan veered off the road to the shoulder in front of them. Macklin hauled open the passenger door with obvious relief.

"That was fast!"

"Get in!" came the impatient reply. "And it helps that we'd looked the place up ahead of time and made the reservations before we portaled."

Kayleigh opened the rear door and slid in, Scout scrambled in afterward, and then he got his first look at Macklin's fiancé.

And tried not to clutch his heart and gnash his teeth because the guy was taken.

Tall—taller than Macklin, even seated—but younger, closer to Scout's age, the man had white-blond hair, intense blue eyes, and cheekbones to die for. And a sort of intensity around his mouth, a thing that said nothing got in his way. Wow. Scout would follow this guy anywhere, including three thousand miles across the country through a hole in space and time.

"Where to next?" Macklin asked.

"Well, we're making a U-turn and going back into town," Jordan said. "We've got reservations at the Holiday Inn there and…." His eyes flickered to Kayleigh and Scout in the back seat, Scout in his white linen ceremonial robes and nothing else and Kayleigh wearing a traditional calf-length cotton dress with clunky practical shoes. "There's a Walmart there so they can go shopping. And we can get something to eat and go back to the hotel and figure out what they're going to do for the rest of their lives."

Scout swallowed hard. Next to him, Kayleigh fumbled for his hand. They laced fingers and squeezed because Jordan was right. They'd just been flung out of their homes and into a world they'd studied about but never lived in.

And then Scout remembered that if it weren't for Josue and his unconditional love or Macklin and his super-dreamy boyfriend, he and Kayleigh would still be out in the woods alone, trying to figure out what to do.

He turned a serene face to Kayleigh and gave a watery smile. "We are so blessed," he said gruffly.

To his relief, because he needed Kayleigh to be okay with what he'd done by pulling her away, she smiled back. "We are."

Kayleigh usually scoffed when he said things like that, but then, she was naturally sarcastic and had grown up in a world that liked its women pliant and obedient. Scoffing was her only defense.

Not now, though. Now she gave him a watery smile and squeezed his hand. "We really fuckin' are," she said. She squared her jaw and turned to look out the window as the woods that had held them, protected them, and also trapped them whizzed by. "The woods don't look nearly as scary from here, do they."

Keeping tight hold of her hand, he looked through his own window, where the streaks of brown against a gray sky seemed strangely alien and very far away. "They don't look like home anymore either."

His chest suddenly relaxed, like the elephant that had sat on it since he'd been born had wandered off, or like the giant rubber band that had swaddled him in rules and must-nots and have-tos for his entire life had simply snapped.

He wasn't aware he was sobbing until Kayleigh tackle-hugged him from behind, and they held each other tightly and cried for the rest of the trip to town.

SEVERAL EXCITING, exhilarating, *exhausting* hours later, he discovered that having an older brother was not as cool as he'd thought it was.

"Would you let go of the spell, Scout?" Macklin snapped. "The whole point here is an unbiased divination!"

"But *shouldn't* it be biased by what I want to do?" Scout argued.

"But what do you want to do?" Macklin asked, obviously trying to hold on to his patience. "The whole reason we started this spell was because you needed help. Remember? I said, 'What do you want to do?' and you said, 'I don't know what I want to do,' and Kayleigh said, 'Let's ask the magic, like we used to do when we were kids,' and that leads us to here, where we're throwing your avatars on a map and trying to make a divination spell, but you *keep seizing the avatar with your power*!"

Scout scowled, but not so much because he was mad at *Macklin.* He was mad at *himself.*

"I'm not doing it on purpose!" he blurted, unable to blame it on Macklin being bossy anymore. Then he looked apologetically at Kayleigh, who grimaced back. "But I think Kayleigh is."

Macklin grinned. "Kayleigh! Doing the thing with the power! That's great. Did you teach yourself?" Women were *not* taught about power in the compound. Kayleigh was supposed to learn history to the 1950s and pagan theology and poetry, but only certain poets. How to use her own power? Certainly not.

Kayleigh gave a relieved smile. "Scout taught me most of it," she said. Her shoulders slumped. "I just… I don't like feeling power*less*, if you understand me."

Well, of course not. For their entire lives the two of them had been told what to do and what not to do, and—even worse—what they could *be.* To finally have a chance to control their own destinies and then cede the control to Macklin? It felt like a betrayal.

Macklin leaned his head back and sighed, scrubbing at his face. They'd checked into their hotel rooms and sent Jordan out for pizza nearly an hour before, and it occurred to Scout belatedly that this day hadn't been any easier on Macklin.

"Look," Macklin said, keeping his patience with obvious and sincere effort. "Let's try it once again. Remember, we're not trying to control you. We're asking where *you* will have the most control. Where does your destiny lie? Think of it that way."

Scout tried—he really did. He watched as Macklin blew on the pebbles he'd had Kayleigh and Scout choose from the wooded area beyond the Walmart. The trip to Walmart had been enjoyable, actually. He and Kayleigh had run around the store in a daze, looking at all the things they *could* own, if only they had the money to buy them. They'd had to repeatedly remind each other that the money in their pocket was limited, and although they'd enjoyed picking out clothes—jeans, T-shirts, shoes, socks, even *underwear* that nobody else had chosen for them—they realized they *still* had to find a way to make a living and that they didn't even have a place to call their own yet. And seeing the cost of things—wow! That had been an eye-opener. Food, clothing, rent, transportation. Scout was already feeling a little bit of that elephant on his chest again, and the weight was rib-crushing.

It was *that* memory that hit him now, unfortunately, just as Macklin made the final toss of the hand-polished, skin-warmed pebbles to throw them on the map laid out on the table in the hotel room.

The pebbles, both of them, hovered in the air, suspended over the map and practically dancing in indecision.

There was a sound at the door, and one pebble launched itself in that direction, while the other one embedded itself in the map and the table underneath, pretty much at their exact location.

"Jordan!" Macklin cried, alarmed.

Jordan stood, the giant pizza box balanced on one arm, and stared at the pebble that had buried itself in the doorframe about six inches from his head.

"I, uhm, could come back later," he said with wide eyes.

"Oh my God!" Scout squeaked. He'd almost killed *Jordan*. Forget Macklin, his brother whom he probably loved. He'd almost killed *Jordan*, the crush upon whom all other crushes would pale in comparison!

"Divination not working?" Jordan asked, his sinful mouth relaxing into a smile as he entered the room and closed the door behind him.

"We're having trouble," Macklin said. He fixed Scout with a grim look. "Releasing control."

Jordan set the pizza box down as Macklin delicately pulled the map free of the rock lodged in the table.

"Mm," Jordan murmured, looking at the hole the pebble had left. "So one of you wants to stay here and kill Alistair, and the other one wants to go to Australia," he hazarded, fixing his gaze on Kayleigh first and then Scout. "Why?"

Kayleigh broke the stunned silence with a giggle. "How did you know I wanted to kill Alistair?" she asked.

"I met that fucker once, and I wanted to kill him," Jordan said grimly. "I can't imagine living with him. Particularly not when all he did was treat you like a broodmare. I mean, can't fault your intentions, but that's not going to give you a lot of control over your life afterwards, so you may want to redirect your rage, right?"

Kayleigh laughed a little more. "Right," she said, shooting a grin at Scout. "Why Australia?" she asked him.

Scout grimaced. "Because murder is wrong." Which was only part of the truth. "Also, because I don't want him to have any control over who I am or what I do. Like Jordan said, killing him would mean he'd control my every action for the rest of my life, whether I got caught or not."

Jordan nodded. "Okay, then. Let's have some pizza. I have an idea." He looked apologetically at Macklin. "To start with, the pebbles weren't the way to go. We're asking the magic for suggestions. With the avatars, it's like we're asking their *power* for suggestions. Remember what we learned last year? The magic holds definite opinions about what's good for us and the world around us. We need to separate the two."

Macklin had the grace—and humor—to look sheepish. "You're right," he said with a sigh. "I can't believe I forgot that."

Jordan wrapped his arm around Macklin's waist and pulled him close enough to kiss his temple. "You grew up with Alistair too," he said softly. "That's a lot of bad habits and bad feeling to unlearn. That's part of adulthood, right? Unlearning the bad and celebrating the good parts of childhood?"

Macklin leaned into him, and Scout watched him visibly relax. "How'd you get so wise?"

Jordan chuckled. "The dads. They're pretty much infallible."

Macklin chuckled in return. He looked up at Kayleigh and Scout and said, "Someday, you'll have to meet his dads. We can all spend our time wishing they'd raised us instead."

Scout's stomach growled loudly in response, and Macklin pulled away cheerily. "And in the meantime, have either of you had pizza before?"

Jordan sighed. "You East Coasters and your pizza. Someday you'll have to come to California to taste *real* pizza."

Macklin snorted, and together they set up their pizza-and-salad feast, along with soda pop, which Jordan and Kayleigh found to be wonderful in spite of Jordan's assertion that pizza needed at least four more toppings to be considered "real" pizza.

By the time they were done, Scout and Kayleigh were stretched out on the two beds, trying to stay awake, and Jordan and Macklin were cleaning up the pizza to put by the coffee maker for morning.

Jordan paused in cleanup and pulled out the map, which he'd folded up, hole and all, and put in his pocket. Scout watched him through hooded eyes as he spread the map on the table and produced a tiny wooden top from his pocket, then spun the top on the page.

His back was to Scout and Kayleigh, so all Scout could see was Jordan's jerk of surprise when the top did something unexpected.

Macklin grunted from across the room and walked over.

"Do that again," he ordered softly, and Jordan did without question, but Scout got the feeling that was only because Jordan wanted to do it anyway.

This time they both grunted in surprise.

Quietly, so as to not disturb the top with his steps, Scout rolled off the bed and approached the map. The top—tiny and wooden and apparently homemade—was perfectly upright, spinning on a little spot off the coast of the Carolinas. Much of the coastline was formed of little peninsulas and tidal islands—Hilton Head being one of the more notable places—but there were smaller islands. Tybee for one, and this one here… almost directly at the border of North and South Carolina.

"Spinner's Drift?" Scout murmured. "Never heard of it."

"Maybe not," Jordan murmured. "But it's heard of you. Spun the top twice, and both times it went directly there."

Scout blinked. "For which one of us?" he asked.

"Both," Jordan murmured. "I wasn't picky with the spellcasting. I just thought, 'Where should they go?'"

As if in emphasis, the top bounced up once, twice, three times, each time landing so emphatically on that point on the map that it had already drilled a tiny hole through the spot.

Jordan spoke softly. "I don't doubt you," he said to the top. "I'm just going to try it one more time to prove to them this is your doing, okay?"

The top gave a sulky little hop and then, much to Scout's surprise, jumped directly into Jordan's waiting palm.

"Where did you get that?" Scout asked.

Jordan smiled softly at him. "My friend Lachlan made it. We were practicing divination spells after we found out about the portals. He got really thoughtful, went home, and came back with ten of these, one for each member of the coven. Plain, well-made, and very susceptible to magic. They're perfect."

He smiled at the top spinning in his palm like a child might smile indulgently at a pet hamster. "Ready to go again?" And with that, he picked the top up by the little spinner and used his thumb and forefinger to whirl it directly on the map. Scout was watching this time. It landed somewhere in Kansas and made a beeline directly to the exact same spot.

Spinner's Drift.

"You think?" Kayleigh asked softly from over his shoulder, where she'd come to watch the tiny top that held their fate.

Scout looked at her and shrugged. "Why not?" he asked. He turned troubled eyes to Macklin and Jordan. "Not that we're ready to leave tomorrow!"

"No worries," Jordan said easily. "We'll set you up, get you at least partially ready for life outside the compound. Don't worry, guys. Believe me, if Macklin had his way, we'd be on a plane to Sacramento right now with plans for you two to have a second childhood at our house. He was so excited when Josue contacted him about helping you. You have no idea."

Exhaustion swamped Scout as he remembered that just that morning, he'd awakened with a vague tickle in his stomach telling him this was the day Alistair would test him, and knowing he'd fail.

The day had taken a lot of strange turns since then, and as lucky as he and Kayleigh knew themselves to be, he was ready to drop where he stood.

"Sorry, Macklin," Scout said through a yawn. "One childhood was hard enough."

"Well, I'll be happy to be your brother as an adult," Macklin said. "Now we're going next door to let you two sleep. Don't forget to charge your new phones. Dropped calls are the bane of modern existence." He said it with a wistful smile, and Scout and Kayleigh were suddenly in his arms for a big three-way hug.

"Thanks, Macklin," Scout whispered, eyes burning. "You didn't have to do any of this, but you and Josue and Jordan—you saved our lives."

"Gotta watch out for family," Macklin said, kissing them both on the temple. "Now to sleep. We'll see you in the morning."

But in the morning when they awoke, they both found texts on their phones, sent at around 2:00 a.m.

Alistair showed up to get Kayleigh back. We portaled to Australia to get him off your tail. Take the car—it's paid for—and make your way to Spinner's Drift. Text us when you need us. If we can't make it, we have friends who can. Love you both—Mack and Jordan

Scout just stared at the text in shock for a moment, and then Kayleigh spoke into the bright silence of the hotel room.

"You can drive, right?"

Scout gave half a laugh. "Remember when Barnaby was supposed to train me to monitor the perimeter of the compound?" Barnaby was a little Alistair, right down to his nasty attitude. Scout had lasted about a month on that detail before they'd had enough of each other. However, thanks to him, Scout could drive automatic.

"Excellent. I say we eat pizza for breakfast, shower, and hit the road," she said. "If they went to all that trouble to get Alistair off our backs, I'd hate to wreck it by getting caught ten miles from the compound."

Scout opened his mouth to protest, to shout, to get mouthy in typical Scout fashion, but he glanced at her and saw her eyes were red-rimmed too.

They had brothers who loved them and who would put themselves out for them. The least they could do was get the hell out of Dodge and do what the magic said.

Spinner's Drift, here we come.

Lucky Find

LUCKY STARED out the window of The Magic of Books, trying to keep the inward flutterings of his stomach to himself.

"New guy's trying to do another magic show," he muttered to Helen, the proprietress. In her late fifties, maybe, and as spry as a teenager, Helen was hard to get a bead on. She wasn't old and bitter, but she wasn't under any delusions that fifty was the new twenty either. She was, if anything, *circumspect*, and given that she'd offered Lucky a job in the little coffee-and-book shop when he had little more than a fake ID and good intentions to recommend him, he'd come to treasure that quality in her. She didn't poke, didn't pry, just let him sleep in the little room in the basement—or on the roof in the summer, when even the cool of the underground stucco hadn't been enough to combat the stifling humidity.

Helen chuckled, bringing her cup of apricot and ginger tea with her as she leaned against the frame of the open french doors and peered into the quad of the little tourist square that made up the business center of Spinner's Drift.

The drift itself was a series of tidal islands, an archipelago, grouped together off the coast of the Carolinas. The main island—the one the business center sat on—was about twenty miles from end to end and not quite round. More of an egg shape. This island—*his* island, as Lucky had begun to think of it—was the biggest. The islands were connected, depending on the size of each one, by a series of tidal roads, bridges, and ferries. The residents kept in touch with everything from power boats to skiffs to off-road vehicles, and while the majority of the population of about three thousand was on the main island itself, another thousand people lived in the houses and cabins scattered across the little archipelago.

Most of those people made their living here, in the three-block section of businesses that overlooked the harbor or in the two resorts that took up much of the rest of the island.

Lucky had been living here in Helen's spare room for the past six months, taking a breath, regrouping, trying to get his shit together, and nothing—*nothing*—had caught his attention in that time like the new magician who did shows from the magic shop across the street.

The shop itself sat right next to a fish-and-chips place, and the owner, Marcus Canby, was smart. The ferry from Spinner's Drift to the mainland—Charleston to be specific—arrived and left during high tide in the morning and the evening. The food service businesses in the square prepared for their rushes around the ferry arrivals. People got there and wanted to eat, or they went fishing or played in the resorts and then got ready to leave and wanted to eat before they left.

And the magic shop put on shows during the peak food hours in the hopes that those who'd had their interest piqued by the show would wander in and buy the equipment that would help them be as interesting and as handsome and as mysterious as the guy currently bumbling, grinning, and faking his way through Marcus's usual stage performance.

Or at least that was Lucky's guess.

"He's getting better," Helen said mildly.

Lucky gave a skeptical snort and rolled his eyes. "It wouldn't be hard to improve," he muttered.

"Oh come now," Helen chided. "Look at him. He's enjoying the hell out of this."

Lucky scowled at her, but his eyes, as always, wandered across the street to Marcus's new apprentice.

He was unfairly watchable.

Six feet tall if he was an inch, he had a slender, rangy body that looked damned good in the sleek black jeans and fitted satin waistcoat that Marcus had given him to wear for the performances, as well as a black leather cloak that was used as a prop sometimes. His shaggy black hair had been trimmed since his arrival back in early September, but even fashionably cut, there was still the hint that it would grow overnight, leaving his narrow, appealing face half-hidden in riotous curls and obscure his *stunning* cobalt eyes under bold black brows. He had a commanding nose, a square jaw, and a little cleft in his chin, which he would finger sometimes when he was thinking.

And his sudden smiles could outshine the sun.

Lucky scowled at himself and tried not to look at Scout Quinton—also known as "the Great Gestalt"—anymore.

But Helen was right. He *was* getting better.

"Oh, he's doing the levitating table next," Lucky said, and while he tried to infuse his voice with sarcasm, he was actually more anticipatory. This was Scout's best trick.

From across the quad, they could hear Scout's voice, supported enough not to be whipped out to the harbor by the ever-present wind.

"Notice, my friends," he said, that grin at the ready. "No strings above, no strings below!"

Marcus came out at this point, a good-natured smile on his weathered face. He was wearing a sports coat—black with planets and stars sewn into it in silver—over a pair of worn jeans. With a showy heave, he lifted his leg up and over the table, and then feigned a pulled muscle from the strain. The crowd laughed accommodatingly, and Marcus popped up spryly and grinned at them all before giving Scout, or "the Great Gestalt," a grand bow and gesturing for him to continue.

"Does anyone from the audience wish to check?" Scout asked, waving his hand over the table and then under it and around. He searched the audience for his shill—usually his sister, Kayleigh, who had brown eyes instead of blue but otherwise was a softer, more feminine version of Scout with a sort of coltish charm and natural sarcasm. Scout frowned when she didn't immediately raise her hand and catch his eye, and Lucky let out a frustrated breath for him. She had gotten a job at one of the resorts, and while Helen let her use a bicycle to get to and from work, the Morgensterns, who ran Morgan Star Recreational Resort and Spa, were known for keeping their employees late and not giving a rat's ass if they had other jobs or not. Some of that had changed in recent months—the youngest heir was making a go at not being a total bastard—but those efforts had apparently not trickled down in time to help Scout today.

Scout bit his lip at all of the eager volunteers, and for a moment, Lucky felt pity. When he'd arrived on the island in September, he'd been *terrible* at this, and now that his showmanship and dexterity with the magic equipment were starting to improve, he was being thwarted by an evil capitalist agenda.

Suddenly, almost desperately, those cobalt-blue eyes that Lucky found so mesmerizing were fixed on Lucky himself.

"You, sir!" Scout called across the square. "Would you care to come be my assistant here?"

Lucky's eyes widened. He and Scout had barely spoken three words to each other in the past month. Not that Scout hadn't tried.

When Helen had introduced them, telling Lucky that Scout was Marcus's new magician and his sister was the new shill, Scout had smiled at him and extended his hand happily.

"Nice to meet you—"

"You'll be gone in a week," Lucky had muttered, turning away and stomping toward his room.

He'd been so unsettled—both by Marcus having an apprentice and Helen's almost immediate affection for the two siblings—that his first thought was that he'd be back on the road in no time.

Who wanted a short, sturdy, untalented barista when there was Scout Quinton in the world?

He'd been so angry. He'd just been relaxing into Helen's tidy little setup, just beginning to believe that he might have found a home. And here comes this handsome, glib stranger with his pretty face and his guileless cobalt eyes to take his place.

In a temper, he'd broken a promise to himself that he'd managed to keep since he'd shown up at Helen's door.

He'd flipped a coin.

"Heads he stays, tail he goes," he muttered, thinking it would be a quick turnaround to tails.

His heart sank when the coin—an old Liberty silver dollar—landed heads up.

Well, shit. He'd started this train wreck; he might as well finish it.

"Heads *I* stay, tails *I* go." He'd flipped the heavy coin with his thumb, his busy brain already packing the few possessions he'd allowed himself to accrue when he caught it in his palm and smacked it against the back of his hand.

And almost sat down on the adobe floor of his little room when it came up heads.

They'd both stay?

For a moment Lucky doubted, but flipping the coin hadn't been wrong yet. In fact it had been right so often it had almost ruined his life. He'd stared at the coin on the back of his hand in dismay, only tucking it back in his pocket when Helen had descended the stairs from the store to give him hell for being rude.

"What were you thinking?" she chided. "He's a perfectly nice young man and—"

"And if you don't want me around anymore just say so," he snapped, and to his surprise, her expression softened.

"There's room for you both, Lucky. Scout and Kayleigh are staying in the apartment below the magic store. You remember both our stores have one. Marcus will keep his cabin in the woods like now. Scout's going to help with the magic shop, and Kayleigh's already got a job working at Morgan Worm's." Marcus and Helen had a years-old contempt for the Morgensterns who owned the resort. As of yet, Lucky hadn't been able to figure out why.

"Fine," he said grudgingly. "I'll try not to be a dick the next time I see him."

"Well, it's not an apology, but I guess it will do."

Oh sure, she *said* it wasn't an apology, but Lucky was pretty sure she *expected* an apology, and as of yet, he'd managed to avoid any sort of moment in which he could *make* an apology. He'd spent the last month dodging neatly out of the room whenever Scout walked in, and he was particularly proud of his ability to hear Scout's voice—which had a deep timbre, even if he often sounded guileless and whimsical—from half a block away.

But he couldn't get out of this.

"Come on!" Scout called across the lunch goers in the crowd. "Let's get our local barista to come help me. I mean, a helping hand, a free cup of coffee, all of it's good, right?"

He got some laughs there with his patter, and Helen cleared her throat.

"Really?" he asked, knowing it was due.

"Was there ever *really* an apology?" she said, turning his word back on him.

He sighed, which was the only answer she really needed.

"Go," she chided. "I don't want to see you until the evening rush!" And with a gentle shove on his arm that precluded any questions about why she would send him on a three-hour break, Lucky found himself trotting across the square to the applause of the good-natured crowd.

"So," Scout said as Lucky clambered up the stairs to the concrete walkway that led into the magic shop. It doubled as a stage, and Scout was adept at running up and down the four or five stairs for emphasis during his tricks. It was something he'd added to the show that Marcus was probably a little creaky to perform. "Would you care to introduce yourself to the crowd?"

Scout smiled at him with a predatory gleam in his eye, and Lucky knew his avoidance had not gone unremarked upon.

"I'm Lucky," he said, knowing the Philly in his voice was showing. "I pour your coffee over at Helen's place." He gave The Magic of Books a nod, and Helen raised her mug of tea in salute.

There was a heartier round of applause, because everybody knew Helen's place, and Scout—the Great Gestalt—gave a grand gesture of welcome.

"So, Lucky, you know what I want you to do, right?" Scout raised an eyebrow, and if Lucky *hadn't* known Scout was hoping he'd confirm the absence of wires or other paraphernalia to make the table look like it was floating, the eyebrow would have done it.

Lucky rolled his eyes and walked over to the little table… and frowned. He knew what Marcus's rigged table looked like: a light aluminum table with a black velveteen tablecloth over it. The tablecloth had silver piping around the edges that held a stiff silver wire in it. The wire held tension like an umbrella frame, so with a pass of the hand, the edge of the tablecloth buckled up instead of hanging down, and the frame was so light that a bare finger under one of the points of tablecloth wire could support the table itself.

Voilà. Floating table.

Lucky wasn't sure if that's how other people did it. He was sure every magician's equipment held very specific secrets—but that's how *Marcus* had done it.

Except this was a different table.

Curious, Lucky waved his arms over the sturdy hand-planed and sanded wooden table. He picked it up, hefting it, and noted that while it still had a tablecloth, the cloth was a simple cotton square with a sun/moon/stars print over it and edged in gold. Pretty, yes, but not "magic."

Suddenly conscious that he still had a crowd, Lucky looked out at them and grinned, lifting the table showily to prove there was nothing to see. Just an ordinary table, folks. No magic at all.

The crowd nodded appreciatively, and Lucky set the table down and gestured for the Great Gestalt to proceed.

For his part, Scout flipped his black leather cloak off his shoulders and clapped his hands together, taking a deep breath.

He held his hand out, fingers up, like a man doing his best to hold the forces of the universe, and commanded the table to rise.

Nothing happened.

Scout raised his eyebrow theatrically and turned a gimlet eye to Lucky, who couldn't help it. He grinned and held his hands out, helpless, playing to the crowd, who laughed.

Scowling, Scout clapped his hands and rubbed them together, then held his hand out, fingers up, and *commanded* the table to rise.

A sudden chill ran up Lucky's spine, and he felt a ruffle of wind in his hair, and the table rocked back and forth, although it had sat perfectly level when Lucky had shown it to the crowd.

Scout—without words—held his hands out and made the "gimme-gimme" gesture to the amused audience, who responded with an enthusiastic round of cheering.

One more time, Scout clapped his hands together and rubbed them, and this time, he held them *both* out to the table, one eyebrow raised, as he glared magic at the ordinary object and *willed* it to float.

Nobody was more surprised than Lucky when it did.

Scout wasn't touching the table. He was, in fact, six feet away from it. The table wasn't under the eaves, and there were no wires, not above nor below.

It was just *hovering* there at the top of the stairs before it started a stately and grand march down.

The audience *oooh*ed appreciatively, and Scout said, "Would Lucky like to check it for tricks?"

Well, hell yes, he would.

There were, in fact, two flights of stairs: the one closest to the harbor, which the table was using as a guide to its descent, and the one leading from the small eating area to the street people had to cross to get to Helen's shop.

Lucky took the other staircase down from the walkway and met the table as it descended, passing his hands underneath it while it was still at chest level, and then over the top and sides of it as it continued lower.

"I'll be damned," he said, ignoring the gasps of the mothers in the crowd. "No strings."

Scout's playfully raised eyebrow should have warned him of what was coming.

"Are you sure?" Scout asked.

"Yeah, I'm sure. Oh my God!"

The table, which had come to rest about six inches off the concrete of the food court, suddenly zipped right back up the stairs to rest at Scout's feet.

Lucky gasped like the rest of the crowd, and Scout waggled both eyebrows at him.

"It seems to like me," Scout said mildly.

And then the table lifted up off the ground again and went zooming around in a wide circle over the concrete apron, over the heads of the onlookers, balancing on the rail of the tidal wall that overlooked the ocean and twirling, the tablecloth spinning out, out, out, out before separating entirely and hovering over the table.

The look Scout gave the table then was not exactly surprise—and definitely not panic. It was more an "I'm gonna kill so and so when I get my hands on them!" as he made a gesture with his fist and called the table back.

Yes, that's exactly what he did. He *called the table back*. It whizzed over the audience's heads fast enough to whistle before planting itself firmly at his feet, the tablecloth floating gently down from about ten feet to land on the surface, now that it was done with its adventure.

Lucky knew he wasn't the only one staring in awe as Scout shook his finger playfully at the little table and then gave a grand bow.

The crowd erupted into applause, and then the table floated up about two feet, inclined itself as though bowing, and floated down again. Scout gave it a startled look that Lucky would put money on as being unfeigned, and the crowd went *wild*.

"Thank you!" Scout called. "You've been watching the Great Gestalt! I perform here twice a day, and anything you'd like to learn about magic, you can find it right here at Gestalt Magic Incorporated!" He gestured to Marcus's shop and bowed again, and the crowd began to disperse, many of them disposing of their fish-and-chips wrappers before disappearing into Gestalt Magic Incorporated. Lucky took the stairs up, beating the crowd, hoping to have a word with the Great Gestalt when he'd spent nearly six weeks avoiding him.

As Lucky drew abreast and people flowed around them, Lucky heard Scout mutter, "Kayleigh, I'm going to throttle you."

Scout's sister circled around the concrete walkway to them, pausing to kiss Scout on the cheek. "Sorry, Scout," she said sheepishly. "I was trying to make up for being late."

Scout gave her a lopsided grin. "I know you were, but I almost had a heart attack when I thought you were going to send it over the water."

She grimaced. "Oh hell no—no control over the water. You'd think somebody would have told us *that* little tidbit, right?"

Scout glared at her, and she noticed Lucky, standing awkwardly near him and soaking up every word.

"It's, uhm, harder to maintain the illusion," she mumbled, clearly lying.

"Kayleigh, my dear," Marcus called over the crowd. "Could you come in and help me? I'm afraid the Great Gestalt has a, erm, business meeting he can't avoid."

Scout looked puzzled as she nodded and followed Marcus in to help him ring up purchases, and then he and Lucky were out on the concrete apron alone, next to a very ordinary but well-traveled little table.

"I, uhm, wonder what that's about," Lucky said, feeling green and awkward.

"They're trying to give us time alone," Scout said glumly, giving him an apologetic look. "Which is stupid because you obviously don't like me, so really, it's sort of pointless."

"I don't not like you!" Lucky blurted, stung by the obvious hurt in Scout's voice. Oh Goddess, his rudeness really *was* coming to roost, wasn't it?

"Sure," Scout said shortly. "You're so excited to talk to me you had to be publicly shamed into coming to help. Never mind. I don't need pity." And with that he picked up the table and was probably going to stalk away, but he'd done his job too well, and the magic shop was full of people.

He sighed and set the table down. "Well shit. I'll ask Helen if she can hold this for me until tomorrow." He gave Lucky a sour look. "No, I'm not going to make you introduce us. She actually eats dinner with Marcus and Kayleigh and me sometimes." His sulk lightened a bit. "She's really nice."

"I know she is," Lucky retorted, feeling possessive. "I stay in her spare room." He sounded churlish and he knew it. "Here, let me carry the table. I know where you can stash it."

With that he picked the thing up again and turned to lead Scout across the square.

"That was really clever," he said as Scout drew abreast. "What you did with the table. I, uh, have never seen the trick done like that."

"Thanks," Scout said, but he didn't sound pleased, and Lucky realized it was on him if he wanted to keep the conversation going.

"I, uh, used to watch Marcus do the act all the time. You've… well, I mean you were awful when you started. You kept staring at the crowd like you'd never seen people before. But you've gotten better since."

"Thanks."

Oh hells. Scout was really going to make him work for this, wasn't he? "And now they can't get enough of you. That must feel good." He half expected another laconic "Thanks," but apparently he'd phrased the question the right way, and Scout *had* to answer.

"I'd never seen that many people before," he said. "Certainly not paying attention to *me.* And never a live show. That first time I dropped every prop Marcus had—twice."

"I know," Lucky told him, lips twitching. "I saw you."

He was hoping Scout would laugh with him, but instead his shoulders slumped with dejection. "Great."

"But hey, you're better now, right?"

"Yeah. Sure."

Lucky didn't have a chance to come up with something to fix the self-recrimination in Scout's voice before they were at the coffee-and-book shop. Helen was dealing ably with the stragglers from the lunch rush, and she nodded Lucky over to the back corner of the store with the table. She gave Scout a penetrating look and an arch of the eyebrow, indicating the table, and Scout shook his head.

"Kayleigh," he said, and she laughed and turned her attention back to her customers.

But Lucky had seen the whole thing and held up a finger to Scout, indicating one minute, then dodged behind the glass case containing the pastries. He grabbed two chocolate croissants and threw them in a pastry bag, then took two bottles of water, which he shoved into the pockets of his cargo pants, and gave Helen a little wave. She shooed him off with a nod at Scout, and Lucky trotted out the door and grabbed Scout's hand, dragging him into the brisk wind of the South Carolina fall.

"Where are we going?" Scout asked plaintively. "You don't even like me!"

"Changed my mind," Lucky dared, not sure why he was suddenly so excited about talking to Scout Quinton. Maybe it was his last name. It felt like a lie, and Lucky was pretty good at sniffing those out. But he thought it was more than that.

Maybe it was the way he'd stood, day after day for a month, trying to master something he clearly wasn't good at while crowds of people watched him make an ass of himself. For the entire month, he'd seemed good-natured and cheerful about his learning curve, laughing and bowing and hamming it up in front of the tourists like he ate that shit up.

And maybe it was the vulnerability he'd shown Lucky about how *not* okay he'd been about being a shitty magician at the beginning and his humility about how far he knew he had to go now.

Whatever it was, Scout didn't put up much of a fight as Lucky dragged him down the sun-bleached streets of the square overlooking the harbor, pulling him to the tide wall and a hidden thruway that led to a little used spot on the beach.

"I've never been here before," Scout said curiously, following Lucky across a hardpan walkway that skirted the sand and bordered the oak and beech trees that covered the untraveled parts of the island. Kudzu fought to take over the forest floor, although the business association spent lots of money beating it back several times a year, and Spanish moss fell gracefully from the trees' outspread branches, blowing like a girl's tulle skirt. Scout led Lucky through a little bit of underbrush to a clearing that overlooked the ocean. In the center of the clearing sat a marble bench that appeared to be kept up. Moss and grime had been removed at least twice since Lucky had arrived on the island, although he'd never seen anybody out there but himself.

"It's a good spot for thinking," Lucky said, pausing to look at the inscription on the back of the bench before plopping down on it. *To Tom, who may someday come home.* Given that the bench looked out to the ocean, Lucky thought that Tom was probably *not* coming home, and he felt bad for whatever parent or sibling or lover kept such a devoted watch over the big blue empty to see if he'd return.

"Yeah?" Scout asked, sinking down onto the opposite end of the bench. "What do you think about?"

Lucky sighed and passed him one of the croissants and, after fumbling in his shorts for a moment, one of the waters. "I think about what I'm going to do with my life once I leave this island," he said flippantly, and he grinned at Scout, hoping he'd share the joke.

But Scout was looking at him thoughtfully. "But you're a transplant, like me and Kayleigh. Why'd you come here if you want to leave so bad?"

Oh ouch. Now see—*this* was why Lucky didn't want to talk to new people.

"Same reason you probably did," Lucky snorted. "Because I didn't have anywhere else to go!"

Scout took a bite of his croissant. "But we did," he murmured softly. "There were lots of places we could have gone. We wanted to know where we *should* go, and we ended up here. Was that what you did?"

Lucky thought of the series of poor life choices and coin flips that had ended up with him on the ferry for Spinner's Drift. "More or less," he said, not wanting to talk about it. Nobody believed him about the coin flips. And the people who *did* believe him? Well, those were people he wished would forget his name.

But Lucky remembered the table, zooming around the square over the heads of the crowd as though it had been on rails, and wondered if maybe—just maybe—Scout would believe him.

"How did you do it?" he asked, taking a bite of his own croissant. "The table, I mean?"

Scout gave him a look of disgust, and Lucky sighed.

"Magic," Scout said flatly. "Pure magic. Are we done now? Have I answered your question?"

Shit. Lucky had done this to himself, hadn't he? First by being a rude asshole and then by not being honest when Scout had tried to speak from the heart. Gah! Lucky's grandmother had tried to teach him better than that.

And maybe that was the place to start.

"My grandmother died," he said baldly, leaping right over the dark, empty forest of grief that the words conjured in his heart. "Her name was Adele McPherson, but we all called her Auntie Cree. Anyway, my parents were bums, and Auntie Cree raised me, and then she died, and suddenly our walk-up in Philly was surrounded by every gangster in Southie who thought Auntie Cree would have wanted him to have it."

"Oh," Scout said, looking at him with compassion. "Wouldn't she have wanted *you* to have it?"

"Well, yeah!" Lucky had to give a bitter laugh. "That's what I thought too! And… well, I have a little trick I do. It's… it's nothing really. Auntie Cree used to call me a lucky guesser. That's why I'm Lucky, right?"

"Makes sense," Scout said, and he was—oh heavens—turning those stunning cobalt eyes on Lucky and drinking in his every word. Lucky felt the lost month acutely. He'd been afraid, in a way. Not just of getting attached to Scout, but of Scout finding him… lacking in some way. Scout and Kayleigh were amazingly interesting, and Lucky? Lucky was a street rat with a little bit of shine.

"Auntie Cree thought so," Lucky agreed. "I was going to junior college at the time, working toward the big leagues. I was going to move up to State at the end of this year, maybe get my degree, teach some school. She thought that was a real nice idea. She wanted me to have a safe place to do it." He gave a shrug like the loss of her dream hadn't hurt. It had been overshadowed by the loss of the one person in his life who'd loved him, anyway.

"So what'd you do?" Scout's voice was still soft, like he was getting why this wasn't easy.

Lucky blew out a breath, because this was by far the dumbest thing he'd ever done in his life. "Well, I pulled out my coin. It's… well, Auntie Cree gave it to me because my grandpa gave it to her. It's a silver Liberty Bell coin, and it's heavy and old and sort of beat the hell up. But I… I'm really good at guessing with my coin, you know? So I pulled the coin out and asked it questions—you've got to choose your questions—but they basically led to which batch of gangsters would protect me and let me live if I gave them Auntie's house."

Scout let out a startled gasp. "You gave it to them?"

Lucky rolled his eyes. "Gangsters. I know you're thinking Al Capone and shit, but this was… this was real. There's all these mean guys with prison tats and semiautos sitting in my Auntie's house getting gun oil on her damned tapestry couch saying, 'Kid, we think you should give the house to us,' but they're all prepared to start shooting each other if I pick the wrong guy. So I let the coin pick the right guy, the one everybody's afraid of, and he nods and tells everybody else to scram. Then he looks at me and my coin and starts asking me stuff about tomorrow's horse races."

"Oh no," Scout said, and Lucky breathed a sigh of relief, because it looked like Scout could tell where this was going.

"I was right every fucking time," Lucky told him. God, he hadn't even told this to *Helen*. He'd just asked for a job and begged her not to ask for his real driver's license. But here, with a guy who'd made a table fly—yes, *fly*, because that hadn't been a damned trick—Lucky knew that if nothing else he had a believer.

"So what'd you do?" Scout asked.

"I…." Lucky shrugged, not sure if he could ever convey the hopelessness of those few months. "Well, for one thing, I got to stay in Auntie Cree's house. I mean, Scaggs Cawthorne didn't give a fuck if I kept my room—he and his boys got the rest of the place, and they didn't treat it bad, you know? They even fucking vacuumed. But God. Every morning, he'd call me down and we'd do the ponies. And every night, Scaggs would call me in and give me a cut. And tell me not to leave town."

"You were trapped," Scout said, reading the situation the same way Lucky had. "How did you get out?"

Lucky shuddered. "Well, word was getting around about Scaggs's secret weapon with the ponies. He was taking his drug and gun money and tripling it every day. And he knew how the coin worked. I couldn't even try to lie to him, convince him it didn't work anymore, my luck had run out. And the coin—it doesn't work for anyone else, only me. So one day, I was trying to get to the grocery store. I wanted to make my grandma's brisket in the worst way, you have no idea. It was like the coin was itching in my pocket to go get a brisket and salt water. I was sitting in the back of the bus, and I heard these two goons talking about how they were going to hit Cawthorne *that fucking night*. I had a pocket full of cash to go to the market—and more, because, I'm telling you, I'd been looking for a way to get out of town since this whole thing began. Anyway, I got off the bus at the market, caught the next bus that took me down to the train station, and I just kept on going. I don't think a soul noticed me going out of town, but I had to leave everything behind. My money, my clothes, shit my grandmother left me." He tried not to let his voice shake. His grandparents' wedding rings—he'd wanted those. Not that he'd ever marry a girl, but… but they'd meant something to him.

"I'm sorry," Scout said softly. "That's hard. Did you hear what happened?"

Lucky grunted. "Yeah, I heard what happened. A rival gang took out Scaggs is what happened. A bunch of dead people and shattered glass in my Auntie Cree's living room. But one of his gang must have squawked about me when he had a gun to his head, because two days later, my coin, it starts getting hot in my pocket. I'm on the train heading west because I've always wanted to go to Disneyland and that's all I've got to go on. My coin is *literally* burning a hole in the pocket of my jeans, so I get up and move to the bathroom so I can flip the damned coin in the stall and start asking it questions to figure out what the damage is. While I'm in there, I hear two guys outside my stall, and they're *looking for me*. I guess someone's got a witchy sister or brother or something who did a spell and rolled the frickin' bones, and they were told to take the train west. So I pull out my coin and ask it if I should go back north. No. East? No. West some more? No. South? And it comes up yes. I'm surprised. I start trying variations—southwest? No. Southeast? Yes. So I make my way down here, coin flip by coin flip. I've got to tell you, I had to ask the damned coin if I'd get busted picking certain pockets, you know? And I felt bad. I felt like shit because my parents were street junkies, and they stole from fuckin' everyone. I swore I'd never end up like them. But every time I even thought about slowing down and getting a job, the coin would get hot, until… well, I ended up here."

"Wow," Scout said, sounding a little stunned. "All of that? You don't talk to me for a month, and you tell me all of that *now*?"

Lucky felt stupid. So stupid. "I… look. I get the feeling you… that table, man. Watching that table today. I know all of Marcus's tricks, right? And you've been getting better at them, but some of them, like the tower-of-crap thing he does with putty? You made that stay upright yesterday in the middle of a gust of wind that blew some guy's toupee off and massacred a nice woman's weave. And I thought, 'Naw. Couldn't be.' But then I saw that table today and…." He shrugged, out of words. "I thought, you know… the coin thing. You'd believe me. Maybe you'd understand."

Scout blew out a breath, stood, and paced to the edge of the clearing to look out of the underbrush to the great ocean.

"I wonder who Tom was," he murmured, just loud enough for Lucky to hear.

Lucky scrambled at the change of subject and then took a breath. Scout was doing what Lucky had done—rearranged his thinking about someone he'd already dismissed. It had taken Lucky a month. The least he could do was to give Scout a few moments.

"I don't know," Lucky murmured. "I worry more about the people who'll miss him."

Scout turned to give him a quick smile. "That's sweet." Swinging his arms, he took a couple of steps, and then stunningly enough, he executed a flawless pirouette, ending with his arms flung out at his side. For the first time, Lucky realized that what he'd assumed were dress shoes were really leather jazz shoes, and he laughed, both in startlement at the dance move and the surprise.

"O-kay…."

Scout shook out his arms and shrugged. "Kayleigh and I were taught dance for physical education. Good for flexibility, but sometimes I *longed* to catch a ball."

Lucky laughed, as he was meant to. "I woulda gotten the crap beaten out of me if I'd even tried dance."

Scout shrugged. "If you'd *tried* it, yes, but not if you mastered it." Very deliberately, he flexed his feet and raised himself to the tips of his toes, so slowly it was almost as *if* he was levitating. But after seeing the table, Lucky knew the difference.

Much like he knew the strength and discipline it took to do what Scout was doing.

"Very nice," he said, whistling. "That's impressive."

Scout inclined his head and executed a full bow from his toes, before slowly lowering his feet flat against the pavement again. "Thank you," he said quietly, and although he paused, Lucky knew he wasn't done. "The table… what you saw with the table? It *looked* easy. Looked like the table just whizzed around, nothing to it." He executed another pirouette, and this time Lucky saw his thigh muscles, his ass muscles, his back muscles, his calf muscles, all work in perfect concert.

And Lucky got it. "Years of training," he deduced.

"Years of training," Scout agreed, and an expression of sorrow—and resentment—passed over his features. "Much like the dance training, actually. Not all of it was welcome or pleasant."

Lucky's mouth made a little O. "I know how to use a gun," he said baldly, not able to meet Scout's eyes. "Not because I wanted to, but because Auntie Cree paid a guy to teach me when I was sixteen. She said if I had a reason to pick up a gun in our neighborhood, I'd better know how to use it."

Scout took a step toward him, and Lucky was forced to look up and meet his cobalt-blue gaze. "So you do understand," he said.

Lucky shrugged, feeling naked. "It was a month of Saturdays," he said. "I hated every minute of it. I-I can't imagine doing it for, what? How long have you been learning… dance?"

Scout blinked slowly and nodded, as though thinking. "Dance? Since I was five years old. Tables? Since I was three."

Lucky sucked in a breath. "Did you hate learning them both?" Good God. Where had this guy been brought up?

"Not always." Scout shrugged. "Like your gun. I hated the expectation that went with it. I hated that I had to, that it was necessary." He grimaced. "I hated that Kayleigh had to do the dance but didn't get to do the… table. Because she was a girl. Because she made dancing fun, and it wasn't fair."

Then Lucky made one of those brain jumps that used to get him strange looks at the public school he'd grown up in but that his Auntie Cree had told him meant he was destined for great things.

"You taught her," he said, remembering that crazy circle the table had made and Scout's determination to call the table back from the edge of the water. "*You* taught her, and you played with… the table together."

Scout nodded, and the look he turned toward Lucky was both clear-eyed and sad. "She's the best friend—probably the only friend—I've ever really had. I…. Never mind."

And now Lucky felt like complete shit. He had no idea where Scout and Kayleigh had come from, but it was pretty clear now that Scout had been lonely and Lucky had looked like a possible ally. "My folks were junkies," he said, not putting any pretty on the truth. "I was super smart in a school where that got you beat up, and pretty gay in a neighborhood where that could get you killed. My Auntie Cree was my best friend, and she… she died. And as far as I know, my coin could start burning a hole in my pocket any minute now. I didn't want to meet anyone in case I had to leave. I'm sorry. I was a coward. You and your sister… you looked nice. But I figured you had Marcus and you wouldn't need a Philly street rat, you know?"

Scout nodded and came to sit next to him, sagging against the cool marble of the bench. "I get it," he said. "Just… just remember. Your coin. That's a very serious secret you gave me. And I gave you one in return. So maybe the next time I come into Helen's for coffee, you can maybe smile at me?"

Lucky swallowed. "Yeah. I'm sorry. I thought if I was a dick, maybe you guys, you wouldn't get attached."

"And once you knew about the… table, you thought maybe you could?" Scout asked dubiously.

Lucky sighed. "I figured you'd understand if one day I just disappeared. So, you know, you wouldn't think I was making up excuses. It's dumb."

Which pretty much summed up how he felt at this exact moment, but the look Scout turned toward him was gentle.

"So you were trying to protect our feelings," he said thoughtfully.

"And my own," Lucky admitted. "I… it's been a while since I had anybody I could trust. I figured I only got one person, you know?"

"Helen?"

Lucky shrugged. She'd reminded him of his Auntie Cree.

Scout nodded. "That's okay. It's a small island, right? And Marcus and Helen are—" He smirked. "—friends."

Lucky let out a sound worthy of a twelve-year-old boy. "Sure. That's what they are. Friends."

Scout shrugged. "Hey, I'm so used to seeing men and women despise each other while they pop out babies like bunnies, I think it's sweet. It doesn't have to look like an R.L. Merrill novel or a Parker Williams book to be a romance."

Lucky scowled at him. "Who in the hell are they?"

"Romance writers," Scout said with a faint smile. "Hey, don't laugh. They got me through some tough times. What I'm saying is that Helen and Marcus can get it on all they want as long as they make each other happy. That doesn't happen often."

"Not for guys like me anyway." He wanted to say "guys like us," but he didn't know for sure. He had to look up those romance writers, maybe, to see.

"You'd be surprised." Scout yawned and stretched and stood. "But that's another story. I'm sorry, and I'm grateful. I'm glad we had this chance to talk, but Kayleigh just worked a full shift, and if she's still helping Marcus, I need to take over. And if she's not, I need to cook dinner, because it's my turn."

Lucky got it, but he was reluctant to let this moment go. He stood too and floundered for a moment for something to say. Talking like this—

honestly, intimately—had been… God, such a relief. He felt like he had to say something, anything, to let Scout know he'd like to do this again.

"I… uhm. Thank you. For being really human. Talking to me like a person when I was a dick. It means a lot."

Scout's eyes sharpened on his face, and Lucky wished he had something better to offer. His build was best typified as Irish bull—broad shoulders and chest, square face, dirty blond hair and muddy green eyes. Nothing special. Back in Philly, nobody wondered that girls hadn't hit on him, because he was that plain. But now, under the gaze of this beautiful man with the very pretty eyes, he remembered that other secret, the one besides the coin, that he'd been keeping since he was twelve years old, and his face heated.

When Scout spoke next, what he said was a complete surprise. "What's your real name?" he asked. "I mean, Lucky's a nickname, right?"

Lucky grimaced. "Justin. But nobody calls me that. Ever. What's yours?" Because who named their kid Scout?

"Scotland." Scout shuddered. "It's hideous. Please keep it to yourself."

Lucky grinned, liking this very much. *This* was the way to end a conversation. He spat into his palm and held out his hand. "Deal," he said, half expecting Scout to recoil and get all squeamish about a time-honored way of sealing a deal in his neighborhood.

Instead, Scout lit up, like Lucky had given him the best present, and spat in his palm like a pro before shaking Lucky's hand.

Their palms touched then, and shit got *really* interesting, really fast.

Souls in Waiting

THE ARC of blue light that surrounded them took Scout's breath away, and he barely remembered his training. But twenty years of constant drills about protecting yourself against hostile power didn't go away, much like the foot and leg strength to do a lift like he'd just done to show off didn't go away either.

He kept his hold on Lucky's hand, scowling into the other man's eyes and nodding shortly. Lucky nodded back and squeezed, and Scout waved his free hand in a seemingly lazy circle around them—a circle of protection, but not a blind one. He and Lucky could see out, but enemies couldn't see *in.* Once the shield was in place, he looked very carefully about, thinking that he'd felt something when he'd set foot in the little clearing, and he was pretty sure that was the boundary of this… neverland that he and Lucky found themselves in.

What he saw made him gasp.

Beyond the clearing, the light made sense. The gold-saturated blue of the bay was giving way to silver in the long shadows of late afternoon in October.

But *in* the clearing, the light was electric blue and a sort of sickly green, and nothing in the area surrounding their stone bench was as it had seemed.

An industrious washerwoman labored over the cut marble of the bench, taking off the scales of moss or sand that accrued over time and taking a small stylus to the inscription, making sure the appeal to Tom continued unblemished through… how many years?

Young lovers, a boy and a girl, huddled in the southeast corner of the clearing, sobbing, hiding from blows that obviously landed, although Scout could never see the source.

A little girl clenched her arms around her knees and sobbed, rocking back and forth on the bench itself, and as Scout watched, the washerwoman passed *through* the child to continue her labor on the bench.

And in front of the bench, a young man, face peaked and gaunt and tearstained, stood staring yearningly out into the ocean, as though willing somebody over the waves to return.

Clearly through the crackle of otherworld, Scout heard the words, *Come back to me, Tommy. Beloved, beloved, come back to me, Tommy my boy.*

Holding the shield while keeping himself and Lucky solidly in the otherworld was stretching the limits of Scout's power. He growled to himself and gave Lucky's hand another squeeze, before releasing his grip and peeling back his shield, almost simultaneously.

With a sizzle, a bolt of electricity sent them both reeling back onto their asses as the sky around the clearing assumed the gold-saturated blue that meant they were solidly back in reality now.

They both scrambled to their feet, chests heaving, and Lucky spoke first. "The actual fuck? What in the actual—"

Scout shook his head and held his finger to his lips, gesturing with his head that they should leave the clearing. Lucky followed him as he led, although Scout could practically hear the gears grinding in the other man's head.

Well, Scout had some grinding gears himself, and surprisingly enough, they weren't from the spirit trap he and Lucky had just discovered.

He'd wanted to be friends so badly! He'd seen Lucky working in Helen's shop the first day he and Kayleigh had arrived in Spinner's Drift, driving the car Macklin and Jordan had left them, a small cache of accrued possessions in the brand-new suitcases in the back of the Oldsmobile Cutlass that, they had learned, was possibly the least cool car in the entire world.

But it was theirs.

Jordan and Macklin hadn't texted them since that first day, but their friends, Jordan's coven, had. In the weeks since Scout had first arrived, barely clothed, in the woods, they'd gotten used to someone they'd never met checking up on them via their phones. They each had their favorites. Kayleigh was partial to Kate, the only girl who texted them, while Scout had a soft spot for Bartholomew, who seemed, even via text, unbearably shy. But as comfortable as they were—and as much as it helped not feeling cut off from family of any sort, even family they didn't know—Scout had been dying to talk to somebody in person. Someone his own age.

Someone male.

Marcus was lovely. He was kind and surprisingly chipper for someone approaching seventy, and he'd pretty much opened his home to Scout and Kayleigh after a long conversation over his counter. He'd seemed to perk up especially when Kayleigh had mentioned their brother's name: Macklin.

"Is he, perchance, with another young man named Jordan?" Marcus had asked.

Kayleigh and Scout had given each other sideways looks. "Yes?" Scout hazarded.

Marcus had nodded. "Karma is a funny thing. You two are welcome to stay in the downstairs apartment. It's got two beds and an attached bathroom. If you help me in the magic shop, learn to put on performances during rush hours, I can work on fixing up my little bungalow in the woods." He'd winked. "I've got to make it special so my girl will move in, right?"

And then he'd introduced them to "his girl," Helen, and had *tried* to introduce them to Lucky. Lucky's subsequent retreat and surliness had… well, it had been a blow to Scout's confidence.

Kayleigh had gotten another job at the resort, since Marcus didn't have that many hours to offer, and she'd managed to make friends there, but Scout hadn't been so fortunate.

Most of the people who watched him perform only wanted to know his magician's secrets, and not all of the people who came into the store to buy were particularly nice.

Scout's hurt toward someone who seemed to be in the same situation *he* was, and who *should* have been an ally if not a friend, had built up until that day, when he'd seen Lucky watching from the doorway of the book-and-coffee shop, and Scout had wanted just a little bit of revenge.

He hadn't expected Lucky to blow out a breath, roll his eyes, and take his punishment like a man. Nor had he expected Lucky to be so… so game, during the performance. Scout may not have been training to be a magician all his life, but he and his brothers and sisters *had* been disciplined to perform. Scout suspected it was because if they ever had interactions with people outside the compound, Alistair wanted them to be able to project aloofness, the smooth ability to get what they wanted without giving anything, not even a smile, in return.

It had obviously been lost on Kayleigh, who had flirted and giggled her way through all her recitals, and Scout, who had been *over*curious if not quiet and bookish offstage, had become flamboyant and expressive while performing. The mothers had loved them. In fact, everybody in the compound had loved them—except Alistair, who had praised the more restrained performances excessively and given Kayleigh and Scout condescending notice at best.

To find a place in which he could make magic, even pretend magic, in front of a crowd and be loved for it? Scout had been a fan immediately. But he'd expected Lucky to roll his eyes and stalk away, leaving him high and dry—again.

Instead, he'd agreed to come on stage and had made a showy production of it, almost like he'd been watching Kayleigh be the shill and had taken notes.

Almost like he'd had a guilty conscience about being a rude asshole.

But it hadn't been until Lucky's story about being on the run, being afraid because he didn't want the little bit of magic he had to be stolen, that Scout truly understood, and then *he'd* had the guilty conscience. He'd spent the last month being butthurt because Lucky had blown him off and hadn't caught on to the fact that Lucky had been achingly lonely and very, very scared.

Scout needed to remember that he may have grown up insulated from the rest of the world, but other people had real problems too.

Sort of like the people in the soul trap, who were an entire other story.

But not distracting enough to pull Scout's inner eye from the tiny freckles on the bridge of Lucky's nose, or the way his hazel eyes had grown large and thoughtful when he'd spoken of his grandmother.

And definitely not distracting enough to dismiss the fact that Lucky had a wide, mobile, expressive, *kissable* mouth that might not mind being kissed.

Because it may have taken a minute for those words to sink in, but Scout had been too fascinated with Lucky for too long for him to shake them anytime soon.

But Alistair had drilled responsibility into him for far too long to neglect priorities, and the thing he and Lucky had just seen qualified.

Finally, they'd traveled back across the thruway and up onto the road of the tourist center. Scout glanced around and saw that the streets had pretty much cleared out, like they did after the second ferry left for the mainland. Everyone else was headed back to the resorts on one of the small shuttles provided by the hotels, and the only people left were locals who had run out of something small between their own big trips to Charlotte for supplies.

Helen's shop wasn't quite empty yet—locals liked their coffee and late-afternoon pastries as much as the tourists, and four o'clock was a great time to peruse a bookstore for either new bestsellers or secret used volumes—so Scout didn't head that way. Instead he walked toward the Gestalt, the magic store, where Marcus was locking up the outside.

"Hello, boys," Marcus said with a smile. "Did you enjoy your break?"

Scout paused, not wanting give all the bad news at once. Being told to go off to play with a potential friend was not an experience he'd gotten as a kid, but he sure did appreciate it as an adult!

"Very much," he said, catching Lucky's eye. "I appreciate the chance to get to know Lucky better. That was very kind."

Marcus's expression turned sad. "So very formal," he said softly. "But you're welcome. Is there anything you need? Kayleigh assures me it's your turn to cook dinner. What did you have in mind?"

Kayleigh had been teaching him how to cook, so relieved that it wasn't only her responsibility anymore that she nearly cried when Marcus or Scout cooked. Getting lunch at one of the kiosks or small restaurants that dotted the island was such a luxury for her after twenty years of being told that being a cook and a broodmare were her only options in the future that Scout dedicated himself to toast and jam for lunch to eke out their finances a little. It had always been his favorite anyway.

"I was thinking ramen with pork and eggs," he said hopefully. It was simple and very satisfying. "There's enough for Lucky. We need to talk."

Marcus's eyes went wide. "About what? This sounds serious."

"About the soul trap down by the beach," Scout said, lowering his voice appropriately.

Marcus sucked in a breath. "Oh dear. You discovered that, did you?"

Scout and Lucky met gazes. "You knew?" According to Alistair, soul traps were a terrible disaster, the paranormal equivalent of a toxic spill, to be cleaned up by only the most powerful wizards in hazmat suits with flamethrowers.

"Well, hard not to," Marcus said. "In fact, it's one of the things that attracted me here—and Helen as well. It's an opportunity to do some good, you see. Couple of old hoofers at our age, getting a chance to do something this big. One of the reasons I took you and Kayleigh in. That much untapped power, with…." He sighed. "I was hoping with a little more… you know, finesse than your people usually have?"

Scout stared at him for a second, not sure if he should throw himself on Alistair's mercy and call him in to save them, save them all from the terrible ghosts who might devour their very souls!

Marcus and Helen were hedge witches. Small potatoes. They knew about wizards—Marcus had spotted Scout and Kayleigh right away—but they weren't part of the community at all. And while Alistair had dismissed hedge witches completely, with prejudice and condescension, Scout couldn't help but remember Jordan. While Macklin had tried to muscle his divination with will and power, Jordan had spun his little top and waited to see what happened. Macklin's approach had been very like Alistair's, which Scout had never understood. But Jordan's… Jordan's approach had been much more organic.

And suddenly he got it.

This little island was insulated. One of the first things he'd asked was whether Kayleigh had to worry about Alistair popping up out of nowhere and dragging her back to wizard central in upstate New York.

Marcus had shaken his head. "No, my boy. Salt water tends to thwart wizarding powers. Hedge witches, on the other hand, tend to be much more connected to the elements. If your lot are all wizards, you have nothing to worry about."

This island was safe. Safe from wizards. Safe from whoever was chasing Lucky. Safe. Bringing Alistair Quintero in here for a couple of ghosts who had, apparently, been here for quite some time would be like dumping napalm on the entire island and burning it down because someone's chicken got out.

"Of course," he said, allowing some of his intensity to recede. "Of course. It's your island. It should be done your way. But, uhm, Lucky may want to be briefed. He—*we*—were pretty rattled."

"Thanks," Lucky said quietly, and Scout sent him a quick smile. Yeah, nobody wanted to admit they'd been freaked the fuck out, but Scout knew it had been both of them.

If it hadn't, he might have taken advantage of the privacy some more.

The thought intruded out of nowhere, but Scout took another look at Lucky, who was looking to Marcus for guidance. His cheekbones were razor sharp—sharp enough to make the planes of his face look broad and the angles surprising. Not a pretty face, no, but interesting. Arresting.

Fascinating.

Scout might like to study it some more.

"By all means," Marcus was saying, pulling Scout back to the present. "Go fix dinner—fix enough for Helen too, and we can eat on the back porch." He threw his head back and tasted the wind, licking the tip of a pink tongue across age-thinned lips. "The wind should die down in an hour or so. It will make for a pleasant evening."

"Of course." Scout turned to Lucky. "Want to come talk to me while I work? I, uhm, suck at the noodle part. Kayleigh makes them out of flour, water, gluten, and baking soda, and I'm hopeless."

"You make noodles out of flour?" Lucky asked, sounding puzzled. "I seriously thought you got them from the store in those little packages."

Scout had seen those packages; Kayleigh had been so pissed that it was possible to eat noodle soup without making the noodles from scratch that he hadn't even wanted to bring it up.

"I've never had that," he said apologetically. "We've been slow-cooking a pork shoulder for hours, so we have broth and pork." He smiled again at Lucky's dazed expression. "Here, follow me. We can talk while Marcus is rounding up Helen and Kayleigh." Wait. "Where's Kayleigh?"

"She ran to the general store for soy sauce, which means you should hurry!" Marcus urged, and Scout took him at his word.

In front of the magic store, by the rail that blocked off the cliff to the beach, was a little staircase. Most folks missed it, because taking it required hugging the railing and then disappearing literally under the store. It probably wasn't easy for Marcus to take these stairs anymore—his knees weren't what they used to be—but the road behind the store was much lower than the road in front of it. The little apartment underneath opened out to a nice patio, and since the streets of Spinner's Drift were practically vacant in the evening, anyone sitting there had an unobstructed view of the beach to one side and the encroaching undergrowth from the island on the other.

It was lush and overgrown in a way Scout had never experienced before, and while it could get chilly in the winter, he knew that snow was rare.

"This is nice," Lucky said as they made their way down the stairs and into the hidden apartment underneath the shop.

"Helen says you have something a little smaller," Scout said. "I have the feeling most of the shops have little apartments over and under them. We lucked out because Helen and Marcus want to live in their little cottage in the woods."

Lucky grunted humorlessly. "Well, they do call me Lucky."

Scout winked at him. "And you have no idea how lucky you really are," he said, making his way to the kitchen. The kitchen wasn't huge like the one in the compound, but Kayleigh had taken a look around and pronounced it "adequate." "Here. Sit. There's soda in the fridge and chips in the pantry. I'm going to go change out of my work clothes."

He indicated the formal waistcoat with the red satin shirt underneath, and he watched Lucky's comic dismay dawn across his face.

"No," he said, grinning, "I do not wear this around the house. Why do you ask?"

Lucky ignored his injunction to sit and instead followed him to the single bedroom with a single bed on either side of the room.

"Isn't that inconvenient?" he asked as Scout slid off his waistcoat and hung it neatly on the hanger. "Living with your sister?"

Scout shrugged and started unbuttoning his red satin shirt. He had a T-shirt on underneath, he admonished himself. There was no reason, none whatsoever, for this to feel quite so intimate.

"I'm gay, and she's so disenchanted with men right now she might as well be," he said. "She's my best friend. It's not a problem."

Lucky *hmm*ed. Scout looked up quickly to see what he was thinking but only saw curiosity in his eyes. "Why's she hate men?"

Scout shrugged and slid off the shirt, then went to work on his suit pants, hanging them up on the same hangar and very carefully not glancing at Lucky, who seemed absolutely fascinated at seeing Scout in his skivvies. Scout had spent his entire life sleeping in a dorm/barracks with all of his brothers and half brothers, and not once had he felt so self-conscious. But he wasn't going to tell Lucky that.

"Kayleigh and I grew up in… sort of a family ranch," Scout said, trying to explain it without exaggeration while he was rooting through his drawer for his jeans, a new T-shirt, and a sweatshirt. He adored hooded sweatshirts—had bought five on the trip from upstate New York to South Carolina—and T-shirts to match. The freedom of jeans or cargo shorts and T-shirts as opposed to a button-up shirt and slacks, which he'd been required to wear every day, was probably in line with Kayleigh's joy at eating something she hadn't cooked. "Everything was very patriarchal. The women were expected to give birth to more people who could… uhm, move tables, I guess, and cook for the men. And everything was about the men. Could we move tables well enough? Were we onboard with the family plan? When I was a little kid, my older brother, Macklin, managed to escape. My father kept expecting him to 'sow his wild oats' and come back to the fold. About a year ago, Macklin fell in love with another man, and basically, they both told Dad to fuck off. Since then, Dad has been *insane* about breeding more—" He hesitated at using the word. "—wizards."

"Table movers," Lucky supplied dryly.

"Yeah, that." Scout winked. "Anyway, the situation hadn't been ideal before, but my table-mover power is… well, I don't want to say weak, because Macklin says I'm pretty strong. And I don't want to say wonky, because… well, it always does exactly what *I* want it to do, but not what anybody else *tells* me to make it do. So, that thing you saw today? That was Kayleigh and me playing around. If Alistair, my father, showed up and said, 'Move that table or I'll blow your brains out,' Kayleigh would have a lot of cleaning up to do."

Lucky recoiled in horror.

That's the way to make it romantic, Scout. Gross him out.

"Would your old man really do that?" he asked, sounding appalled.

Scout found his sweatshirt and set it on the bed before rooting for a T-shirt that wasn't white. In the barracks, they'd had to keep their clothes neatly folded and in the appropriate drawers, all in a row. His way wasn't as efficient, but, well, it was giving Lucky more time to look at him, and the thought was making him sort of tingly.

"Let's say I *was* thrilled to get kicked out of the house, but it was also inevitable. I did the two things that would get me disowned. One was like boys better than girls, and Dad found my favorite romance novels to prove it, and the other was not be able to perform to spec. I was supposed to do a particular trick for him, and I guess my magi—erm, table moving wasn't up to his standards, so next thing I know, I'm standing ten miles from home, barefoot in my ceremonial robes."

"Yikes!" Lucky said, obviously sincere. "How did you get Kayleigh to join you?"

Scout chuckled. "It was the damnedest thing. The trick I was supposed to do was open up a portal. It's one of the biggest things you can do because it disrupts time and space. Anyway, Alistair asked, I couldn't perform, and I end up alone in the woods. Then I discover that one of my other brothers had prepared for this very moment. I've got a phone, I've got cash, I've got my brother Macklin's number in my pocket—I am *free.* And the first thing I think of is Kayleigh, because as trapped as I was, she was, like, a thousand times more trapped. She was going to get married to some asshole she's never met who would expect her to pump out a few puppies and cook for the rest of her life."

"Oh wow," Lucky said faintly. He looked genuinely sympathetic for Kayleigh, and that earned him points right there. "That's… wow. So what'd you do?"

"Well, I thought about Kayleigh, and I summoned my… uhm—"

"Call it magic, Scout. I can deal with magic."

Scout gave him his biggest smile and found his jeans, aware as he did so that Lucky had been listening to every word he'd said, but he hadn't taken his eyes from Scout's body as he'd done so. Scout felt that tingle amplify and wished he had more muscles or a six-pack or a chest. He thought when he'd hit his twenties, he'd fill out—Macklin had a broad-shouldered build—but no. He'd stayed tall and slender, with only his definition to show his strength.

"So I summoned my magic and thought miserably that I wanted Kayleigh there, and boom. There's the portal I couldn't call to save my life. I yanked Kayleigh through it—willingly, there was hugging, I'm a good brother—and now we're on the run. Alistair didn't give a rat's ass about *me*, but *her* marriage was supposed to seal some sort of power deal. My brother Macklin and his boyfriend have been zipping around the country keeping Alistair busy for the last few weeks. I think they've got Jordan's friends working on a way to block Kayleigh from Alistair forever so she can really be free of him."

He gave Lucky a sober look. "So like your coin—if your coin ever gets warm in your pocket, you'll know someone's looking for you. Jordan's friends are casting spells to protect Kayleigh. If their spells ever turn on them, we'll get a phone call about Alistair and…." He shrugged.

"You'll be on the next ferry," Lucky said with satisfaction.

Scout pursed his lips thoughtfully. "Maybe. Or maybe my magic decides to stop being chickenshit and keeps her safe. Or even better, she figures out balefire—I mean, she's got enough justified rage, believe you me—and then Alistair returns home with his hair all crispy and decides this is not a place he wants to come anymore."

Lucky snorted into his hand. "Really? You spend your life afraid of the guy and you think that's gonna happen?"

Scout couldn't help grinning. Lucky had been trying so hard not to laugh. "See, now, a year ago I would have thought that's not a possibility. But that's because I didn't know what happened last Samhain, uhm, Halloween."

Lucky blinked. "What happened?"

"Well, we all knew that Alistair was pissed at Macklin. I guess he'd had Macklin *and* Macklin's boyfriend in our house against their wills. They kept escaping—it pissed him off. So he was going to visit them at midnight, California time, All Hallows Eve, when his power was crackling around their heads and he could scare the shit out of them. Now, we don't know exactly how this happened, but apparently they'd been under siege by all these animals—birds, squirrels, snakes—and he'd been fucking around with them when they'd been doing some serious spellcasting. So they'd done it. They'd broken the spell at midnight, and all the animals were there, wandering around, getting pissed and frightened, and Alistair showed up, trying to bring the wrath of the Goddess to them, and…." He started to giggle, because this part always made him giggle. "We were wrapping his wounds for days. There wasn't enough gauze in the house. Apparently turkeys and owls and squirrels can be mean fuckers if they've been messed with. Anyway—" He sobered. "—a year ago, I wouldn't have been so cocky. But he's human. He's a fucked up, mean-tempered, tyrannical nightmare of a human, but he's a person."

It hit him then why Lucky would be so in awe, and it apparently wasn't the magic. "Once you realize your enemies are people," he finished, "I think they're not so scary."

Lucky grunted. "People don't scare me. *Guns* scare me, Scout. But people *with* guns are twice as scary!"

Scout didn't laugh. He felt Lucky's fear to his very bones.

"We'll work at keeping you safe," he said simply. "Guns *are* scary. People with guns are scary. But *you* don't have to be scared—not all the time."

Lucky looked away, and Scout shivered and stepped into his jeans, only to hear a little whimper emerge from Lucky's throat.

"What?" he asked.

Lucky shrugged. "Just… you know. Appreciating the view."

Heat swept up Scout's body. He'd been enjoying the covert glances Lucky had given him, but to hear it actually said *out loud*—ooh, that was something.

"Thank you," he mumbled, knowing his neck and throat were probably blotching and absolutely helpless to stop it. "I, uhm…." Without looking in Lucky's direction, he stripped off his white T-shirt and reached for the blue one he'd thrown on his bed.

It wasn't there. With a frown he glanced around the room and saw that Lucky had picked it up and was dangling it from one finger, teasingly.

"Can I, uhm, have that?" he asked, burning with embarrassment—and want.

"Sure," Lucky murmured, moving in closer but pulling the shirt to his own chest. "Just reach out and get it."

Scout did, and Lucky used the opportunity to pull Scout closer.

Scout swallowed and looked away, very conscious of their bodies, aligned nicely. Lucky was shorter, but his shoulders were broader, and his tight, flat stomach was about even with Scout's groin.

Scout was very, very aware of this.

"You, uhm, don't even like me," he said apologetically, in case Lucky had forgotten.

Lucky grimaced. "I didn't want to get attached to you," he clarified. "That doesn't mean I haven't *watched* you. Uhm…." And Scout was charmed by the two crescents of color that stained Lucky's broad cheeks and sharp cheekbones. "I like the way you move."

Scout bit his lip. "I couldn't even get you to look at me when I got coffee." He'd tried too, chatting blithely to Helen, talking about all the different coffee flavors Kayleigh wanted to try and getting input. Lucky had steadfastly ignored him, answering in monosyllables and setting his purchases down on the counter so there wasn't even a chance of their fingertips brushing.

Lucky met his eyes, a rather devilish smile twisting at his lean mouth. "I looked at your ass when you walked away," he admitted. "Does that count?"

Scout laughed softly. "No," he chided, but he didn't back away. "I've never kissed anyone before, you know. I pretty much told you Kayleigh and I got raised in a monastery. What makes you think kissing me's such a good idea?"

Lucky swallowed and skated his fingertips along Scout's cheekbones. "'Cause I ain't never kissed anyone before either. I got raised in a place where if you got caught kissing another guy you'd get your face beat in. But you're not gonna beat my face in."

Scout cupped Lucky's chin with his fingers. "I like your face," he said sincerely. This was the absolute truth and part of why Lucky's coldness had hurt so much. Scout *did* like his face, and he'd liked the respectful way Lucky had spoken to Helen and the vitality in his sturdy body. It had seemed absolutely unfair that this person who had so many qualities Scout *liked* had been determined to have absolutely nothing to do with him. "But I don't want to be kissed just because we're the only two gay men on the island."

Lucky made a rude noise. "Have you *seen* the resort crowd? No. No, you haven't. Because if you *had*, you would have seen all the tourists hitting on you, and yes, a lot of them are male." He twitched his shoulders then, an almost unconscious gesture of arrogance, at the same time he bit his lip in uncertainty, and Scout's stomach dropped off a ten-meter board, backflipped, jackknifed, and did the twist. "I think we should kiss for the same reason anybody kisses. 'Cause we been eyeing each other for the last six weeks and now we got no secrets to keep."

Scout gave a lazy smile, his blood thrumming in his ears with anticipation. "Oh, I might have some secrets lef—"

Lucky kissed him.

Scout caught his breath, and that let Lucky's tongue in his mouth, and *wow*, that was a *good* thing. A *really* good thing. He returned the tongue stroke with one of his own, and Lucky made a helpless sound, so at odds with his sturdy Philly "I got this" that Scout deepened the kiss.

Oh wow. This was… this was *good.* This was what the romance books said it should be. They weren't, either of them, experts, but it didn't seem to matter. They tasted, they learned about lips and teeth, they explored with tongues, and it just kept getting deeper and deeper.

One of them groaned, and Scout couldn't tell if it came from his own throat or Lucky's, but then Lucky palmed the naked skin of Scout's back and Scout shivered, viscerally aroused and startled at the same time.

Lucky pulled back anxiously. "I didn't… did I scare you?"

Scout's entire body felt flushed. "I… I don't have a shirt on," he said gruffly. "I'm… uhm, kissing you without a shirt." Part of him wanted to be *naked* already and was thrilled at the head start, but a part of him *really* wanted his shirt back.

Lucky smiled shyly and picked the shirt up off the bed where he'd dropped it. Scout took it from him and pulled it over his head, giggling—*giggling*—when Lucky stroked his stomach.

“Not fair,” he said, reaching for his sweatshirt. It got cold in the apartment near evening, and Marcus had already warned them that they’d be depending on a space heater in the winter to keep their toes from freezing. Also, because part of the apartment was half dug into the cliff that overlooked the ocean, it could flood during hurricane season, which explained why the floors were mostly nonskid tile. He pulled the sweatshirt over his head, and when he could see again, Lucky hadn’t moved back much. He was looking out from under his lashes, and it only took Scout a minute to know what he wanted.

Gently, sensing that Lucky was still skittish and that the kiss had meant something to both of them, he lowered his head and took Lucky’s mouth again, once, twice, a third time. He pulled away and bumped his nose along the side of Lucky’s jaw.

“Now we’ve both been kissed,” he said softly. “Maybe we’ll both be kissed again.”

Lucky’s smile told him it was the right thing to say.

“Maybe,” Lucky said, his shoulders twitching with that cockiness that had probably been dying to come out since he was born. “Depends on what you feed me for dinner.”

Scout laughed, pleased. Had he known this was the Lucky behind the surly façade? It felt like he should have. It felt like he should have known this was the Lucky that had been waiting for him all along.

When The Trap is Sprung

LUCKY WATCHED Scout—*Scotland*, and he could understand why Scout hated that name—move around the kitchen, talking easily about any subject Lucky asked about.

And Lucky was torn between wondering why he hadn't trusted Scout sooner and wondering if he was crazy for trusting him now.

Part of him really wanted to ask about that thing they'd seen on the beach, the "soul trap," but part of him had parked that big ugly killer-clown van in the back of his mind and was concentrating on watching Scout's fluid, dance-like movements as he chopped vegetables, rolled pasta for noodles, and prepared broth.

He claimed to be new to cooking, but Lucky was pulled forcibly back to coming home from high school and watching his Auntie Cree in the kitchen. Auntie Cree had been old school—men didn't cook in her house—but Lucky had liked watching her. There was a sense that this was a performance, like a ballet, and that the final show was the meal. Lucky had grown up eating ramen noodles from the grocery store, because Auntie Cree couldn't cook *all* the time, and whatever Scout was making now, it wasn't the ramen from the store.

And as interesting as watching Scout move was hearing him talk. He talked like he was surprised that somebody was listening but he'd been wanting an audience for his entire life. Lucky, who'd spent *his* entire life hoping nobody heard him say fuckin' boo, became caught up in his stories of the place he'd grown up. It was almost like a Disney movie, but not perfect. Lucky could hear the deep thread of loneliness in the stories of Scout and Kayleigh meeting by their favorite tree so they could read a book in some fuckin' peace and dream of a life of their choosing.

Lucky could relate. He'd been having that dream his entire life. Until he'd shown up in Spinner's Drift, he'd thought it was just that: a dream. But he'd shown up in July, and these last months working for Helen, seeing her warm smile when he woke up, not worrying about what the wrong person would see if they caught him on the bus or—worse—if this was the day Scaggs decided that money on the ponies wasn't worth letting Lucky sleep in the room he'd had since he was a kid.

All of it had given Lucky a feeling of freedom, of power, and a sort of half-hidden joy.

He liked it here. He knew it would get chilly after hurricane season, but right now, in the beginning of fall, it was crisp and breezy but not cold. Certainly not the soul-sapping cold that Philadelphia could muster. February in Philly could suck the life out of a fire-monkey, if there were such a thing.

He'd seen summer here, and it was hot and sultry, but it was an island, with lots of wind, and the beaches had white sand and long slopes. The only place he'd ever really gone swimming before coming to Spinner's Drift had been the public swimming pool, but Spinner's Cove, on the other side of the big island, was like what people imagined when they thought of coming to a resort to catch some sun. He'd bought a pair of water goggles from the Sand and Surf and had spent his time off from Helen's learning to swim out past the breakers. He couldn't spend *too* long there, though, because his Irish-pale skin *would* burn in spite of all the sunblock in the world, so he had sweet memories of the late afternoon shadows stealing over Helen's store while he flipped through old magic texts, wondering if anything in them was as real as the coin in his pocket. If the old magic texts failed him, there were wide worlds of adventure or mystery stories, and he'd allowed the sound of the wind and the seagulls and even the laughter and excited voices of the tourists to seep into his bones and wash away some of the fear that had lived there for maybe most of his life.

Something about how he felt must have come out in his words, because Scout paused after he'd assembled all his ingredients and set the water to boil.

"You should stay here," he said quietly, leaning back against the counter and wiping his hands off on a towel. "No matter what happens, you should stay here. I think the island likes you."

For a moment, Lucky took that at face value. He knew *he* certainly liked it here, but then it occurred to him. "Why? Why do you think it likes me?"

Scout raised his eyebrows. "Well, because it showed you the soul trap this afternoon."

Lucky scowled in return. "I've been there a thousand times. Why wouldn't the island show me that until now?"

Scout tilted his head to the side, a faint smile on his face. "You really love that spot," he said softly.

"Well I *did*," Lucky said passionately, not quite able to contain his betrayal. "I didn't realize it was… all full of pain and grief and shit!"

"But you *know* pain and grief and shit," Scout said, giving Lucky a glance of compassion. "You know how to move beyond it. That's… important, I think. I think that's going to help us."

"But I had no idea all that was going on until you *touched* me!" Scout retorted. "It's like we spit on our hands and smacked them together and *boom*! I can see ghosts!"

Scout gave an apologetic shrug. "That was me, I'm afraid. I think you've got… well, like a magic tool. Your coin—or your ability to use the coin—gives you barely enough magic to get a peek into the world. It gives you some influence. You can't make a table float, but maybe that's lack of training. For all we know, if you'd been learning cantrips and spells as a child, you'd be a full-fledged mage. Or even a powerful hedge witch. Or maybe just a guy with a coin, which is pretty powerful itself."

"I still didn't see nothin' until we touched."

Scout shrugged again. "I've got more magic," he said. "We touched, and you had the affinity for the place, so my magic let me see it, and I had the extra magic, and that's what let you see it too."

Lucky regarded him through narrowed eyes. "So what you're saying is that it was both of us."

Scout grimaced. "Well, yeah. But you could have been down there with Kayleigh just having a convo. The magic conduit was necessary but not personal. This was personal to you, I think."

Lucky snorted. "I could have lived my entire life without seeing that much misery," he said. Then he let out his irritation on a sigh. "But, you know. Then we kissed and that was pretty good, so I guess everything's a trade-off."

Scout's laughter caught him by surprise. For all that Scout was a slender man, this laugh—this laugh should have come from a daddy bear, someone with a bit of a beer belly and apple cheeks and a trucker's cap on backward.

"What?" Lucky asked defensively. "What'd I say?"

Scout just shook his head and went back to fixing dinner, still chuckling to himself, and Lucky leaned against the counter that separated the kitchen area from the living room area and tried not to sulk. But when Scout had to circle around from the kitchen to get something on the far corner of the counter, he paused long enough to lean up against Lucky's back.

"Don't be mad," he murmured in Lucky's ear. "Maybe with a little more practice, the kissing will be better than pretty good."

Lucky couldn't help it. He smiled and turned his head, rubbing his lips against Scout's happily.

"Couldn't hurt."

He felt Scout's low chuckle against his mouth before the kiss started properly, and this time he had Scout's warmth against his back. Everything faded into the background except Scout's dreamy kisses and the feeling that he was safe and secure in this little kitchen and in the arms of the man who was cupping his jaw and getting ready to kiss deeper.

The sound of the door from the outside stairs opening pulled them apart, and Scout retrieved the item on the counter, a strainer, and was back behind the stove when Kayleigh strolled into the living room.

"Smells good!" she chirped. "Scout, you're getting good at thi—oh." Her voice cooled considerably. "Hi, Lucky."

Lucky grimaced. Yeah, he wasn't proud of himself for how he'd treated the two of them.

"Hi, Kayleigh," he said. "Sorry I was a douche when we first met."

Kayleigh, apparently, was not as easy as her brother. She put her hands on her hips and stared at him, her brown eyes trying to bore into his soul. "So why are you not being a douche now?" she demanded. "Or probably more accurately, why are you still being a douche now but pretending to like my brother, who's a sweet summer child and too nice for this world."

"Ou—" Scout began.

"I'm not pretending shit!" Lucky protested.

"—ch," Scout finished, after making the word three, four syllables at least. "Kayleigh, I'm not that naïve."

She rolled her eyes. "Sure you are. You've been hit on by eleventy-twelve guys hotter than this one in the last six weeks, and this is the guy I come home and find you kissing?"

"I have not!" Scout argued.

"I told you!" Lucky chortled. "I *told* you that those resort guys were hitting on you, and you kept saying no they weren't. My God, she's got you pegged, don't she!"

"They weren't *hotter* than you," Scout declared triumphantly, and Lucky and Kayleigh both rounded on him.

"A*ha*!"

"I mean," Scout stammered, "that nobody hotter than you has tried to hit on me."

"Oh God," Kayleigh muttered. "Give it up, Scout."

"I mean nobody on the island has hit on me," Scout amended, looking baffled and miserable and dear.

"Sure they haven't," Lucky said, deciding he'd had enough. "We'll believe you." His eyes sought out Kayleigh's to see if maybe they were on the same side now.

She scowled at him, so maybe not. "No, seriously, *Sucky*, I need a better explanation for why you were a total douchebag to us for a month and now you're in here all primed to break my brother's heart."

"Kayleigh…." Scout covered his eyes with his hand and then moved it quickly, probably remembering he'd just chopped up shallots for the noodles.

Her eyes widened as she watched him run water in the sink so he could stick his eyes under it, but her scowl didn't lighten up one iota. "Look at him, Lucky. If I don't look out for him, who will?"

Lucky sighed. Those gangs that had sat in his living room? Most of them had been thick with brothers and cousins. Whatever weirdo cult bullshit Scout had been describing, it couldn't be argued that he and Kayleigh had each other's backs.

"I hear ya," he said, trying for honesty. "I… I really like your brother, okay? I had my reasons for being a douche, but they weren't worth making you both feel like crap. I'm sorry."

She eyeballed him up and down. "What were your reasons?"

"He's being chased by the mob," Scout told her, "because he's got a lucky coin."

She blinked once, but not in disbelief. "Can I see it?"

"Yeah." Lucky pulled it out of his pocket. "But you can't touch it. It… it gets hot when someone not me tries to touch it." He chuckled nastily.

"Scaggs Cawthorne's lieutenant got a big ugly burn on his palm when Scaggs told him to take it from me. It's the only fuckin' thing that kept me alive."

Kayleigh's eyes widened, and he snuck a look at Scout to see what he thought of this.

"Good," Scout said, nodding. "Karma is very cool with magic. In fact, there's one school of thought that says magic is the ultimate karmic leveler. It was practiced to even the odds from the very beginning, and that's why dark magic users are so seriously fucked. The entire purpose of the element of magic is to make sure the little guy has some recourse when he's getting his ass kicked."

"Show me the magic," Kayleigh said, undeterred by Scout's little lapse into philosophy. Wow, she was tough.

Lucky took the coin and set it up to flip. "Is there something you need to know?" he asked.

"Ask it if Alistair's still looking for us," Scout said.

"You told him about *Alistair*?" Kayleigh asked disbelievingly.

"Heads he is," Lucky told him, caught up in the patter. "Tails he ain't." He flipped the coin. "Heads. Fucker ain't given up yet."

"Easy one," Kayleigh muttered. "Ask it if he knows Jordan's coven is intervening." She looked up at Scout. "I'm worried about them. I don't want them to get caught. He could strip away everyone's power—"

"Except Jordan and Mack's," Scout said complacently. "Ask it."

"Heads Alistair knows about the coven, tails he don't." And flip. "Tails it is. Your friends are safe."

He watched Kayleigh's shoulders relax. "Okay, then. Does he know we're here?"

"Heads he knows, tails you're safe," Lucky pattered. The coin flipped, and he put his palm out to catch it, and it didn't fall. Just hovered in the air a little.

"Huh," Scout said, sounding as surprised as Lucky was.

"Uhm," Kayleigh said.

"Sweartachrist it ain't never done that before," Lucky muttered. He frowned. "I think we asked it the wrong question." He reached into the air and grabbed the spinning coin. "C'mere, you." He set up to flip. "Okay. Let's be simpler. Heads he knows, tails he doesn't." Flip. "Tails it is. Alistair doesn't know you're here. Okay. That's good, 'cause he sounds like a *dick*. Now, heads you're safe and tails you got something to worry about out there that could hurt one of you."

Flip.

"Tails," he muttered. Well, shit. "Okay, heads it's Scout, tails it's Kayleigh." And heads. "Kayleigh, you're in luck. Scout, you got to leave."

Scout snorted. "Hell with that. I like it here. Ask it if leaving will make me safe."

Lucky stared at him. "Are you stupid? Something's after you! Of course you're not safe!" God—this guy! Couldn't he see he needed to get the hell off this island? Lucky thought of something happening to Scout's lithe body—and happy, sort of dreamy personality—and his balls got cold, they honest to God did.

"Well, ask it!" Scout told him. He was browning meat in a skillet while he spoke, and Lucky thought he had to have some serious skill there to be doing fancy shit for dinner while he was bossing Lucky around.

"Okay, smart guy. Heads, leaving makes you safe. Tails, you're still in danger." Flip. "Tails. Fuck. Okay, then. Is Scout in danger because of that thing we found today? That… that whozit. The soul trap. Heads, the soul trap is a danger to Scout, tails it's something else."

And the coin hovered in the air again.

Well, shit. He snagged it again, like he would if he was getting cute with the flip. "Heads, the soul trap is the most dangerous thing Scout has to worry about, tails if it's something else."

And heads.

"So we gotta concentrate on the soul trap, and then we gotta worry about the other thing. And it's not your asshole father. Fantastic. Great." He turned to Kayleigh. "Are you happy now? I was having a decent day. I was getting to know your brother, and he's a good guy, and now I'm scared out of my mind for him. I hope you're happy with yourself. I blame you."

Kayleigh stared. "Scout, I cannot fucking *even* with this guy. Do something."

Scout appeared to consider her words carefully before saying, "Lucky, you need to set the patio table because it's the only thing that'll seat the five of us. Kayleigh, get the black and white candles from the closet and set them up in a pentagram around the table. We're going to need protection from magical forces, so figure out a setup, okay?"

She rolled her eyes. "You're impossible. I can't believe you're the only family member besides Macklin I can actually stand." And with that she stomped off, presumably toward the bedroom closet.

Lucky turned to Scout in irritation, actually understanding Kayleigh's ire. "That's it? Set the table and throw a spell around it?"

Scout smiled prettily at him. "Dinner's almost ready. I've cooked my heart out for you guys. The least you could do is eat!"

"Augh!"

"Dishes are in the cupboard by the fridge," Scout told him, happy as a clam. "Silverware is in the drawer underneath."

"You suck!"

Scout turned red. "You don't know that yet," he mumbled, and then Lucky felt his own ears get hot, and he had no response to that but to put his coin in his pocket and go get the bowls.

LUCKY HAD always thought Marcus and Helen were sweet and courtly together, but that's because he'd never once seen them exchange so much as a kiss on the cheek. They usually communicated almost wordlessly, with tilted heads and raised eyebrows and speaking glances. At least in front of him.

But at Scout and Kayleigh's place, Helen knocked on the door with a bottle of wine and was setting it on the table when Marcus came in bearing flowers. Without a word, without even rolled eyes, Kayleigh went to get a vase, and they had wine and flowers when they sat down to eat.

Lucky had never had wine before.

"Not even communion wine?" Helen asked, curious.

Lucky shrugged. It was true much of his neighborhood was Catholic. Even the gangsters went to confession, although that was often because someone in their family was a priest.

"Auntie Cree stayed away from church," he said, thinking about it. "She told stories about the fair folk instead." He thought of his coin, and his cheeks heated. "I guess, given the magic in the family, there may be a reason for that." He glanced at Marcus. "Helen told you about the coin, right?"

Marcus inclined his head. "She did indeed. It's not the only case of small mechanical powers I've seen. I've always felt like there should be more of them."

"Like you should start a school or something," Lucky said, thinking he was being a smartass.

To his surprise, everyone at the table took him seriously, pondering for a moment.

"The book-and-coffee shop would make a perfect place for it," Helen mused. "The problem would be getting the word out."

"Maybe make a specialty shelf of some of the magic books," Marcus suggested. "People often look in small book stores when they have problems with things not brought up in the mainstream."

"Isn't that what the internet is for?" Lucky asked, semisarcastically.

"You had a lot of *luck* with that, uh, *Lucky*?" Kayleigh asked him sweetly.

"You don't let shit go, do you?" he retorted. "I said I was sorry!"

"But you never satisfactorily explained why you did it," she replied. "I get it. You've got the lucky coin. Good for you. Why did that mean you had to be a dick?"

"He didn't want to get attached," Scout replied for him, defending him like a knight in shining armor, actually. "He was being chased by the mob the same way we're worried about being chased by Alistair. I guess he figured out we had the same sort of secret and we'd understand if he had to take off."

Lucky tried giving her his gamest smile, but she shook her head in disgust.

"Fine. But what's he doing here for dinner?"

"Trying to get in your brother's pants," Lucky snapped, causing both Marcus and Helen to spit out their noodles. "Do you mind? It was working."

Kayleigh gaped at him, and he turned back to his own noodles, which were, in a word, delicious. "Sorry, Scout," he muttered. "I feel bad about that, but she needs to drop it."

"She does indeed," Marcus said softly, catching Kayleigh's eye. "For one thing, her dinner is getting cold, and Scout really outdid himself, Kayleigh. And for another, we have more important things to discuss, but perhaps we can bring them up after dessert? I don't know if you noticed, but I brought berry shortcake and whipping cream."

Kayleigh swallowed tightly and sent Lucky a dark look. "I'm just saying, if he hurts my brother, shit's gonna get real."

"Why would I hurt your brother?" Lucky asked, puzzled. "He's been nothing but decent to me."

"Fine." And with that Kayleigh took a bite of her noodles, and Lucky could actually see some of the tension drain out of her muscles. "And dinner really *is* good, Scout. I'm sorry I didn't say anything before."

"No worries," Scout said cheerily. "I'm just glad I'm getting better at it!"

"Practice helps," she said with a small smile. Then she turned to Lucky and made an attempt at civil conversation. "Do you cook?"

Lucky shrugged. "Irish food. I make an amazing corned-beef brisket, and I'm hell on a potato. After that it's shit like mac and cheese and hot dogs or tuna casserole." He shuddered. "Everyone's crazy about tuna casserole—everyone but me. I'm saying, if tuna had been meant to be floating around in cheese and mushroom soup, the ocean would be a very different place."

Scout wrinkled his nose good-naturedly. "Did we ever have tuna casserole?" he asked Kayleigh.

Kayleigh shuddered. "No, Scout, no we did not. Because Alistair, for all his faults, was never that crazy."

Marcus chuckled. "That's probably the nicest thing I've ever heard said about Alistair Quintero."

Lucky's eyes popped open. "*Quintero*. That's what's wrong with your name. You changed it!"

"Not much," Scout said with a lift of his shoulders. "Mostly we didn't want to bring attention to it—sometimes a whole name, spoken out loud, can call someone from a long ways away. Also, the name scares hedge witches, and it should, because Alistair's a dick to them, but we don't want a thing to do with him, so there you go."

"I didn't even know there was such thing as hedge witches," Lucky said curiously.

"That's funny," Helen told him. "It sounds like your Auntie Cree was one. Did she ever leave beer for the wee folk?"

"Yeah," Lucky said, "and a little bit of honey and bread in the corner."

"Anyone who rubs a stone for luck or knows the names and purposes for flowers has the potential to be a hedge witch," Helen said.

"Sometimes they generate real beliefs, real potions, real magic, and sometimes, just believing they have power over their own destinies is magic enough. And most of the time, hedge witch magic is small and personal and of no consequence to Alistair and his ilk. He's busy training wizards and mages and breeding more. But that said, if any hedge witch gets above themself and brought to Alistair's attention, he can make life… uncomfortable for them."

"What can he do?" Lucky asked, more out of curiosity than anything else.

"Well, common practice is to strip a hedge witch's power," Helen said grimly, looking at Marcus for confirmation.

Marcus nodded. "Oh yes. It's cruel. Unnecessarily so."

"Do they have to do bad shit with it?" Lucky asked. He could see that. If you abuse something special, you shouldn't get to have it anymore.

"From what I can see," Scout said glumly, "they mostly just have to bring it to a wizard's attention."

"That was rather our take on it too," Marcus said softly. "Which is one of the reasons Helen and I settled here. The salt water creates a barricade when the tide is up, and something about the island… well, it does rather hide magic users from the mainland."

Lucky frowned. "Except my magic told me to go here," he said.

"Ours too," Scout supplied, and Lucky looked at him sharply, wondering about that story.

"Well, perhaps some of us are invited," Helen said, giving a smile that was a little too serene.

Lucky scowled at her. He loved the old woman—she was feisty, sarcastic, and he'd once seen her stop a shoplifter in his tracks with a little incantation and a wiggle of her fingers. The guy hit the doorway, started to sob, dropped the paperback he'd tried to pocket, and ran wailing down the street like some asshole had kicked his puppy.

He'd also seen her trip a purse snatcher right on the street.

What she never was—and never had been—was serene.

Lucky and Scout met gazes over the dinner table, and Scout winked. Lucky's scowl couldn't hold up against that; it just couldn't. He was too… too *happy* right now to snap at Helen, and Scout's wink seemed to indicate that it would all come out in the end.

"You'll tell me, right?" he asked anxiously. "When it's time."

Helen gave a thoughtful nod, as though she knew how many times Lucky had found out the shitty thing at a shittier moment.

"Lucky, I've got flaws, and one of them is keeping things too close to my vest. I've got some amends to make from keeping too many secrets and leaving people to clean up my mess. Don't worry. Right now, I just want to enjoy my dinner and hear about everybody's day. Eventually, we'll talk more magic, I promise." She turned to Kayleigh with a smile. "Now, my dear, please tell me you have some gossip about the Morgensterns. I need to know old Garth Morgenstern is still as much of an asshole as he's always been."

Kayleigh harrumphed. "*Such* an asshole," she muttered. "I mean, his son, Callan, seems to be trying to fix things. I know it was Callan's doing that I could get off today to try to make Scout's show. But Garth had a big board meeting there today, and I got stuck clearing dishes and food away while they all smoked cigars and talked about ruining the planet." She scowled. "I mean, seriously. They had plans to decimate this protected wildlife refuge in Florida, and not one of them felt bad about bribing the contractor. I'm pretty sure they put the guy in so much debt his family would have lost their house if he didn't break the law for them. It was gross."

Incongruously, Scout chuckled. "Uhm, *had* plans?" he asked slyly.

Kayleigh gave a smile that was all teeth. "*Had* plans," she replied and all but licked her whiskers.

"Oh, Kayleigh," Marcus admonished. "You must be careful."

"Don't worry, I was," she said, not at all contrite. "It was a very subtle spell. They probably all got a little talky after lunch, and by the time they went back to their hotel rooms, they were calling their wives and confessing to all the times they cheated or grabbed ass or something, and by the time they wake up tomorrow, they'll all be absolutely unable to do anything they know is wrong without holding a press conference about it."

"You're so good," Scout said with admiration. "I never would have thought that deviously. I would have done something dumb and gotten caught."

The look Kayleigh sent him was fond. "Naw. You would have tried to cast the same spell I did, and it would have gotten twisted somehow, and by tomorrow, all of the same guys who are going to be sweating through their suits tomorrow would be all sloppy happy instead. They'd all have a bro hug, cancel the deal, go snorkeling together, and resolve never to destroy the environment again. It would be beautiful, big brother. I have no doubts. It just wouldn't be…."

Her pause indicated this was a long-standing script they read from.

"What I planned," Scout said, laughing.

They talked some more, and Lucky got to tell his version of what happened with the table and then hear that Kayleigh had tried to seize control of it when Scout started the trick.

"You were so good," Kayleigh said, nodding. "I was all high from my little success with those numb-brained assholes at Morgenstern's, and then you—you didn't just get control back, you played with me. We played tug of war with it, and I had all the slender kids who loved math, and you had the three-hundred-pound bruisers who lifted their houses in the morning as exercise."

Scout rolled his eyes. "It was a table, Kayleigh, not world peace."

"But I'm saying," she responded, nodding her head sagely, "someday it *could* be."

There was general laughter around the table, and when it was time for dessert, Kayleigh and Lucky cleared the table in grudging concert while Scout went to the refrigerator and got the berry shortcake from the fridge and whipped up some heavy cream with sugar and vanilla in the time it took them to do the dishes.

Then they all sat down with a heaping bowl of whipped cream, berries, and a cake so light it practically floated, and Helen and Marcus met eyes.

"Okay, for starters," Marcus said, looking at Scout and Lucky, "tell us what happened today. Don't leave any detail out, no matter how small."

Lucky looked over at Scout. "Okay, so I'll start. I saw the table thing today, and it hit me that I might not be the only one on the island with a secret. And I felt like a douche, because I should have been nicer to you guys, but, you know, I didn't want to get attached. So I took Scout to that bench—"

"Tom's bench," Helen said softly.

"Yeah. His bench. Anyway, I've always liked the place. I felt like… like something there understood me. And it was private. Not many people go there. So I took Scout, and we had a talk, and… I don't know. I thought it went pretty good." He looked at Scout and willed him to agree, because as much as he wanted to talk about Tom's bench and the soul trap, the things they'd said to each other, the way they'd said them—that felt private.

"I was happy," Scout agreed. "And we did that thing kids do when they're sealing a pact? Spit on our hands to shake on not being dicks."

"Yeah, that," Lucky said. "And then our palms connected and shit got… weird."

"Describe weird," Marcus said ruminatively.

Scout took over, and boy, did he remember everything. From the color of the light when their palms connected to the spell he'd cast to keep the window open so they could memorize what they saw. He remembered every ghost, from the expression on their faces to the clothing they wore to the grief that brought them to that place, and he gave a detailed accounting from beginning to end. When he was finished, he looked at Lucky.

"Did I forget anything?"

Lucky shook his head. "Not that I can remember." He took a breath. "But… but I think there was a, you know, a connecting emotion between all the ghosts there. It's not like you left it out. It's like, you know, you didn't notice it. There was… I mean, all of them were stuck there for one reason or another. Those kids—the couple—getting beat there. I think they got beat to *death* there. Or at least one of them did. The woman scrubbing the bench? Her life stopped when Tom, whoever he was to her, went away. The little girl crying was watching the horizon for the beginning and end of her world. And the guy sitting on the bench—it was the same thing. Everybody we saw, their hearts stopped somehow because of something that happened in that clearing."

There was silence around the table then, and Helen spoke next.

"I think you put your finger on the pulse of it, Lucky. That's the very nature of a soul trap. It's a place in which something *so* heartbreaking happened that it attracted all the souls affected by the heartbreak."

"Wizards say the only way to get rid of them is to strip the place they're in of magic," Scout said. "It's usually—" He glanced apologetically at Kayleigh. "—not great for the actual natural environment surrounding the trap either."

"What happens if we just leave them be?" Lucky said, appalled. As sad—as *heartbroken*—as everyone seemed to be, he thought that they'd rather be sad than to not exist at all.

"That area will keep attracting more and more misfortune," Helen told him. She smiled grimly. "That side of the island used to be much busier. I imagine that bench would have seen much more traffic and much more tragedy, but the Morgensterns built their monstrosity in the 1920s, and it pulled people away from that little memorial. Only those of us who live here and gather on the quieter beaches actually know it's there at all."

"But we can't just… annihilate the place," Lucky said, giving Scout an accusatory look. "And we certainly can't call your old man in. He sounds like a fucking disaster."

"He is, mostly," Scout mumbled. "And I didn't say that was *my* plan. I just said it's what I was always told to do." He gave a tentative smile. "I mean, Kayleigh and I aren't exactly poster children for doing what we're told."

"Indeed you are not," Marcus said with a faint smile.

"So what do *you* want to do?" Kayleigh asked.

Marcus and Helen exchanged glances. "Well, we always thought that soul traps were… well, they're an opportunity to do some good," Helen said after a moment. "But as for what kind of good, that depends on each soul. It would mean we'd have to do some research. Find out who Tom was, perhaps. Find out which spirits would be hanging out at the bench. And then, quite simply, talk to them, see what we can do to lay them to rest. Perhaps it's simply moving their bones, or maybe it's discovering a crime. The two of you saw four different mysteries on that bench—maybe more. If we could… could unravel each mystery, lay the souls to rest, perhaps the place would only be haunted by memories and not by souls anymore."

Kayleigh's mouth had formed a little moue of enchantment. "Really? So like solving a mystery? And casting spells and… like, taking all our power and *doing* something with it? Can we do that?" She turned to Scout. "Can we? Can we?"

"Can Lucky help too?" Scout asked, and Lucky grinned at him, as enchanted as Kayleigh but by something else entirely. "Lucky, do you want to help? Do you want to do this? We could look up old spells and research families and—"

Marcus held up his hands. "Stop, my children. I need you to hear us out."

Walking Home

SCOUT VOLUNTEERED to walk Helen and Lucky home, which was mostly across the quad, only to be met with an arch look from Marcus.

"Helen will be staying with me in the cottage tonight," he said kindly. "But you may walk Lucky back to his flat if you like."

Scout was pretty sure he blushed like a cartoon character. Cartoon characters were something he and Kayleigh hadn't had much experience with—their television viewing had been limited to nature documentaries and the history channel—but the two of them had been making up for lost time since they'd arrived at the island.

"Kayleigh and I were going to watch cartoons tonight," he told Lucky after Marcus and Helen left. He sent Kayleigh a hopeful look. "Do you want to stay a bit and join us?"

Lucky looked… surprised.

"Uhm… cartoons?"

"We're trying to make up for the cultural deprivation of our youth," Kayleigh said with a straight face. "Tonight, it's *Despicable Me*, one and two, although I understand there are more with those cute little yellow things in them."

"Minions," Scout supplied. "Muahahahahaha!"

That earned him another one of those sort of gooey looks from Lucky, and Scout figured he had an in.

"Uh, sure. I wasn't doing nothing but a book anyhow." Lucky took a deep breath and gave a fair attempt at grace. "I guess this is what I missed by being an ass hat when you first got here, right?"

"Yeah," Kayleigh said, absolutely unmerciful. "Try not to be a dick next time"

"Understood."

Scout and Kayleigh ran to their room to get some of their favorite purchases: big fluffy blankets meant exclusively for snuggling under when they were on the couch. When they came back, they turned on the television that Marcus claimed had come with the apartment but that Kayleigh insisted he'd had installed the day they'd moved in, and hit the remote.

"You've got a streaming service?" Lucky asked as Kayleigh made herself comfortable on one corner of the couch and Scout took the opposite side. The furniture was all wicker based with woven cotton pillows done in blue or green, and while it might not have been as sturdy as the oak stuff at the compound, Scout was so much more comfortable on it.

This furniture didn't judge him if he forgot to take off his shoes or if he was wearing the wrong outfit with dinner.

"We've got a couple," Kayleigh said, surprised. "Marcus has them at the cottage, and I guess we're certified users." She managed to look a little embarrassed. "I sort of get the feeling that he felt responsible for giving us a crash course in modern life when we got here. We were damned near Amish, except not as sweet and not as…." She waved her hands around under her fluffy pink throw.

"As useful," Scout supplied dryly. "At least the Amish can milk a cow or churn butter or build barns or something. We couldn't do any of that, *and* we were damned near unemployable." He gave Lucky a hopeful smile as he stood in front of the couch and scanned the furniture in the room. There wasn't much—the couch, a chair that was part of the set, and a giant beanbag chair that was on top of a plush area rug. "You can sit with me," he said, batting his eyelashes. "The throw's pretty big."

He held the throw off his lap and gestured next to him, gratified when Lucky sank down on the cushion.

"Are we snuggling now?" Lucky asked suspiciously. "I'm not sure if I know how to snuggle."

"I think you just need to lean back against me under the same cover," Scout said, wrapping his arm around Lucky's chest, "and then put up with all our stupid questions about the movie and remember that we're almost Amish."

Lucky snorted. "You do know the Amish would probably burn you witches at the stake, right?"

Scout gave a delighted cackle. "Well, we're more mages, but yeah. Anyway, just…." And he hated the vulnerability in his voice, but, well, things you couldn't change. "Don't laugh at us, okay? There's lots of things we don't know."

Lucky wriggled back against him and said, "Yeah, well, one of the things you don't know is that these are two of my favorite movies. So no laughing at you guys, but push Play. I want to hear you laugh."

"Why?" Kayleigh asked suspiciously.

"Because he laughs like Santa Claus, and it's really weird coming out of a skinny dancer guy. I could listen to him laugh forever."

Kayleigh blinked her amazing brown eyes at him, and her face softened for the first time since she'd nearly caught the two of them kissing. "Okay. You might not suck. Go ahead and sprawl a little. You can have both our blankets. It gets chilly in here."

Scout gave her his happiest smile over Lucky's head. She rolled her eyes and pressed Play.

Lucky was a *wonderful* person to watch a movie with. Scout had never thought about that as a good quality in a potential companion, but it turned out to be key. He could explain all sorts of things: the James Bond trope, the supervillain, even Girl Scout cookies, which were parodied in the film. By the time they'd finished the movie, Kayleigh wanted to watch it again, because she was pretty sure it would be even funnier the second time, now that they knew more.

Scout agreed, thinking the same thing, but he forgot that Lucky had the morning shift at the coffee shop. Not that Lucky complained, but about a quarter of the way through the second viewing, Scout realized that Lucky's sturdy, vital weight against his shoulder had become limp and heavy, and that the man had fallen asleep on him.

I'll wake him when the movie's done, he thought, and that was the last thing *he* remembered before he fell asleep.

A few hours later he woke up lying flat on the sofa with Lucky tucked against him, still sleeping in his arms. They were covered with both the couch throws, and the only light was the ambient light through the sliding glass window to the patio. For a moment, that's what dominated his thoughts, the feeling of that warm, trusting body in his arms and the way his own body wanted to touch it more.

Naked.

Mmm…. He stretched, pushing himself even closer, gratified when Lucky wriggled back against him. Nice. So nice.

Hoping Kayleigh had gone to bed, he started to glance around the room to see what had woken him up. Something… something tickled on the edge of his brain. There had been a whisper. His name.

The moon was full with only a few scudding clouds for company, illuminating their living room almost brighter than it had been when the television had been on. For a moment, Scout allowed his eyes to drift closed again, with the vague thought of setting an alarm for Lucky when he had to get up to pee, as he often did in the middle of the night.

Then he saw it—a faint cloud of light particles, coalescing in the center of the room.

His eyes flew open, and his first thought was to shake Lucky awake so he could see the magic too, but a figure in the center, blurry, wrapped in pixilated tulle, held transparent fingers to the suggestion of lips, and Scout was suddenly paralyzed. He couldn't move. He couldn't speak. He could only stare at the figure bobbing gently in the center of the room.

It was gesturing for him to follow it, and without knowing quite how, he did.

He and the ghost light skimmed the ground, the sliding glass door yielding like water to his touch but leaving him dry. They bobbed down the street, the cobblestones smooth as soft concrete under his feet, no threat of twisting ankles to make him mind his step.

Down the tide wall, much as Lucky had brought him, out the thruway, and they were on the beach, heading for Tom's bench, and he was suddenly afraid.

The last time he'd been there, he'd been there with Lucky, and they'd been okay. But this time he was alone, and it was dark, and nobody knew where he was. He hesitated, and the cold iron burn on his wrist told him that the presence, whatever it was, wanted him to come closer, and so he did, close enough to peer into the bench clearing from the outside.

Close enough to see the four separate tableaux, the grieving washerwoman, the heartbroken young man, the disconsolate young girl, the terrified couple, all of them living their same separate hells again and again and again.

But unlike last time, he was not *inside* the tableau, trapped with those in its throes. He was outside, and he saw a dark thing with many arms, like a tree, and a yawing mouth where its face, neck, and torso should have been.

Terrible and huge, it stretched those treelike arms around the clearing, hugging it close, and Scout realized that *this* was the thing keeping everybody trapped. *This* was the presence keeping these poor souls stuck in their worst moment, their helplessness, for time without end.

And now it was looking at him, its entire form an absence of light. Around it, stars twinkled and the moonlight bounced off the water, but inside it was simply void—no starlight, no moon, not even the memory of the sun. It was vast and empty, and its presence seemed to suck all of the warmth, all of the remembered laughter, out of Scout's very marrow.

Its posture changed, and Scout knew it had seen him and his ghostly companion.

He turned to run, only to find that cold-iron grip around his wrist had tightened.

Free them came the voice in his head, and as he turned back to the soul trap, his friendly light diffused itself through the clearing, and for a moment he saw….

A happy mother, who had once swung her brown-haired, brown-eyed son in a playful arc while he screamed "Again, again, again!"

An excited child, playing the same game with a boy who must have been the son grown older. The boy stopped their whirling circles, and they fell to the sandy ground, laughing while she planted kisses on his cheek and they giggled.

The little girl, grown now, turning her face up to a kiss from her first lover, which he gently delivered.

Two young men, one of them the boy with the mother and the sister, sitting on the beach in front of what was now the clearing, leaning shoulder to shoulder as they stared into a clear night sky.

Free them! came the voice, panicked now, just as the presence clamped down on the light from the visions and then turned, roaring, toward Scout.

Scout screamed and tried to run, but he was wrapped in the iciness of a capsizing winter sea.

HE WOKE up screaming and gasping on the couch, limbs flailing as he shoved the hapless Lucky off the edge.

He was soaking wet, so cold he could see the blueness of his own fingers, and the couch was awash in seawater. Seaweed fanned the ground.

"Holy fucknoodles!" Lucky shouted, scrambling to his feet. "What in the hell…?"

But Scout was shivering too hard to even speak, and as Lucky drew near, he pulled Scout's hands into his, rubbing them furiously to bring back some warmth.

"Oh my God, Scout. What happened?"

Scout was vaguely aware that Kayleigh had rushed in and was breaking out old towels and the mop to try to control the mess, her voice rising to hypersonic levels as she demanded to know what was going on.

Scout could only shake his head, accepting Lucky's touch gratefully, aware that every rub of Lucky's hands helped to bring the feeling tingling back into his extremities.

"Scout," Lucky said gently. "Scout, man, you've got to open your hand up, okay? Open up… relax…. Oh. Oh damn. Kayleigh, come look at this!" he called frantically.

Scout managed to focus on the object Lucky had pulled from his clenched fist.

"What in the hell…?" Kayleigh murmured. She took the ring—for that's what it was—from Lucky and peered at it. A simple circle of gold, like a wedding ring, it said *Tom's.*

"Oh wow," Lucky said, breathing out his awe as they all stared at the thing in Kayleigh's palm. "Scout, what did you do?"

"I had a dream," he chattered. "And now I'll never be warm again!"

"Shower," Kayleigh said decisively. "Now. Lucky, get over your maidenly modesty and help him out of his things. I'll clean up the mess, and we'll figure out what to do when we're done." She sighed. "I really love this couch. I hope it dries off."

Scout found himself being half dragged, half shoved to the bathroom, and when they got there, Lucky was surprisingly confident about undressing him as the water ran hot.

"S-s-s-omehow I-I-I thought this would be…." His teeth chattered particularly hard when Lucky unbuttoned his jeans and then shoved them down his hips.

"Yeah, well, I had dreams about romance too," Lucky muttered. "And I was having them on that couch until you disappeared and then reappeared wearing half the ocean. Now lean on me and lift your foot out of your jeans. God, your feet look like they've been through wars. Dancing ain't for the weak."

Scout did as ordered, sighing blissfully when Lucky pulled back the curtain and helped him into the shower cubicle. Oh God, oh God, oh God. He was shaking so hard he couldn't even risk speaking, and his vision went dark with the pain and relief of warmth returning to his limbs.

Finally, just when the water was starting to cool off a little, he felt like he could stagger out of the shower on his own power, but Lucky was there for him with a big fluffy towel.

"Your sister's got the space heater going in your room," he said, rubbing Scout's limbs down and scrupulously avoiding looking at the rest of his body. Well, on the one hand, Scout had *liked* being checked out when he was changing that afternoon—he could admit it—but on the other hand, he wasn't flirting right now. He was vulnerable and a little helpless, and he appreciated the respect.

Lucky kept that firm, sturdy arm around his shoulders, helping him to the room and sitting him on the bed while he found a new pair of briefs and some warm sweats. It wasn't until he was dragging the sweatpants up Scout's thighs that Scout found words.

"Stay," he muttered, finally registering Lucky's hands on his skin. "Borrow my pajamas and stay with me tonight. I-I promise I won't follow any more fairy lights into the darkness. Just…." His teeth started chattering again.

"Yeah. Stay. I got it," Lucky said. He patted Scout's cheek like he would a little kid's. "Although what you need me for when you got your ferocious sister, I'll never know."

Scout captured Lucky's hand as it rested on his cheek. "You're not my sister," he said, some warmth suffusing his body. "I don't want to… to hit on you now, but…." It was so embarrassing to say.

"You don't want me to leave either," Lucky acknowledged humbly. His thumb skated restlessly over Scout's cheekbone, and Scout's eyes drifted closed. He was sitting half-naked on his bed, and he slumped a little, sideways, as though only the ice in his body had been keeping him upright.

"Here," Lucky said, as though he'd spoken. "Let's get you dressed and under the covers. I'll see if your sister needs any help, and then you and I will resume the snuggle."

He followed through on his words with actions, and Scout recalled a period of lying in bed, shivering badly, before he heard the hum of the space heater his sister must have broken out from the closet. Then there was some rustling in the room, and Lucky's sturdy body slid in bed behind him. Lucky wrapped his arm around Scout's chest and his leg around Scout's thighs, and finally—*finally*—the shivering abated, and Scout's exhausted, racing mind began to slow down.

The last clear thought he had before he fell asleep was that there *had* to be an easier way to get Lucky in his bed.

Worry

LUCKY WORKED the coffee shop counter on autopilot, and while he was sharp enough not to get swamped in a bog of mistakes, he was preoccupied enough to be brought down to earth in the rudest of ways.

"Oh my God, he *is* hot! The Great Gestalt, right?" said a female voice, young and giggly and belonging to a girl who was maybe eighteen, getting coffee with her friend.

"Yeah! Just reading in the back of the store!" The friend was a little older, and male. Maybe a brother or cousin. "He's even hotter in person!"

"Should we, like, go get his autograph?" asked the girl.

"We should at least go see what he's reading," said older cousin. "I mean, I like old bookstores, don't you?"

She laughed again, and Lucky tried not to be jealous of a teenaged tourist with the giggles. Scout had gotten kicked out of the house for not being interested in that kind of thing, but the older cousin… that was something else entirely.

For one thing, he wasn't giggly. He had a rich-guy's voice—sort of like Scout's, actually, but snootier. And he was cute. Tall, blond, green-eyed, clean cut, very sporty in a rich-guy way. His name was probably Tad, Lucky thought uncharitably, or worse, Justin.

Except this guy would wear that name like Lucky never could.

"Hi," said his next customer, another teenager, this one a rather shy, gawky boy. "I'd like, uhm, a caramel frappe or whatever you call them. Something sweet that doesn't taste like coffee that'll, uhm—"

Lucky had to spare the kid a brain cell. He wore his hair long enough to cover his eyes and looked desperately uncomfortable. "Wake you the hell up?" he asked, feeling acute sympathy. He needed six of those himself.

"God, please?" the kid begged.

"Sure. Coming right up."

He tried to keep focused as he made the kid his sugary caffeinated goodness, but it was tough. Kayleigh had been the one who'd shaken him gently that morning, telling him apologetically that his pocket was beeping and he probably needed to go get ready for his job.

He'd rolled out of bed and double-checked to make sure Scout was cocooned safely under the stacks of blankets. He was—pretty much only his nose and mouth peeked out from under the covers—and Lucky dropped a kiss on his swaddled forehead before scurrying out of there and heading for his flat under the store. The last thing Kayleigh had said to him was that they'd be in around eleven, so when he was ready to take his break, they could talk.

He hadn't been ready to see them walk in at ten thirty, both of them looking tired and frowzy but okay.

They'd ordered their coffee—large, with cream and sugar but nothing fancy—and then Kayleigh had dropped a kiss on Scout's cheek and run out of the store with a wave. Lucky assumed she'd gotten an unexpected shift at her own job, and then the weekend ferry had docked, and Lucky had been too busy to even go back and ask Scout about it. Usually the Saturday morning rush died pretty hard by eleven, but Lucky was very aware that Scout had to go perform at twelve.

He wanted his break before then, and he *didn't* want Mr. Super-hot Rich Guy and his giggly cousin to have a chance to go seduce Lucky's innocent, awkward, super-sweet magician with the dancer's body and the dreamy eyes.

If Lucky had any idea how to work those moves himself, he was damned sure Scout wouldn't have been distracted enough by ghosts in the living room to follow them out to the damned beach.

He'd finished up the kid's frappe and gotten him change when he realized that finally, *finally*, there was no more line and Helen was working on restocking.

"Go say hi, Lucky," she said softly. "I can tell you want to."

Lucky had relayed the whole "Scout disappeared and then reappeared with half of the Atlantic," story as they'd opened that morning. She'd been concerned, but he'd been very aware that everything from his body language to his voice had been borderline hysterical.

Finally, Helen had stopped him cold by saying, "Lucky, he was fine. Remember, Scout and Kayleigh deal with big magic all the time. It's not quite so scary for them."

Lucky had glared at her, and she'd reconsidered.

"Was this why you didn't want to get attached?" she asked after a moment, her voice hesitant.

He'd shifted uncomfortably and remembered the first time he'd met Scout—or really, had run away from meeting him.

"People are hard," he'd said at last, miserable. "I'm pretty sure you only get one."

Her face softened. "I think that's dangerous," she said after a moment. "I thought like that for the longest time. And then… then I got in a fight with my one and I thought I had none. I wronged a lot of people—an entire coven of witches, it turned out—because when I realized I couldn't deal with my own mess by myself, I just left them. Deserted them, because I knew that my mess would destroy me. They fixed it themselves, and I… well, I've got a lot of karma to make up for since then. Don't make that mistake, Lucky. Don't limit yourself to only one person. Embrace as many as you can, and remember to forgive. Trust me. You'll be happier if that's a lesson you can learn."

Lucky had stared at her then and had wanted more details, but at that point people had started to come in, and he'd been locked with that, with Scout and the feel of Scout's body against his, and his worry, all swirling around in his stomach.

Sure, he may have wanted the big triple-caffeinated dessert thingy, but the odds were even that it would also make him throw up.

Which was why he was judicious when he chose the bran muffin for himself and the chocolate croissant for Scout before he practically jogged to the back of the store.

What he found there made him relax a tad.

Scout was hunched over a book, so close it looked like he was about to fall asleep between its pages, and Mr. Clean-cut Snooty-voice was trying desperately to get his attention.

"Uhm, there's a light over here. Uhm, Gestalt? I mean, that can't really be your name, right? But you're welcome to come sit here with my cousin and me."

Lucky slowed as he neared the end of the bookshelf that led to the reading niche just to see what Scout's reaction would be. It turned out Scout was one of those people who could read through bombs going off around him. He hadn't noticed the flirty rich guy at all.

Right when Lucky was about to pop his head out from behind the bookshelf, the girl gave the flirty rich guy an impatient kick in the shins and a meaningful glance. He scowled at her, but then, after a furtive look around the reading niche, blinked three times at the torchiere lamp that sat behind Scout's table. The lamp clicked up about three notches brighter, and Scout's shoulders relaxed. Lucky could hear an actual sigh of relief coming from him as he yawned and rubbed his eyes and then went back to reading.

Lucky looked back to flirty rich guy, who grimaced sheepishly at his cousin and shook his head, and Lucky suddenly understood.

No, Scout wasn't paying him any attention, but he'd needed the extra light, and flirty rich guy could fix that with his one small magic. So he did.

Lucky swallowed, suddenly feeling like a heel. Scout had proven himself oblivious to pretty much everybody *but* Lucky, and Lucky had to trust in that.

"Here," he said, going to flirty rich guy and his cousin. They both startled guiltily, as though afraid they might have gotten caught doing something wrong, and he pushed on through, pretending he hadn't seen a thing. "I've got an extra bran muffin and an extra chocolate croissant from the counter. You guys game?"

"Ooh, those look good," the girl said, smiling at her cousin. "Yes, please. Are you sure it's okay?"

Lucky nodded and set the pastries down at their table. "I'm gonna go get my boyfriend a refill and bring him his own breakfast. You guys enjoy."

With that, he turned and put his hand on Scout's shoulder. "What do you want to eat?" he asked gently, and Scout blinked up at him as though he were coming awake from a long sleep.

"What you just fed them," he said softly. "But if you're out of chocolate, I'll take almond."

Lucky opened his mouth, not sure what to say, but Scout blinked and squeezed the hand on his shoulder. "Go get our breakfast, Lucky. I'll be here when you get back."

When he returned, after making sure to pay for the two comped pastries, he slid his and Scout's on the table in front of him and looked over to where lightning guy was sitting—alone now.

"Where's your cousin?" he asked.

Lightning guy shrugged. "Your modern romance section, I suspect." He gave Scout a meaningful look, and Scout winked at Lucky.

"I may have mentioned we saw his little trick," Scout said quietly. "And that we had a theory."

"Little magic," Lucky said promptly, trusting Scout. "Little tools in the magic chest. Some of us have 'em. It was nice of you to help him out when he wasn't giving you the time of day."

Lightning had the grace to blush. "I had no idea he was taken," he mumbled, looking uncomfortable.

Goddammit. Lucky might not be able to hate this asshole.

"Well, it's new," Lucky conceded. He gave Scout a fond look. "And he wasn't making it easy on you." He sighed. "I'm Lucky. Nice to meet you."

He stuck out his hand, and snooty rich guy shook it. "Piers," he said, and Lucky grunted.

"Can't I just call you Lightning?" he asked. Or "snooty rich guy." Because Piers. Seriously? No.

"The name is not my fault," Piers said, grimacing. "So sure. Lightning is fine." He smiled a little. "I might actually prefer it."

"This here's Scout," Lucky said. "Shake his hand. We can't talk about the book now anyway."

Piers smiled winningly and stuck out his hand, which Scout shook dutifully.

"Why can't we talk about the book?" Scout asked. He glanced at Piers—*Lightning*—and frowned before looking at Lucky. "Trust him or not?"

Lucky gave Piers a smile that was all teeth and then disappeared behind the bookshelf and took out his coin. "Heads we trust him, tails we don't."

Heads it was.

He came back from around the bookshelf and said, "Tell him, Scout. I got seven minutes left on my break, and I want this over with."

"You'll need more than seven minutes!" Scout blurted, and then at Lucky's exasperated look began to talk. "The book I'm reading is about ghostly apparitions and their meaning," he said. "And yes, they're real." He grimaced at Lucky. "That's what I saw last night. Here, look."

He held the book open and shoved it across the table at Lucky, who scanned the text. It appeared to have been typed and published on an old linotype press with handwritten notes in the margins.

The illustration he was looking at consisted of a sprinkling of dots with a suggestion of a human figure in the center, made up of a denser application of dots.

"That's what appeared to you when you were asleep?" Lucky asked. He shivered—*that* would have freaked him out.

"It's a Wisp, I think. The book isn't great at naming things. Just says, 'Hey, this is what it looks like and sort of what it does.' Anyway, it says here they show up in the twilight stages between sleeping and waking," Scout told him, running his finger along the text. "And that's where I was. And it appeared and wanted me to follow it. I-I guess I… uhm, my sleeping self? My unconscious self? Followed it."

"So it felt like you were still behind me on the couch," Lucky said, thinking. "And then what happened?"

"Well, it took me to the place, and—" Scout started to thumb through the book quickly, obviously looking for something he'd seen before. "—I saw the four tableaux, the different pictures of people locked in grief, and then, standing over them, I saw this."

"Bwah!" Lucky said it, and Lightning echoed it over his shoulder.

"That's terrifying!" Lightning gasped, his lean, tanned body shuddering all over. "You saw that?"

"I think it attacked him, didn't it, Scout?"

Scout swallowed, visibly shaken, his Adam's apple bobbing with distress. "Worse than that—it *saw* me. It turned and *saw* me, and *ate* me, and submerged me in the ocean!"

Lightning made a sound of disbelief, and Lucky turned to him, as deadly serious as Scout had been.

"No, seriously. One second he was lying right behind me and warm and breathing, and the next he was in the same place but sopping wet, like he'd been dumped on the couch with half the ocean. There was seaweed on the floor, and his fingers were blue. It was that fast."

Lightning sucked in a breath of absolute surprise.

And belief.

"That's… that's terrifying," he said, looking from Lucky to Scout and back again. "What do you think happened?"

"It's a long story," Scout said, his hand clenched on Lucky's knee in an unconscious reaction to fear. Lucky put his hand over Scout's and squeezed, unsure how he'd gotten so comfortable being Scout's wooby so quickly. He decided he didn't hate it. Scout had this perfectly nice Lightning guy willing to hit on him—or mother him—and the person he'd looked to had been Lucky.

And Lucky didn't want it to be anybody else. In fact, he might rip anybody else's throat out, which was why he was glad Lightning hadn't been a total douchebag.

"And we don't have that much time," Lucky said, reminding him. "You go on in half an hour, and I've got to get back."

Scout sighed. "Will you be off when I'm done?" he asked hopefully, and Scout hated to dash that hope.

"Sorry. Helen needs me until pretty much when the boat leaves on Saturdays, but you can come in the store and talk while we're closing down."

Scout's crestfallen expression brightened a little. "It's Kayleigh's turn to cook," he said. "Movies?"

Gah! He was so cute! Lucky kissed his mouth, hard enough to mean it but not sloppy, because they didn't have time for sloppy no matter how much he wanted sloppy and all over the place and handsy.

"Movies," he agreed. "This time, we watch *The Incredibles.* It'll be *great*!"

Scout's happiness practically radiated off of him, and Lucky was about to turn to walk away when he noticed Lightning looking a little depressed.

"How long you here, rich boy?"

"Until the Thanksgiving holidays—I hope," Piers said, shuddering. "My cousin—Larissa, you saw her—is…." He let out a sigh. "She has a stalker," he muttered, obviously sure it was too outlandish for them to believe. "And he's… he's violent. She barely got away last time, and the police won't do anything. Our parents have money, and I sort of dropped out of school and took my trust fund and swept her here." He shuddered and checked over his shoulder to where he could see her long swing of dark brown hair around the corner. "The Morgensterns are friends of my parents, and I don't know what else to do to keep her safe while my folks try to get this guy taken care of."

Lucky held up a finger. "I'll, uh, be back in a second."

Thank you, thank you, magic coin.

He came back and murmured in Scout's ear, "Stalker doesn't know where she is right now, but he's searching for her. Coin says we've got about three weeks."

Scout pulled in a breath and nodded. "She's safe for now," he told Lightning. "But I think the lot of us have a *lot* to talk about." He looked at Lucky with a sigh. "Later."

Lucky kissed him again—for luck—and went back to helping Helen behind the counter.

This time he was fully awake, if not more worried than he had been before. But he kept remembering the one thing that should have been completely irrelevant in all of that.

He'd used the word "boyfriend," which, in his mind, was completely unwarranted and premature. But Scout hadn't batted an eyelash.

SCOUT WAS left looking at their new friend, unsure if that's how friends were made.

Lucky had been different. Scout had been intrigued by Lucky from the very beginning. He'd seen that sturdy, purposeful figure, that vitality, and had been attracted—had wanted to know him better.

Their conversation under the waving cypress trees had been awkward and bitter and revelatory in a way that had not been entirely comfortable.

But what had been left when Lucky's defenses had been stripped away had been everything Scout had ever dreamed of, and the night before, without the supernatural out-of-body journey, of course, had been the simplest, most perfect romantic moment of Scout's life.

He knew why Lucky had come bustling into the back room, throwing his energy around and using a word like "boyfriend" when they were still too new for that. It was because Lucky didn't want to share.

Scout was fine with that. Piers—Lightning—was a very nice kid, in Scout's opinion, but in the romance area, Lucky didn't have anything to worry about.

The Wisp, on the other hand, and the angry thing guarding the spirit trap, however… well, Scout was worried.

"So, uhm, how does he know my cousin will be safe?" Lightning asked, intruding on his thoughts.

Scout looked up from his book distractedly. "He's got ways," he said vaguely, and then realizing that Piers and Larissa might need more than that, he added, "The same way you probably have never had to walk into a dark room in your life."

Lightning shrugged his shoulders. "My father didn't believe in night-lights. I got scared. I don't know. I guess I started to make my own."

Scout's distraction changed to focus. "You have one of those too?"

"One of what?"

"One of the 'toughen up and be a man' fathers?"

Lightning grunted. "I wish I could say you're way off base, but…." He shrugged. "At least he's okay with the gay thing. And he and Mom were one hundred percent behind my idea to keep Larissa safe until they could have PIs track down her stalker. But yeah. He was tough on us."

"Well, you're lucky," Scout told him, casting a glance through the bookshelves to see the *real* Lucky serving coffee to a sweet little old couple who practically lived on the island during the cooler winter months. "Not everybody is fortunate enough to have a father who cares."

Lightning followed his gaze. "I take it you're not speaking just for yourself?"

Scout shrugged. "Let's say this island has a way of attracting people who don't want to be found." He looked back at the book again and sighed. "I really hope when I'm done here, I won't take away some of the protection it offers."

"What are you trying to do there?" Lightning asked.

Scout was going to brush him off, and then he paused. Scout and Lucky could see the soul trap; he wondered if anyone else could too. Could Kayleigh? Could Lightning's cousin? Could Lightning himself?

"Actually," he said thoughtfully, "after I'm done with work and Lucky's done with his shift, maybe you and Larissa would want to help us in a little experiment."

Lightning smiled, clearly excited to be included. "That sounds great! Would it be…?" His voice dropped, and he looked around furtively, as though total strangers might have suddenly appeared around them. "Would it, you know, involve something like my light thing?"

Scout nodded. "It might indeed," he said mysteriously before taking a sip of the coffee Lucky had left him.

Lucky had added a pump or two of something that Scout had never thought of. It was, of course, delicious.

"HE'S IMPROVED even more," Helen remarked as they watched Scout's performance from across the quad.

"I thought it was just me," Lucky said, pleased. It wasn't like he, Lucky, had magical kisses or something so that suddenly Scout was as outstanding a magician as he probably was a mage, or whatever it was that Scout and Kayleigh *were* that could do the things he knew Scout and Kayleigh could do.

"Except it *is*, isn't it?" Helen asked, giving him a thorough once-over. "Look at him. He's got a confidence he's been lacking. Did you give him that?"

Lucky shook his head, not so sure. "Naw, I think he's always had that. Maybe he's sort of figured out he can do more than he thought."

"Well, that's confidence, Lucky." She looked at him kindly. She was wearing a Beach Broad T-shirt today, one of many snarky shirts that Lucky had seen, and he wondered again at her backstory. "Why are you so reluctant to take any credit for his new attitude?"

Lucky grunted. "Because I'm unreliable at best, Auntie," he said, the old habit of calling women like his grandmother Auntie not going away anytime soon. It had been a title of deference—not given to *every* older woman he knew, but to the ones whose word had carried weight in the neighborhood. "You know that I may have to kite the hell out of here, and it would suck to leave him alone if I'm giving him something he needs."

"Well, maybe he's enough of a mage to help you out of your jam," she said. "Did you ever think that?"

"I don't want to use him like that!" Lucky protested, almost embarrassed to realize he hadn't even thought of it.

She sighed with exaggerated patience. "Lucky, you obviously care for him. It was apparent from the very beginning, even when you were avoiding him and Kayleigh like mad. You watched his show every day, honey. And I saw the way you two smiled at each other when he walked into the store. You can be many things, *Justin*. Surly, irritable, pessimistic. But I didn't think dishonest was one of them. You and that boy mean something to each other already, and that meaning is making him better at his craft."

"Isn't that… I don't know. Doesn't that violate the rules of something? Like we're supposed to be all independent and actualized and shit?"

She snorted delicately. "I don't think it's bad if another person brings out the best in us. As long as we remember it's there should they leave."

Lucky shuddered, remembering the panic of finding Scout gone the night before—and the terror of having him back, but freezing and incoherent with cold and fear.

"What?" Helen asked. "What's that look?"

Lucky was quiet for a moment as Scout tried a pass of his hand over three metal balls in his other hand. In the past, he'd been able to get the three balls to stand up in his palm, one on top of the other, spinning enough to see across the quad.

He did the pass of his hand, and the three balls remained static on his palm, doing nothing. He narrowed his eyes and looked out into the crowd. Kayleigh was there this time, and Scout saw the minute shake of her head.

Scout's eyes narrowed, and his hair rose up in a crackle of electricity that the entire crowd could see. Then he looked out across the quad and gave Lucky a smile of bared teeth and bravado and winked.

Very slowly, as deliberate as Scout's toe-stand the day before, the balls rose, one after the other, until they performed their delicate dance on Scout's palm. Then Scout gave a grim smile, a sort of gutsy, Philly, nobody-fucks-with-me smile that did *amazing* things to Lucky's body from half a block away. Under Scout's narrow-eyed concentration, each of the stainless-steel balls rose—not far, about three inches apiece—until they were *hovering* over the palm of his hand and there existed a visible space between each one.

The crowd caught its collective breath, and as a united whole, erupted into applause.

Lucky was the only one who saw the near miss.

The three balls jerked as though wrestling from Scout's control, and Scout made a decisive gesture with his free hand to call them back. There was a silent back-and-forth—Lucky could read it in the clenching of Scout's jaw and the furtive, terrified look he sent the crowd—and Lucky suddenly understood the very real peril.

He'd seen those props in the magic shop. They were the same "stress balls" anybody could get in a novelty store: weighted, chrome plated, and smooth.

If Scout gave up control they would cease to be props and instead become three very heavy projectiles, hurtling through a sea of soft flesh and brittle bone.

He wasn't trying to keep his dignity here; he was trying to keep his magic trick from becoming a mass-casualty event.

The crowd must have sensed something. Perhaps, they thought, another trick, and Scout didn't let them down. With a dramatic gesture of his hands, he rose to one toe, his other pointed at his knee as though he were about to start a pirouette. He swung his foot, looking as if pulling momentum into his body, when Lucky knew that all his momentum was going to have to come from his torso and arms, but the entire time he was staring at the chrome balls that he held under his control by force of will alone.

And then, swinging his shoulder but keeping his hands fixed, the balls between them, he began to whirl.

Lucky could never figure out if he used magic to propel himself in a series of pirouettes or if the pirouettes helped to steady his magic, but Scout did them both, swinging his leg and his shoulders and keeping the balls scrupulously in his control. One, two, three, and with a grand rotating gesture of both hands, he whirled the spheres around, using the momentum built up by whatever opposing force had been fighting him, and hurled the projectiles over the heads of the crowd, over the guardrail of the tide wall, and far, far out into the empty water.

Lucky was still staring at him when he saw Scout give a little twist to his fingers to set the balls aflame, and the crowd *ooh*ed and *ahh*ed as they trailed rainbow fire in their wake like meteors, exploding into puffs of red, yellow, and blue smoke at the horizon.

People were still applauding as they marched onto the ferry, and Marcus sold out of the "galaxy balls" in about five minutes.

And Lucky had to run downstairs to change into a fresh T-shirt, because his own was sopped with sweat just *watching* something like that.

Fallout

AN HOUR after his performance, when the crowd had finally cleared from the magic store and Marcus had locked up, Scout walked into Helen's, and Lucky almost knocked him over.

Scout hadn't been expecting it—Lucky had seemed so grounded, so imperturbable. He'd thought maybe a peck on the cheek or a worried glance across the coffee shop, but what he got was Lucky ripping off his apron in the middle of taking an order and barreling into Scout with the fierceness of an angry bear. The hug went on until Scout was pretty sure his bones cracked.

"Uhm…." And he wasn't sure what the fuss was about, but oh wow. Being held like that, flush against Lucky's sturdy body, held like Lucky would never let him go—that was heady stuff. "What's wrong?" he asked weakly, wrapping his arms around Lucky and holding him back.

Lucky's grip relaxed enough that he was no longer uncomfortable, and Lucky groaned.

"I saw that," he whispered gruffly. "I saw what you did. You were a fuckin' hero, man, and those things could have gone right through you, and I am not okay."

Oh.

Kayleigh and Marcus had known. They'd felt the magic crisping through their hair and had been close enough to see Scout's muscles tremble with exertion as he'd been fighting to keep control of the balls. When he'd started to pirouette, building up enough momentum to use all that force to slingshot the spheres into the ocean, Kayleigh had been the one to add the fireworks to make the trick look more like a trick and less like an attempted murder.

None of them had spoken at the end of it—there had been too many people around—but Scout had been consumed with who had done it and why, and if it had anything to do with the presence around Tom's bench. He hadn't thought how Lucky would react, much like he hadn't been ready for Lucky's practical nursing the night before.

But much like the night before, feeling that warm body next to his, offering comfort, offering strength, had been the most magical thing Scout had ever encountered and the most amazing magic he'd ever known.

Lightning wandered in behind Scout, bumping into him and sending him and Lucky stumbling a few steps toward the counter.

"I'm fine," he whispered near Lucky's ear. "I really am. It's okay. You don't need to worry. Go take care of the line, and Piers and I will hang out in the back, okay?"

"Get in line," Lucky ordered gruffly, backing up to retrieve his apron. "I'll get you guys something."

Well, that was also a plan, and judging by Lightning's relieved smile as he did that, a considerate one. Kayleigh and Larissa went back to reserve a table, and when they got to the counter, Lucky shoved a tray of four hot chocolates—complete with whipped cream and cinnamon—at them.

"Tell your sister I'd kill for Italian, lasagna or meatballs or something. I mean, I'm not trying to run her life, but I am saying…."

Scout smiled and touched his hand. "I'll put in a good word," he said when Lucky waved off his money.

Helen looked over and winked, and Scout took the tray to the back. He set it down and sank wearily into the stuffed chair that appeared to have been saved for him.

"That was rough," Kayleigh said, probably the first words either of them had spoken about the chrome sphere incident. "What in the hell happened?"

Scout scowled. "I'm tempted to say that one thing we've been investigating, but I don't think so. I think it was Alistair."

Kayleigh's eyebrows shot up. "Is he coming here?"

Scout shook his head. "No. And I texted Bartholomew this morning. He said Alistair's retreated back home for the last few days. I'm betting he's there, trying to figure out where we are, and while he probably can't track us on the island, he does have a bead on my magic. So he doesn't know what I was doing or where I was doing it, but he could certainly fuck with the forces to make sure it didn't turn out as planned."

Kayleigh started chuckling, low and evil.

Scout glared at her. "What? It's only a matter of time before he figures out a way to find us. I don't want to leave here! I *like* it here!" He looked down the book racks to where Lucky was waiting on a little old lady with the patience of a frickin' saint. "I like the people here," he said miserably.

"We don't have to leave," she said, lower lip thrust out.

"But Kayleigh—"

"No! Fuck that! I don't want to go. And you know what? You beat him today."

Scout stared at her. "That's impossible!"

"No, it's not!"

"Kayleigh, you remember how we ended up here, right?" He gave Piers and Larissa a green smile, wishing they weren't doing this in front of them. "I wasn't powerful enough to keep in the compound. You remember that. You were there!"

"It was bullshit," Kayleigh told him fiercely. "It was all bullshit. Alistair fed it to you about the time he realized you were looking at the wrong pictures on the internet. Kept telling you that you were too weak to be a wizard, to get used to failure. I heard the way he talked to you. You always sort of tuned out of it, but I know it seeped in somewhere. And it was a lie, and he knew it."

Scout shifted from foot to foot. "I failed the test," he said quietly, trying to remind her of that day—him, standing in front of the entire population of the compound while Alistair screamed *Conjuro!* in his face and Scout held his hands out and not a breath of magic stirred. He'd already been thinking about his exit plan, because in his heart he'd already been gone.

"You didn't care about Alistair's stupid test, Scout. When it was time to break me out of there, you did exactly what he said you were too weak to do, and you did more than he's ever asked of anyone else. You didn't just create a portal, you went through it and pulled me out. You beat him two months ago, and you beat him today."

He blinked at her. "Marcus's chromatic spheres say differently," he muttered, thinking those were coming out of his paycheck.

"No, they say exactly what I'm saying!" Kayleigh argued, hands on her hips. "He tried to get control of your magic today—did he succeed?"

"Almost!" Scout admitted, his heart thundering all over again. Those spheres had been a hair's breadth from being jerked out of his control. "And the scary thing is that he didn't give a fuck what I was doing—he could have *killed* someone."

Kayleigh's oval of a face relaxed a little. "But you didn't let that happen. You took the thing he made you into—all those ballet lessons, all those magic lessons, all those 'everyone else is better than you' lessons—and you spun it into something…." She shook her head.

"Beautiful," Lightning said, looking at his cousin. "Wasn't he beautiful up on stage?"

Larissa, who had been following the conversation with a puzzled look on her face but following it just the same, nodded to agree. "Oh yes. That was fabulous. I… uhm, until I heard you arguing right this moment, I never would have guessed you didn't mean to do exactly that."

Scout nodded, grateful that if they were doing this in front of total strangers, at least the strangers didn't suck. "Thanks, Larissa." He grimaced and looked to the front, to where Lucky and Helen were finally getting a chance to clean up after the rush. "I just don't like the idea that Alistair can peek in on my magic whenever I'm not paying attention. It's bad enough wondering if he's going to find us for real. The magic thing is… intrusive. He kicked *me* out, right? If we hadn't had Josue and Macklin, we could have been screwed. This is—" He waved his hands ineffectually. "—childish and stupid."

"Well," Kayleigh said with a snort, "that's Alistair. What do you think all of that subjugate-women bullshit is if it's not childish and stupid?"

"I need to cook up something that will give me a warning, even if it's only the hair rising on the back of my neck. I swear to Goddess, if I knew it was coming, I could deal."

Kayleigh *humph*ed. "I can do that," she said. "Remember, I spent all *my* magic finding alarms that would let me know someone was going to catch me working magic at all."

Scout snorted. "Yeah. You're right. Childish and stupid—that's dear old Dad."

Kayleigh nodded decisively. "So let me figure out an alarm system. You can beat him if you have some warning. You already did."

Scout doubted that. It seemed a little too optimistic to hope the boogeyman of both their childhoods could be as easy to beat as throwing balls out to sea, but they had other concerns. Alistair didn't give a damn about the poor souls locked in the Tom's bench clearing, and he certainly didn't care about Lucky and Piers and Larissa. Scout and Kayleigh were the best chance the island had of getting rid of its soul trap. And of hopefully keeping the protective spirit that was helping them all out at the same time.

EVENTUALLY THE coffee shop emptied out, and Scout and Kayleigh moved to help Lucky clean up the back with the books, keeping a few specific ones out for themselves. Larissa and Piers watched them curiously for a moment, as though surprised they'd help when it wasn't their job, and Scout turned to Piers.

"C'mon, Lightning, the quicker we help Lucky out, the quicker we can go run my little magic experiment by the bay."

Piers brightened and started helping, before stopping to look abashed. "We, uhm, probably should have helped just not to be assholes, shouldn't we?"

Scout stared at him, surprised. "Well, it *is* a nice thing to do."

Piers nodded. "Uhm, you get very used to privilege without thinking of it."

Larissa grunted and stood up, putting their hot chocolate mugs on the tray. "*We* do, Piers. Something tells me Scout and Kayleigh have had some privilege, and they've worked hard not to let it affect them."

Piers nodded and began to stack the books Scout had been looking at. "So noted," he said mildly.

Scout acknowledged them both with a nod and went back to cleaning the store rapidly. He wanted… well, everything.

He wanted to go see if Piers and Larissa could see the tableaux at Tom's bench. He wanted to hold Lucky's hand on the way there.

He wanted to have new friends come watch movies, although he hoped he wouldn't go wandering about following Wisps again tonight!

And he wanted to see if maybe Lucky would sleep next to him again.

Oddly enough, of all the things that had happened in the past twenty-four hours, that was the one that seemed to mean the most. Lucky's sturdy body, relaxed and trusting in his arms.

His entire life, whenever he'd tried to do magic, he'd always been distracted by the whys of it. Why was he trying to imbue essence in an inanimate object? Why was he trying to create a portal? Why was he levitating three chrome balls in the air and pretending it was a gimmick?

The whys got him every time.

But there was no why in the feeling of Lucky in his arms. It was as if the rest of their messy, complicated existence was mere noise, and what life boiled down to was that pure moment of contact between two people. Scout's need for that focus, for that contact, for all of it, seemed to grow with every passing breath.

Finally they'd cleaned up. Marcus joined them, and Scout told his "swimming in seaweed" story for the zillionth time, this time when Marcus, Lightning, and Larissa could hear him.

When he was done, he gestured to the neatly stacked books.

"So what I think happened is that a Wisp wanted me to see the bench from a distance. Wisps are like… well, they're lost spirits, but they're also spirit guides. They sort of exist outside place and time—"

"I know what a Wisp is," Helen said with a touch of exasperation.

"I don't," Lucky said. "So let him explain."

"But he's doing it wrong. I know the book he got the information out of, and it's incomplete," Helen told him, scowling. "Wisps used to be human. They often knew something nobody else did. Sort of like Cassandra from the old Greek myths. They spent their life's energy trying to convince somebody—or even entire communities—that they were right, that the community had to beware, and they died not sure if anybody got the message."

Scout rubbed his chest. "That's awful," he said, looking at Marcus for confirmation.

Marcus nodded. "It is. Part of what drives Wisps is the hope to help people not make the same mistake they made. It's… it's a combination of pride and sorrow, I think. So, whatever this Wisp wanted you to see, it was trying to warn you and keep you safe."

"Well, it did a shitty job of it," Lucky muttered in disgust. "Do I have to remind everybody about him being half-drowned when he showed back up on the couch?"

"No, Lucky," Kayleigh snapped. "I cleaned up the seaweed, remember? And that's the part I'm worried about. The Wisp was obviously trying to show you whatever it was that had power over the soul trap. What are we going to do about that?"

"We're going to research it!" Scout said in exasperation. "But all of us there. So, you know." He could feel his face heat up. "So if the ocean tries to eat me, you all can grab me by the ankles." He gave Larissa and Piers a smile with too many teeth. "Bet you're thinking this is *so* worth the free hot chocolate, aren't you?"

Larissa and Piers grinned at each other. "This is totally the best thing we've ever done," Larissa said. "It's like… like an amusement park and a murder mystery all rolled into one."

"You guys might not be able to see it," Scout warned, but Lightning just grinned.

And around them the gentle yellow lights fighting against the long shadows of the afternoon went bright and blue, like cage lights in a garage at midnight.

"Nice," said Marcus, smiling at Piers. "My boy, if Scout doesn't take to magic, I believe you've got some tricks to show me!"

"But I like magic!" Scout protested, and Lightning and Marcus laughed.

"I'll teach you the tricks anyway," Lightning said, blinking and allowing the lights to settle back to normal. "You're the only crowd I can really brag about it to."

"But first," Scout prompted, "let's go see who can see what at Tom's bench."

He let Lucky lead the way, but Lucky made sure to keep his hand the entire trip. When they got there, Scout found he was clutching it tightly. He wanted to do this. The prospect of finding new magic, of solving the mystery, was exciting like he never thought it could be. But he wanted what came afterward too.

He wanted to hold Lucky's hand—hold Lucky's body—on the couch in front of the television again.

He wanted more kisses.

All those furtive years, dreaming of things he wasn't supposed to have, and here he was holding the hand of a magnetic, interesting man who seemed especially protective of Scout himself, and they didn't have time to hold hands?

It wasn't fair.

Which was why, as they drew near the clearing, he pulled Lucky aside to allow the living to invade the spirit trap while he and Lucky… took a breath.

A breath that involved Scout's mouth on Lucky's and Lucky's sharp, happy intake of breath welcoming the kiss. The others were looking around the clearing itself, checking out the bench and the view while Marcus told them what he knew of the place—which was the same thing that Scout knew—and Scout was… lost.

Lucky put his hands on Scout's hips and drew him closer before twining his arms around Scout's neck. Scout plundered his mouth, pulling in everything he knew about kissing and learning from the things Lucky was trying to teach him. Finally they had to come up for air, and Scout balanced his forehead on Lucky's.

"Is this normal?" he panted. "I seem to want you a *lot*. Like, an unreasonable amount. Do people crush like this?"

Lucky whimpered. "You think I know? I spent my whole life trying not to want somebody like this. I figured eventually I'd get a kiss and a blowjob and all the good stuff, but I didn't think it would feel so… so…."

"Huge," Scout breathed. "Necessary. I thought like, maybe, getting chocolates. That was nice. I could get behind candy. But I don't need candy to breathe!"

"I never thought I'd kill anyone who wanted my candy," Lucky mumbled before taking Scout's mouth again.

This kiss was even more frantic, more urgent, and Scout ran shaking hands through Lucky's collar-length hair, suddenly wondering how he'd never known he could need somebody like this. Marcus's voice, calling them both over, was the only thing that kept them from sinking into the foliage and Scout finding out what else he'd been missing, stuck in a compound with fifty of his closest family members, very few of whom wanted to be there with him.

"Come—erm, on our way," Scout replied weakly, and Lucky's broken chuckle reassured him. He wasn't the only one who wanted quiet time alone together. Good. They could do this, he thought, as long as there was being together at the end to look forward to.

He and Lucky stepped through the boundary that marked the clearing, and a frisson of something… dire swept up Scout's spine.

He turned to Lucky, who frowned and nodded. "I felt it too. I never noticed that when I was here before."

"He's right," Helen said, prowling the nooks and crannies of the clearing. She walked through where the two lovers had been recoiling from violence and stopped, shivering. "Whatever was here that is keeping these spirits locked in their pattern, it's gotten stronger since I first came to the island."

Scout and Lucky exchanged glances, and then they both looked at Kayleigh, Piers, and Larissa.

"Us," Piers said, musing. "I mean, it might not *be* us, but… well, it's kind of obvious. We're all running from something here, right? And that's got to carry an energy with it. Hiding from—well, in our case, evil."

"Oh yeah," Lucky said, nodding.

"Alistair qualifies," Kayleigh said on a snort.

"So," Scout mused, "either we all attracted evil to this place or we activated the thing that traps energy—"

"Aren't you the optimist," Helen said, obviously skeptical.

"I don't think of myself as a receptacle of evil!" Scout defended. "I haven't done anything wrong! Lucky hasn't either! Piers and Larissa are the definition of victim here." He crossed his arms and glared at the older woman, who pursed her lips and nodded.

"You're right," she said on a sigh. "You are. None of you deserve to be running from something. None of you deserve to be pursued by forces that want to harm you. I came here because I needed to renew my faith—in people, in the world at large—and you all just saw my saltier side, I'm afraid. Carry on, Scout. You were doing some first-rate logic there, and I shouldn't have interrupted."

To Scout's surprise, Marcus reached out his arm for her, and as private as they'd seemed to be, she went, allowing him to draw her against his side as though they'd been married for years and years.

"Look who can learn," he mocked gently, and she gave him an annoyed look.

Scout wanted to know more, wanted to know their history, how they'd come to be here on this small tidal paradise. But that wasn't for now. Now was for figuring out the spirit trap on the island and seeing if the thing that kept the spirits in was also the thing keeping the bad forces *out*.

"Last night, when I was, uhm, *lured* out here, for lack of a better word, there were two things working," he said, pacing. "One was… well, benign, I guess. It was known as a Wisp, and its job has always been to take people to safety. Except the Wisp didn't take me to safety—or at least it didn't take me to a place that was safe for *me*. I ended up here, and there was a big dark force wrapped around this place that really didn't want me here. So I want to see what everyone *else* sees. Maybe with some more eyes, we can figure out what forces are working outside the clearing, and maybe get a better idea of what's working *inside*."

"And how do you plan to do that?" Marcus asked. He had his head tilted as he had during most of Scout's "magic" lessons, inviting Scout to hazard a guess or make his best try. Unlike Alistair, who had demanded studying, answers, and rote memorization, Marcus seemed to value critical thinking above everything else.

"Well, Lucky and I saw the spirit trap by touching hands—we spit on them first, but, uhm, I'm not sure if we have to—"

Larissa, Kayleigh, and Piers all had their palms up in front of their mouths and were eyeing each other as if to see who would spit first.

Scout laughed. "I take it you all are in?"

"When I was twelve, I had a séance in my room with my best friend," Larissa said excitedly, "and the Ouija disk floated in the air for about thirty seconds before falling to the board and cracking in half. Until now, I didn't think anything cooler than that would ever happen to me."

Piers looked at her sideways and snorted, so Scout got the feeling there was more to it than that.

"Were you having a sleepover?" Kayleigh asked, enthralled. "I've read books where people do that, but I never had one myself."

Larissa gave her a big-eyed look and then looked at her cousin. "Uhm… Piers?"

Lightning gave his cousin a game smile in return. "Honey, we're not with our usual crowd, okay? Run with it."

Larissa shrugged and spat in her palm, and everyone else followed suit.

Scout shook Larissa's hand first.

The results were, well, less than spectacular for Scout. He could see all the shadows while holding her hand, but far away, as though filtered behind layers and layers of tulle. But the look on Larissa's face was enchanted, and Scout gave her a moment to look around before gently releasing her palm. Curiously enough, the shadows didn't fade, and as Scout squinted, he realized that he could see them without help, now that he knew how to look.

"You saw that?" he queried.

"That was *amazing*," she said, hopping up and down on her toes and making her ponytail bob. "Piers, you've got to try it. It's… you'll see!"

Larissa was probably mildly gifted; the séance she'd talked about proved that. But Piers's trick with light was a little more serious, and as Scout clasped hands with him, Piers looked around appreciatively—and shuddered.

"Is the light changed?" he asked, squinting around. "It's… there's an ambient illumination here that's neither sun nor moon. And I don't think it's healthy."

Scout glanced around the clearing too, and while the washerwoman still scrubbed, the young lovers still quailed, the little girl still mourned, and the man on the bench still yearned, he saw that Piers was right. The quality of the light was almost polluted, a noxious brown/green film that coated the entire tableau.

"But do you see the spirits?" Scout asked curiously.

"Oh! Yes. They're… they're brilliantly lit. Like the principal actors in an old movie." Piers glanced around again, frowning. "In fact there's, you know, lighting themes." He tried to turn his body to get a better look at the lovers when his hand parted from Scout's.

Scout stayed rooted in the ghostly tableau, and Piers moved far away, as though their physical closeness had been the anomaly and he was actually far enough away to need a telescope to be seen. Curiouser and curiouser, he thought, *Alice in Wonderland* style. Without Piers's touch, the expressions on the spirit's faces grew contorted somehow, and as Scout stared at the nearest one, the washerwoman, it appeared that her eyes hollowed and her skin and muscle shredded until she was left a moving corpse, lost in the administration of her one task, the cleaning of the memorial bench.

He took a step toward her, and another, only to be brought up short by a very real hand on his shoulder.

He stopped hurriedly, the spirits in the trap losing focus a little, although the light remained exactly as Piers had said—toxic and ambient.

"Lucky," he said softly, smiling. The memory of their kisses moments before suffused him, sending a rush of blood under his skin and making his vision of the spirt trap rosy somehow. "Sorry—what was I doing?"

Lucky's own expression was concerned as he stepped into Scout's personal space. Suddenly the spirit trap was both clearer and less consuming. All of Scout's being was focused on Lucky's warm, living body. "Well, you and Piers disappeared, and then Piers came back, and we could see you partway." Lucky grimaced. "I got worried. I thought, you know, you might need a hand getting home."

Scout felt the smile on his lips, the sort of serene sense of well-being that was centered on the man touching him. "Their expressions," he said, not sure he could explain this without it becoming a horror movie. Maybe it had been—tattered skin and shredded flesh certainly wasn't a fairy tale—but it had also been… technical.

Something magical had happened, and magic had rules.

And one of those rules was that using it took energy, and Scout was suddenly very tired, very hungry, and very ready for a break.

"Scout?" Lucky said, his look growing more concerned. He moved closer until Scout could feel the warmth of his body. "Scout, what about their expressions? Scout!"

Scout's knees buckled, and he literally fell into Lucky's arms. For a moment, the world around them whirled, and then they were both alone on the beach, looking at two other lonely figures sitting on a sand dune near the water's edge.

The stars hung above them, brighter than Scout had ever seen stars in a night sky, and the world around them was even darker.

One of the figures was tall and slender, and he was gazing off into the indigo horizon where the ocean met the sky under the watchful gaze of the moon, while the shorter, stockier figure rested his head on the other one's shoulder.

Oh, thought Scout in wonder. *They're lovers.*

"Tom," said the smaller, sturdy one, "do you really need to leave?"

"I'll be back, Henry." The lean figure with the distant eyes dropped a kiss on the top of Henry's head. "I just… a cottage here. That's all I want. A place where we can be bachelors, right? Nobody will ask questions. But I've got no gold and you've got no copper. A few years, that's all. I make my fortune, save my earnings, and then it's you and me and a small bit o' beach. Don't you want that?"

"All I want," Henry said softly, "is you."

The lovers on the beach kissed then, the touch of their lips so full of yearning that Scout thought his stomach would burst with it, and then Lucky's arms tightened around his shoulders *hard*, and Lucky bawled, "*Scout, get your ass back here*!" into his face.

Suddenly they were on their knees in the here and now, dead center of the little clearing, the late afternoon sun stretching long shadows overhead.

Lucky was shaking his shoulders with unnecessary force and snarling, "Would you fucking *breathe* already?"

Scout nodded, aware that his lungs hurt, and it felt like he hadn't filled them in too long a time. Spots danced in front of his eyes, and he thought with wonder that he might be too weak to get up.

"That," he said, "was the damnedest thing."

And then he passed out.

Shelter

YOU COULD tell a lot about how you felt about somebody when you were hauling their dumb ass a half mile from the beach to your dumb apartment.

Lucky and Piers had decided on Lucky's apartment because there were fewer stairs to the ground floor and because it had carpeting that made it a little warmer, and Scout was freezing.

Those seemed to be key factors in the decision-making, but the truth was, after watching Scout shake hands and share magic with everybody else on the island, it seemed, Lucky wanted some quiet for his favorite magician, and he unabashedly wanted Scout to himself.

Yeah, yeah—magic, investigation, oh my God, everybody's fate seemed to hang on that teeny tiny plot of land, but this was the second time Lucky had seen Scout get sucked away via magic, and he was just fucking *done* with it. He'd put off getting to know the guy for a month and a half because he hadn't wanted to get attached. Apparently he'd been getting attached while trying not to, and wasn't that a kick in the ass! Whatever it was, Lucky wanted Scout safe, and he wanted some time alone with him, and yeah, he was curious about what Scout had figured out at the clearing, but that wasn't his priority, not now.

Scout—and Scout only—was the focus of his irritation, his worry, and his care.

Helen let them into Lucky's small flat before following the rest of the party to Scout and Kayleigh's apartment for what was probably going to be snacks and a confab that would rival a military ops debrief.

"I'll tell you what we find out," Helen said softly as Piers and Lucky deposited Scout on the bed in the corner of the cozy little studio. "And Marcus and I will be by early tomorrow to see how he's doing."

Lucky grunted. "Fabulous. I love earlier than 5:00 a.m.…." Because he and Helen opened the shop at six.

"I mean early as in eight," Helen replied, ruffling Lucky's hair. "Marcus will help me with the coffee shop tomorrow. I think you and

Scout have earned some sleeping in tomorrow morning. You can come in for the rush, if you like, because I think Scout still needs to perform."

Lucky squinted at her, shaking out his hands. "In what employment universe?"

She laughed, keeping her voice down so as not to disturb Scout. "In the one where I own the store." On a sober note, she added, "Scout did a lot tonight—and he needs someone to look after him. Kayleigh can take the magic store. Marcus and I will do the coffee shop, but given what Marcus and I saw from the *outside* of Scout's little experiment, Scout needs to save his strength for the trial ahead. And we need to do a lot more research so we know what that trial will be. So take some time—dinner, breakfast, all the luxuries."

Lucky snorted. "Yeah. That's pure hedonism, right?"

Her eyes softened. "You've been fighting this attraction for a month and a half, Lucky. Take a little time to give in to it, okay? If nothing else, talk to him some more. He seems to really like you."

Lucky sighed. What the hell—he already trusted Helen, right? "All that time avoiding him," he muttered. "I just… I didn't want to miss him when he left. Now that I want to be with him, he's almost left me twice. What kind of fair is that?"

She kissed his cheek, which was something his Auntie Cree wouldn't have done in a million years. "The kind of fair that says you're the one who can call him back," she said softly. "Maybe that's why he seemed so drawn to you."

Lucky snorted. "Him? Drawn to me?" But even as he said it, he recalled Scout's cobalt eyes searching him out over the quad when Lucky and Helen took their break every day to watch him do his show.

"He's got very pretty eyes," Helen said softly. "And we've all seen them pinned to you. Every time he got his coffee and you brushed him off, they grew wider and sadder. Don't fight it, honey. Sometimes love's like that."

And while Lucky was still remembering to shut his mouth, Helen nodded to the six-feet-plus of good-looking rich guy who had helped Lucky drag his sort-of boyfriend the half mile to Lucky's apartment.

"Come along, Piers. Kayleigh and Marcus are making dinner. Would you like to join us?"

"I think Larissa is already there," Piers said, nodding acceptance. "Thank you." As he walked out of the tiny studio, he gave Lucky a level look. "And remember," he said gravely, "if you decide you don't want to give it a try, you're not the only one who watches his show."

Lucky's eyes narrowed. "I grew up in Southie, and I'll cut you," he said with absolute sincerity, but Piers only laughed as he followed Helen out the door.

Lucky was so relieved to have them gone he leaned against the door, his gaze taking in his small apartment in one go.

Like Scout and Kayleigh's basement place, the walls were brick, but the hill the shops were built into had moments of granite so absolute they'd been left as foundations for the stores above. The placement of the slab rendered Lucky's place about half the size of Scout's flat. He liked it. The kitchen area had a fridge, a stove, a microwave, and some counter space. Helen had bought cookware for the place, and he'd indulged himself in trying to make his Auntie Cree's favorites since he'd arrived on the Drift. Helen and Marcus had enjoyed his brisket very much, in fact, and he had to admit to himself that he'd been having fantasies of making it again for Scout.

The kitchenette took up one corner of the studio, and the bed was on the adjacent wall. The other corner had a television with a streaming box, and a couch. Lucky had agonized what to do with the couch, but finally he'd conceded that the apartment was just not that big. If he ever wanted company over, he'd have to make the television visible from the bed *and* the couch, so he'd angled everything so the bed was part of the conversation pit.

Seeing Scout curled up on his side on top of the covers, he had to admit he still wanted a movie and popcorn night with Scout and his sister, and maybe even that Lightning guy and his cousin too.

People his own age who didn't want to kill him were turning out to be sort of a kick.

But he didn't want all those people here *now*.

He also didn't want sand in his bed, which meant he was going to have to help Scout off with his boots and his clothes.

The boots weren't so bad; they were a little big, and Lucky thought Marcus might have steered him to a thrift store to put together his performance outfit. His undershirt could stay on, but the nifty waistcoat and red satin shirt had to come off—lots of laces there and some fancy buttons as well.

Lots of chances for Lucky's fingers to brush Scout's chest through his T-shirt as he was doing those laces.

Lucky had already decided he liked the slender muscle of Scout's body, but by the time he was done unlacing the waistcoat and tugging Scout's jeans down off his long legs, he may have been spoiled for every other body type.

Everything about Scout made Lucky want to touch, and if pressed he would have confessed to some lingering strokes of his palms down the back of Scout's thighs and his calves, squeezing the calves a little as he neared the end just because he liked having that done himself.

When he'd tucked the blanket up under Scout's chin, he saw that Scout's piercing eyes were trained on his face.

"What?" he asked gruffly.

"Glad to wake up here," Scout said. He gave a sweet little smile. "I… something about that last image we saw made me appreciate what I had here."

Lucky grunted. "We're not talking about that now," he ordered. "You're napping, I'm making dinner, and if we're super good, we may get to watch some movies tonight and cuddle."

Scout brightened. "Cuddle?"

"Yeah." Lucky moved close enough to cup his cheek. "Cuddle. Like last night. But no magic mystery tours of the beach, okay? I've had enough tours of the beach. I just want…." Well, why not? "You. I just want you. No mysteries tonight, okay? No magic. Just dinner and us."

"That's funny," Scout said softly. "That's what I was thinking all day. That I knew there was stuff to be done, but I really only wanted to be with you."

Lucky scowled. "Then why all the… folderol!"

Scout's snort of laughter made his cheeks apple under his eyes, and Lucky wanted to absolutely devour him. "Oh my God! Lucky! That word. Who says that?"

Lucky's face heated, but still he laughed. "My Auntie Cree, I guess. She worked hard—really hard. Every day. And I asked her once if she didn't want me to get really rich to take care of her. She said, 'I don't want all the folderol, my boy, but I surely wouldn't mind a new dishwasher.'"

Scout chuckled, like Lucky had meant him to, but his eyes remained soft. "Did she know? That you liked boys, I mean?"

Lucky shrugged. "I didn't try to hide it from her. But one day I watched a… I guess he was a rent boy, I watched him get the shit beat out of him, and when I told Auntie Cree that we should call the police, she told me that the cops would only come help the guys beating him. She looked at me for a long time and said, 'You'll have to leave this place before you've got breathing room to be happy, my boy.' I think that's why she wanted me to have the house so bad."

Scout raised his hand and pushed the hair from Lucky's eyes. "I'm sorry," he said. "It must have been so hard to get pushed from your home."

Lucky shrugged, uncomfortable. "How about you and Kayleigh? Any regrets?"

"God no." Scout rolled his eyes. "It wouldn't have sucked so much, you know, if Alistair hadn't wanted me to fail so badly. He knew I was gay. and you have to understand. The compound is one big breeding program, like racehorses, but with Alistair's good stock, as he would say. To Alistair, Kayleigh's only function was to be married off to another wizard to produce a third son of a third son."

"Is that a big deal?" Lucky knew his eyes were huge, but he couldn't fathom that. Yeah, sure, his neighborhood was overrun by gangsters, but if they wanted you dead it was because you pissed them off—not because you weren't the third son of the third son or whatever.

"Well, yeah. See, Dad has three wives and a couple of other women, and each one of them was… well, prolific. Kayleigh and I have twenty-four siblings and half-siblings between us. And Alistair was the leader of the compound, but there were at least six other wizards there, and their women and their children and…." Lucky shuddered. "But Dad's the most powerful, and he's had a couple of third sons. My half brother Macklin was supposed to be the kind of wizard that comes along once in a generation or so—the third of a third of a third. It was a big deal."

Lucky wrinkled his nose. "Was? What happened?"

Scout gave a soft snort of humor. "Well, Macklin submitted all his test scores to local colleges by computer, won a fuckton of scholarships and grants, disappeared from the compound on his eighteenth birthday without even a 'See ya, bitches!' and went on to live a really awesome life. He tried sending us letters—he was close with Josue, our half brother, and I used to worship him. Alistair apparently kept his letters from us, and Josue, who's not a great wizard but is so good with human business dealings that the compound can't afford to lose him, got mad enough to force Alistair to let him keep in touch." Lucky wasn't sure if Scout was aware of the rather sweet wonder that crossed his face when he spoke next. “So like I told you. Alistair banished me, and Josue made sure I had money and a phone and Macklin’s number. And I was so frantic about leaving Kayleigh behind that the trick I couldn’t do—the one that got me banished in the first place—was the first thing I did to get her back.” He grinned. “She jumped through that portal so fast it was like, ‘Hug Scout! See the way out! Get the hell out of there!’ No holding back for Kayleigh, right?”

Lucky thought of Scout’s irrepressible sister and had to agree. “So you guys had the big house, the compound and everything, and servants—”

“Well, servants and women,” Scout said grimly. “Which sounds terrible because it is. The wives and sisters kept house, basically, for all the men. I’ve read up on cults, and you know? This was the real thing. The only difference is that the male oppressors really *did* have supernatural powers, instead of just pretending to like they do if you’re *not* a wizard.”

“Yikes.” Lucky stared at him again, leaning into Scout’s touch.

“Yeah.” Scout pushed up off the bed and brushed his lips across Lucky’s before falling back against the pillows. “It was like, Kayleigh and I read *voraciously* before we got out. We sort of knew how the world should be, and we knew *that* was not it. We’ve made some missteps since we got out. I had this notion that I could wash dishes in diners as we crossed country, and boy, did Macklin’s friends set me right on *that* one. But mostly, we’ve enjoyed ourselves, you know?”

Lucky nodded, his lips tingling from the simple brush of Scout’s mouth against his. “Uhm,” he said, feeling dumb. “I-I mean, I know I had to stay hidden, but I had opportunities, right?”

Scout nodded. “Yeah.”

“I was waiting for someone who… who made me feel safe. Made me feel like I was real. And important. And you tick those boxes.”

Scout’s grin was a tiny bit wicked. “So very glad to hear it,” he said, looking sideways in apparent embarrassment. He met Lucky’s eyes again after a moment. “I didn’t have anyone specific in mind. I think some guys were interested before you. You keep saying so, Kayleigh said so, and she’s really good at blowing off interest in *her*, so I think she probably knows. But you. You caught my attention. It was just… I saw you and thought, ‘Yes! He’s what I wanted and didn’t know it!’” Scout’s face fell. “Except you got scared, I guess.”

Lucky nodded. "And all those weeks of being afraid to talk to you, I couldn't take my eyes off you. I watched every performance."

Scout buried his face in the pillow. "I was so bad at first!"

"Good God, were you," Lucky agreed fervently. "And I don't get it now. I mean, you are *actually magic* and you couldn't pull off a magic trick to save your life!"

Scout appeared to think about it. "It's just… for the show, it's all about the illusion, right? The magic I've got, but that *belief* that gets other people to believe what I tell them—that's what I seemed to be missing. Although…." He wrinkled his nose and held out his hand. "The magic is so-so at best. I mean, I *did* get kicked out of the compound for being a so-so wizard."

Lucky snorted. "I'd listen to Kayleigh on that score if I were you. I think you got kicked out because your old man's an asshole. I think the only thing that's wrong with your magic is you don't have a mean bone in your body. Sounds like your old man was the kind of guy who would *tell* the magic what to do. You're the kind of guy who would *ask* it to do something for you. I mean, that thing you did with the balls—that didn't look like small potatoes to me!"

Scout gave a halfhearted shrug and yawned. "I'm sorry," he apologized, his eyelids fluttering. "I'm not sure why I'm so…."

And then he snored.

Lucky laughed softly and stood, kissing his forehead before moving to his refrigerator and deciding on Tater Tot hash for dinner. He set the pan to heat with the oil in it and dumped the small bag of Tater Tots into it before adding the chopped-up remains of the last brisket he'd cooked. After putting a lid on that, he checked to make sure Scout was still asleep before grabbing some clothes and making off for the small bathroom cubicle, which was right behind the bed.

The place was barely big enough to change in before getting into the shower, but Lucky still managed, going for a quick rinse off to get rid of some of the coffeehouse from his hair and hands. He liked his job, sure—but he didn't want it clinging to his skin when he woke Scout up for dinner. He dressed in pajama pants and a sweatshirt, because Scout and Kayleigh's place wasn't the only place it could get cold.

He emerged just when the Tots were getting crispy on one side. Flip everything over, add a few eggs, grab some fruit on the side to keep ya regular, and voilà. Dinner was served. He plated everything up and set the plates on the bedstand before moving one of his two stuffed chairs close enough to use the bedstand as a table too and turning on the TV. He was about fifteen minutes into *The Incredibles* when Scout yawned, stretched. and then sat up in bed and reached for the food. For a few moments they ate in silence, and then Scout set down his plate.

"That was really good," he said softly. "What are we watching?"

Lucky looked over his shoulder and grinned. "*The Incredibles.* It's about a family with superpowers."

Scout was staring at the television set, as joyful as a child. "That's amazing. I… a happy family. I, uh…." He bit his lip shyly. "I, uhm, was sort of promised cuddles."

Lucky couldn't stop smiling. "Let me pick up the plates, okay?"

When he'd situated the dinner dishes, he crawled into the bed behind Scout, pleased beyond anything he'd ever imagined. With a little plumping of the pillows, he was raised up enough to see over Scout's head, and he could hold that lean dancer's body close to his own and stroke a slow hand along the tight muscles of Scout's chest and stomach.

For a little while, he was content with a lazy caress over Scout's T-shirt, but when Scout made a greedy little whimper and wriggled back against him, Lucky took a liberty and snuck his hand underneath the soft fabric.

Scout sighed luxuriously, and Lucky leaned over to chuckle in his ear. "You know, Scout, I think it's a good thing you found me. You're easy. You should know that."

Scout gave a low chuckle and pushed into Lucky's caressing hand. "So you're going to protect me from myself?" he asked.

Lucky found he was shifting his hips, grinding up against Scout's backside through Scout's underwear and his own pajama pants. "No," he whispered. "I'm gonna take advantage of ya, but I'm gonna do it with love."

Scout let out a long, slow breath and pushed back against Lucky's hips, grinding against Lucky's swollen groin.

Lucky hissed and thrust forward again, letting his hand wander a little lower, under the waistband of Scout's briefs, appreciating the silkiness of the happy trail against his fingers. Scout made a tiny "Ah!" and Lucky's chest was suddenly almost as swollen and achy as his cock.

God, he was so sweet! Beyond precious, and Lucky was suddenly not sure if this was the right thing. He wanted Scout so much, but Scout by his own admission was practically freshly hatched, and here Lucky was, grabbing him with greedy hands—

Scout, impatient with the lack of motion, reached under the waistband of his briefs and moved Lucky's hand to his bare, erect cock, and Lucky almost came even as he squeezed Scout in his palm.

"Oh yes," Scout breathed, and he rocked his hips back again as Lucky rocked his forward. Lucky took over stroking, any protests from his conscience silenced by the onslaught of pleasure—and of need—roaring through his bloodstream.

Scout clutched at his wrist, begging. "Yes. Oh yes… more… that. That thing you're doing. Yes, that. Oh God, Lucky. Please!"

And Lucky was close—so close. Scout's little cries drove him on, made him rock faster, grind harder, while maintaining his stroke on Scout's cock.

It happened quickly—so quickly. Lucky's thumb caught on the ridge on the underside of Scout's cockhead, and Scout cried out, his fingers tightening on Lucky's wrist. A scald of hot come lathered Lucky's fingers, and he thought, *I did that! I made him feel like that!* And his own cock hit the back of Scout's thigh just so and—

He groaned, bucking against Scout's body, sinking his teeth into Scout's shoulder as he came.

For a moment, harsh breathing filled his ears, and he wasn't sure if it was his or Scout's. His heart thundered, making his chest tight, and as his body floated down from orgasm, he felt a shaft of doubt. Oh God, did Scout even want that? Did he screw up? It was hardly hearts and flowers and—

Scout pulled Lucky's hands out of his pants, and Lucky fought the urge to run far away in complete and utter embarrassment.

Then Scout turned in his arms and took his mouth, tenderly but confidently, and Lucky answered the kiss. Gah! He wanted all of this, all of Scout's taste, all of his touch. A little voice sounded in the back of his mind that said he was the only one he wanted to touch Scout *ever*.

The kiss went on, seemingly forever, but Lucky thought it would never be long enough. Scout's hands were now as busy as Lucky's had been, and after Scout wriggled out of his briefs and his shirt, Lucky found those hands running across his chest under his sweatshirt.

"You going to leave this on?" Scout asked with a pout, and with some wriggling of his own, Lucky was naked and under the covers too.

They paused for a breathless second, both of them naked, skin to skin under the bubble of the warm blankets. It was like being in their own world.

"This is real magic," Scout said, his eyes luminous in the light from the television. "This feels like it can move mountains."

Lucky caught his breath, so drawn into Scout's belief, his fervor, and the bone-deep conviction that what they were doing here in the dark was important, so important, to the fate of the world around them.

Then Scout's mouth was on his again, and the world around them ceased to exist.

They tumbled in a flurry of bold, questing touches and kisses that grew more and more heated. Lucky's hips were doing that thing again where he arched his groin against anything he could touch when Scout broke off from the kiss and said, "I've got a thing I want to try."

"A thing?" Lucky muttered to himself as Scout deserted him for the warm cocoon of blankets that covered them both. "A thing? What sort of thing—"

Scout's mouth closed over Lucky's cock without any ceremony whatsoever.

"Oh my God, am I stupid," Lucky breathed.

Scout's response was to bob his head just a little, his mouth closing over the bell, and Lucky let out a full-throated groan.

"Oh that's no fair," he said, and Scout *chuckled*, which was like the flutter of a thousand butterflies, all of them dancing on his cock.

"Augh! Scout! What're ya—"

And Scout lowered his head some more, this time allowing Lucky's cockhead to rub against his palate. "God, that's good."

Scout did it again, but deeper, and Lucky quit talking. He squeezed his eyes shut, and Scout squeezed his lips over Lucky's base, and Lucky whimpered, completely at his mercy.

It was a good thing Scout was a good guy.

He allowed the blowjob to get wet, messy, slurping along Lucky's length and licking if things got too sloppy. Lucky didn't care. He'd stopped with the words and was down to nonsense syllables as Scout teased, licked, and sucked every bit of skin and every pleasure point on that important piece of flesh.

When Lucky was at the point where all he could do was thrust his hips and *fuck*, Scout kept only the head in his mouth and squeezed with his fist and Lucky's orgasm swept over his body, leaving him helpless and grateful that the whole thing was in Scout's hands.

His climax took every brain cell he had.

He arched into Scout's mouth, the deliciousness of the pressure there making it effortless to spurt come into the warm, safe haven of it.

Scout grunted, but not unhappily, and Lucky actually felt his mouth work as he tried to swallow.

Another spurt and Scout tried to keep up, but Lucky kept going, his balls tightening and his stomach cramping as he emptied himself into Scout, lost and drained and needing Scout in his arms again to tell him it was all okay.

In a moment, he had his wish. Scout scooted up along his body and placed his hand possessively on Lucky's abdomen, under his navel. Lucky looked at him in the light from the television and smiled because his mouth was glazed and he had *Lucky's come* running from the corners, and then Lucky blushed because the thought was so unashamedly carnal.

"What?" Scout asked, smiling wickedly, and Lucky hid his face against Scout's shoulder.

"You look… sexy. Sort of… uhm, debauched, I guess."

He was unprepared for Scout's shy cackle. "Awesome. I look like someone who's at least touched another human in a sexy way. That's very, very cool."

Lucky gazed at him again, thinking that he wanted Scout, wanted his taste, his tongue, his—

Scout kissed him, come and all, and Lucky tasted his own earthiness on Scout's tongue and moaned, wanting him again, even though his erection was still working to catch up.

"What?" Scout gasped as Lucky broke away to kiss his way down Scout's body. He paused at Scout's nipples and licked, enjoying the way Scout's fingers tangled in his hair and simultaneously pushed and pulled.

"I want to eat you," he said, almost wincing because it sounded creepy but unable to stop himself from sucking a pert brown nipple into his mouth.

"I wanna be dinner," Scout moaned, and he wrapped his legs around Lucky's hips and thrust.

Oh God. He was hard again, and Lucky only tore himself away from a nipple because Scout's hard erection awaited. There were delights in between—the soft skin of his stomach, the silky hair of his happy trail—gah! He could have lingered there for a moment or two. Even Scout's navel seemed to be a portal to a magic world.

But Lucky really did have one goal, and by the time he got to it, the covers were thrown back, he could see it was swollen and purple, and the end was glistening from come and precome. Lucky didn't hesitate but opened his mouth and swallowed it as deep as he could.

He sucked, pulling the salt and the come from the skin and taking it down. Scout moaned some more, tugging at his hair at the same time he arched his hips to thrust even deeper. Lucky slid his mouth up, using his lips as a shield, and got to the head, exploring with his tongue and his palate, listening to every grunt or groan Scout made, paying attention to those hands in his hair like they were his game controller and he was the guy on the screen.

His only goal was to make Scout come.

Soon Scout was thrusting into his mouth again, gently, fingers tightening in Lucky's hair. Lucky grasped his erection in his fist and squeezed, finding a rhythm, lost in it, the feel and the taste and the pressure and the—

"I'm gonna…!" Scout exclaimed, and then he thrust a final time, a rending groan ripping from his throat as Lucky tried desperately to swallow.

He succeeded a little and failed a little, finally allowing Scout to push him off with a grunt of sensitivity. With a half roll he slid to the side, staring his new best friend in its one eye, and gave it a long stroke along the softening vein while licking Scout's come off his mouth.

"Hey, buddy," Scout rasped playfully. "*My* eyes are up here."

Lucky found himself burbling with laughter as he scooted up, turning toward Scout so they could pull the blankets over their shoulders and tell secrets.

"You're amazing," Scout breathed, looking dreamy and even sexier. "Kiss me."

Lucky did, their lips fitting together so easily, the kiss was heating their blood without effort before they knew it.

Scout fell away from it with a little sigh then, and Lucky realized his eyes were half-closed.

"You're tired," Lucky said softly, pushing Scout's hair back from his face. He remembered belatedly that Scout had needed to be mostly carried home and poured into the bed.

"I'm sorry," Scout mumbled. "It hit me out of nowhere. I wanted to do all of that again. Twice. And there were more things I wanted to try. With you. No resort guys, okay? Just you."

Lucky grunted. "I threatened to cut Piers. I know that sounds dumb, but, you know—"

"Philly. Yeah, Lucky, you're tougher than he is. We know." Scout giggled slightly so Lucky couldn't take offense. "Maybe just say we're a thing now. You can, you know, use the B-word, even though it's super early. That way, nobody questions it. You don't have to get mad. Everybody knows—"

"You're mine," Lucky said throatily, kissing him into silence.

Scout answered the kiss languorously, obviously into it but fading fast into a well-earned sleep.

"Okay. You're mine," Scout mumbled, and then that adorable little giggle. "We're each other's. You don't know, do you? One day it's all good, and the next scary things happen. Let's be boyfriends now. We can stop whenever we need to."

"No," Lucky murmured, hearing the catch in Scout's voice even as he said it. "I can't."

"Me neither," Scout said. "So we won't. We'll be boyfriends until we have to quit or until forever. You'll see. Not scary. Only scary thing is not doing this again."

"Mm." Lucky found he was tired too. He reached over Scout's body for the remote and turned off the TV and the lamp, and then snuggled down on Scout's chest.

"This is awesome," he said, meaning it. Everything. The entire evening. Watching TV with someone who enjoyed it, Scout's company, the touching, the lovemaking, and now this, Scout's warm body, holding his in the dark.

Lucky had never had a best thing before, but he was pretty sure *this* was what made up a best thing.

He wanted more of it. He wanted it to go on forever and ever.

But first, he wanted to wake up in the morning with Scout in his bed. That could be his new best thing.

He closed his eyes on that note, listening to Scout's even breathing because he was already asleep.

Questions and Theories

SOMETIME IN the night, Scout had awakened, needing to use the bathroom. He slid on his briefs and a T-shirt on the way back to bed and discovered Lucky had done the same, probably in deference to the chill.

But after that he slid back in bed next to Lucky, learning the pros and cons of sleeping in the same bed with another human.

Pros: Warmth, touch, soft noises when you rubbed his back

Cons: Mild snoring, which could be ignored

Scout closed his eyes to the sound of Lucky's mild snoring, remembering the days of sleeping in a barracks with all those young men, not one of whom he could open his heart to. Most of whom snored far worse than Lucky.

He was so happy he was surprised he didn't glow in the dark.

When the sun hit his face in the early hours of the morning, Lucky was folded over his back like a big thermal blanket, and Scout huddled deeper into his warm and welcoming body to ward against the chill in the air.

Then Kayleigh's voice penetrated his happy fog.

"Give it up, Scout. It's morning, you're busted, and you totally need to hear what we figured out last night."

Scout grunted into the mattress before squinting through the obnoxious sunlight. "Kayleigh, I thought you loved me," he said, hurt.

"I *do* love you, big brother," she said, laughing softly. "In fact, I love you enough to have brought you and whatsisface *donuts*—from Donut Do Dat—since Helen hasn't started cooking pastries yet."

"Mm…." Scout fought against the exhaustion pressing his eyes closed. "Coffee?" he asked carefully.

"Yes," Kayleigh said on a sigh. "Lucky's got a coffee maker. I started some here. He's also got the good creamer and some ice and a blender. I'll totally make you a coffee drink, but first you need to *wake up*."

That did it. Reluctantly Scout opened his eyes and rolled out of bed, trying to put his brains together as he did so. "It's so early," he mumbled.

"It's eight o'clock," she said, giving Lucky a furtive look behind Scout as Lucky grunted and sat up. "And Helen and Marcus thought you might be super tired—Lucky too—because apparently you did big magic yesterday, which we all have to talk about. But first? Coffee, donuts, and I tell you what we discovered."

"Toothbrush," Scout muttered. "Water on the face. Pants."

Kayleigh smirked. "Do you want me to ask why you're not wearing any?"

Scout tilted his head to stare at her. "We were *sleeping*," he defended crankily.

He didn't want to face her hearty guffaw, so he stumbled to the bathroom with Lucky on his heels.

"God, she's relentless," Lucky muttered, handing Scout a clean toothbrush from his cupboard. "It's like trying to argue with a pit bull. You might win that argument, but she's still got her teeth in your throat, so who cares?"

"She's right, though," Scout said on a yawn while trying to put toothpaste on the brush. "We're both usually up earlier than this. Eight o'clock here is like… I don't know. Luxury hours. We really must have been tired last night."

Lucky's lascivious chuckle brought heat to his cheeks—and his chest and even his inner thighs.

Slowly, still scrubbing with the toothbrush, Scout turned his head to meet Lucky's eyes.

Lucky waggled his sand-colored eyebrows above his hazel eyes, and Scout fought off a pleased smile, mostly because he would have drooled toothpaste everywhere.

"Ya think, Scout?"

Scout hid his face by turning to spit and rinsed his mouth out before finding a towel to wipe off with. When he was done, he found Lucky had taken a step into the tiny bathroom and was standing next to him at the sink, close enough to lean on.

So Scout did.

Lucky leaned back.

"Last night was awesome," he said, enjoying Lucky's arm around his hips.

"Did you mean it?" Lucky asked, and Scout gave him a quick look because he sounded almost frightened. "What you said last night?"

Scout smiled slowly. "Yeah," he mumbled. "I… uhm… we can use the word until it doesn't fit anymore. I want to wake up next to you, a lot. I… it was the best way to wake up."

Lucky's smile practically took over his entire face. "I want to kiss you," he confessed, "but I haven't brushed my teeth yet. Now shoo. I left a pair of pajama pants on the bed for you, so we can wait to dress until after we shower."

Scout kissed his cheek. "That's a good detail to remember," he said. "Thank you."

Lucky shrugged and started spreading toothpaste on his own brush, but he looked pleased. "It's my first sleepover," he said with dignity. "I wanted to do it right."

Then he started brushing his teeth, and Scout took that as a signal to leave.

He remembered to touch Lucky's hip softly on the way out, because he figured that's what good boyfriends did.

KAYLEIGH WAS true to her word, and by the time he'd put on the pajama pants and the sweatshirt he'd worn the day before, the coffee drinks were ready on the kitchen island by the open donut box. Scout took one of four stools that surrounded the island, letting it double as a countertop and a kitchen table, and took a happy bite of a donut. "Mm, this is good. I mean, Helen's still the best, but, you know…."

"A change," Kayleigh conceded. Then she took a surreptitious look toward the bathroom, where Lucky was still getting ready. "So… how was it?"

Scout grinned. "It was awesome. I highly recommend it if you ever get the chance."

"Not with him!" she muttered, and he rolled his eyes.

"With the human being of your choice!" he retorted, keeping his voice low. "I'm just saying…." He gave a happy shrug. "Not overrated."

She winked and leaned her head on his shoulder. "Good. Glad to hear it. It'll give me something to shoot for."

Lucky entered the room, hopping into his pajama pants as he did, and in another thirty seconds he was sitting kitty-corner to Scout with his own donut and coffee drink.

"This is good," he said through a full mouth. "Thanks, Kayleigh."

She sighed. "Well, yeah, apparently I can't be shitty to you without being shitty to my brother, so go figure. But now that you guys are fed and caffeinated, I need to tell you what we figured out so when Helen and Marcus get here, you guys can talk magic stuff, and we can figure out what to do with it."

Scout frowned. "Wait a minute," he said, trying to remember something. "Did *you* see the spirit trap? Lucky sort of intervened because I was getting lost and—"

"Marcus showed me," she said cheerfully. Then her voice dropped. "Okay, so you know how Alistair used to trash-talk hedge witches all the time, right?"

Scout regarded her. "Bullshit?" He was only making certain; he was pretty sure they'd come to the same conclusion.

"Bullshit," she confirmed, taking a drink of her own coffee. She looked into the cup for a moment, ruminating. "See, what I think—and this is all conjecture, mind you—is that wizards and mages and hell, even luck mechanics like your boyfriend here were born with magic. Some of them were born with a whopping lot, like Macklin and you, and some of them were born with a middling amount, like Josue—"

"I don't have a whopping amount," Scout intervened, scowling. Depending on his magic could get them all in trouble.

"There are three chrome balls in a low orbit around the planet that would beg to differ," Kayleigh replied with a sniff. "Anyway, hedge witches were either born with their own and not schooled in it, or not born with any. Either way, they started to tune themselves into the forces of nature—the resonances of crystals, for example, or the power of color to influence mood, or the properties of herbs. So they started putting these forces of nature together and—"

"Spells, incantations, and summoning magic for their own use," Scout said, delighted. "Kayleigh, you're so smart! I never would have thought of that!"

Kayleigh rolled her eyes. "He so would have," she said to Lucky. "Anyway, Marcus has been working on magic summoning for his whole life, and he and Helen lit a single black candle, sprinkled some sage, and had me tie a knot in string before clasping their hands, and whoosh! I could feel the magic pouring through me, just like when I came through your portal, by the way. And there we were, in the spirit trap, and we could see all the things, I think, that you could see. So when we all gathered at the apartment last night, Helen brought some books on local history and spirit traps, and we started reading. Piers called it a study session and said it reminded him of law school, which I guess he dropped out of to protect his cousin. Anyway, so while you were—" She gave them a sideways look. "—*sleeping*, the lot of us found out some stuff that could help."

Scout grinned at Lucky excitedly, but Lucky's expression was a little more controlled.

"Did you find out who Tom is?" Lucky asked bluntly. "Because Scout and I got a little glimpse into something last night that could explain a whole lot about him."

"Oh, we did," Kayleigh said triumphantly. "We did indeed find out who Tom Marbury, born on the island in 1851 to Christine and Ambrose Marbury, died in 1873 on the mainland from cholera was. We know what happened to his parents, his sister, and his cousins. And we know he sailed off in 1871 to make his fortune working for Johnson Morgenstern—and yes, that name should sound familiar—and when word came that he was never coming back, his childhood friend, Henry "Spinner" Corey, worked his entire life to erect that bench in his name."

She paused to take a breath before sipping her coffee, looking very pleased with herself, and Lucky said, "Didja know Henry and Tommy were a thing?"

She spit out her coffee. "Really?" she asked, after grabbing a paper napkin to wipe off her mouth.

"Really, really," Scout said, grinning at Lucky because his timing had been impeccable.

"So Henry was pining for his lover," she said thoughtfully. "Oh my God. That's so sad." Her forehead wrinkled with compassion, and then her eyes grew thoughtful. "Do you think, maybe, he's the spirit on the bench?"

Scout nodded, meeting Lucky's gaze. "I'd put money on it," he said.

"The look in his eyes," Lucky murmured, turning to regard his coffee intently. "He… he was just staring out to sea, waiting… and his guy never came home."

They all shivered, and Kayleigh let out a long breath.

"Tom's mother must be the one keeping the bench clean."

Lucky made a wounded sound, and Scout turned to watch him. "That hurts?" he asked before looking worriedly at Kayleigh. "I… we… our mothers weren't tender," he said after an unhappy moment. "We were treated well enough, I guess, but we had nannies and teachers and…." He stared at Lucky for a long moment. "Do mothers really love their children enough to pine like that?"

"Don't ask me," Lucky said shortly, still studying his coffee. "My mother didn't care enough to clean herself up, much less keep a big hunk of granite clean, as a ghost."

Under the table Scout felt for Lucky's knee and squeezed gently. "Even when you were a baby?" he asked.

Lucky swallowed and shrugged. "We were a happy family when I was a kid," he admitted. "And then… I don't remember much, but I guess they started on the drugs, and one day my Auntie Cree showed up, and I hadn't been bathed and hadn't started kindergarten, and I hadn't eaten in two days, and she just… just took me. I remember my mother yelling at Auntie Cree, screaming not to take her baby, but…." Another shrug, this one smaller. "She never went into rehab. She never came back for me. My father neither."

"So the mother thing," Scout said, looking at each one of them for confirmation. "That's a big deal. She loved her boy. She devoted time to his memorial. She's heartbroken."

"But she had a daughter!" Kayleigh cried, and Scout and Lucky both looked at her.

"She did. That was the little girl crying in front of the bench. She was just staring out to sea, weeping unconsolably. If mom had the time to scrub the damned bench, why wasn't she hugging her baby?"

"I don't know," Scout said, feeling small. He knew this anger in her. He understood too well where it came from. Kayleigh had been treated as less than the boys in the compound all her life. Her only value had been as a servant or a broodmare. Just as Scout felt the void of a mother deeply, Kayleigh would feel the preference of a mother twice as deep. "I would have comforted her," he said, giving her a small smile.

"Yeah, but Scout, you would have been the one lost out over the sea."

He grimaced. "So seriously, that Tom guy should have stayed home, right?"

"Yes!" Kayleigh and Lucky both said in tandem, and Scout gave them both a game smile.

"So Scout doesn't leave the island. I get it. But…." Scout bit his lip. "That couple in the corner—somebody was coming after them. I think one of them was Tom's little sister, grown up, but the boy? I don't know who that was."

"Well we didn't say we had it *all* figured out," Kayleigh said, blowing out a breath. "But knowing who Tom was—and that Henry was his lover—that went a long way to help solving the mystery, right?"

"Yes," Scout said decisively.

"But what does that do?" Lucky demanded, pulling himself into the conversation with an obvious effort. "I mean, so we finally know the people who are stuck in the trap. What happens then?"

Scout paused for a moment and then smiled slowly. "We talk to them," he said, because it seemed to be the most natural thing in the world. "One after the other, we talk to them. Find out what their sadness was. See if they can't change something—overcome their grief, regret a mistake, find a single good moment of their lives and cling to it to get out of that trap."

"But…." Lucky flailed. "Scout…. Scout, they're *dead*! How are we going to talk to them?"

Scout thought about it for a moment. "Well, you know how the visions get more and more real every time I go there?"

They both nodded, looking apprehensive.

"Well, why don't we try doing the same thing we did yesterday, except I grab you, Kayleigh, and you, Lucky, because you're both the most powerful next to me, and we have Helen and Marcus do hedge-witch stuff to connect us to the past, and then we see what happens. What do you think?"

He smiled at them both eagerly, willing them to jump into this idea with the same excitement that had grabbed him.

He wasn't prepared for Kayleigh to shove her stool away from the counter and stalk toward the door. "*You* explain it to him!" she snapped at Lucky.

Lucky, for his part, was doing the same thing, except heading for the dresser back by the bed. "I'm gonna take a shower," he muttered. "I got nothin'."

Scout was left alone at the island, Kayleigh's excellent coffee drink melting sadly in one of Lucky's big plastic glasses and a box full of donuts staring at him in judgment.

"What'd I say?" he asked the donuts, but the box wasn't talking, so he grabbed another donut and munched disconsolately.

He figured he had some thinking to do anyway.

HE WASN'T done thinking by the time Lucky came out of the shower, but he *was* positive that he wanted to know what he'd done wrong.

"What?" he asked, walking to where Lucky was toweling off his hair. He'd put on clean briefs and a T-shirt in the bathroom, but had conceded to the absolutely tiny confines of the space by slipping into his jeans as he stood by the dresser.

"I don't want to talk about it," Lucky muttered.

"But if I did something wrong, I want to know what it was!" Scout said helplessly. "Kayleigh flounced off, you got your tighty-whiteys in a bunch, and I'm—"

"Clueless," Lucky snapped. "You're fucking clueless!"

Scout stared at him helplessly. "But isn't it *your* job to give me a clue? You can't just say, 'You fucked up' and not explain to me why. That's stupid. How does anybody fix themselves if they don't understand what got them into a jam?"

"You make my head ache," Lucky muttered, and Scout almost stamped his foot.

"Maybe that's the flip side of getting blowjobs," Scout retorted, trying to keep his dignity. "On the plus side, blowjob. On the minus side, you have to explain what ticked you off."

Lucky's eyes narrowed. "Oh my God."

"*What did I do*?"

"Okay, you wanna know what you did?" Lucky put his hands on his hips and tried to glare Scout into self-awareness, but little did he know that Alistair had pretty much glared any shame Scout had ever possessed right out of him. Lucky's glare was oddly… tender. Vulnerable. He wasn't glaring because he *hated* Scout; he was glaring because Scout had hurt him in some way.

"Yeah," Scout said, nodding. That was a boyfriend goal, since they were using that word. Don't hurt your boyfriend. "I do!"

Lucky snorted and shook his head. "Scout, when you held Larissa's hand, your body got a little transparent. That was a little freaky, not gonna lie. But then you held Piers's hand, and Kayleigh actually *screamed* because while we could see *Piers*, you *disappeared*. I could see a thin, ghostly outline of you, so that's why I could step in and grab your shoulder when Piers came back and you didn't. But see? Piers came back, and you and me, we disappeared. And while you and me were on the beach, you were getting thinner and thinner. I had to shake you to get you to come back with me." He grimaced. "What happens if we can't bring you back?"

Scout took three deep breaths. "But you *did*," he said, trying to reason his way through. "You *did*. And, you know…." He bit his lip and felt his cheeks heat. "That was even before, uhm, last night. I, uh, I mean, I think we'd be even *more* bound after last night, right?"

Lucky blinked at him. "Why would you think that."

Scout bit back the hurt. "Because what we did was important!" he said earnestly. "And it was *emotional*. I mean, the whole reason your touch kept me solid, kept me anchored in the here and now, was that I care about you. Last night helped make that more real too."

Lucky's lower lip wobbled, and he looked to be on the edge of relenting. "But Scout. See? This is why I didn't want to get attached. What if you disappear on me one day? I-I mean, I *am* attached, and if you just *fade* into the past or get sucked into some sort of dark hole, I'll be *more* than attached. Did you ever think of that?"

Scout stared at him, and for a moment, the earth buckled beneath his feet and he was freefalling into an unfamiliar space. For years, he and Kayleigh had dreamed of being outside of the compound, where they could meet "real" people and have "real" relationships and use their magic however they damned well pleased.

But this look—this haunting vulnerability—on Lucky's practical, plain-featured face, that was because of *Scout*. Scout had made him feel helpless. Scout had threatened to disappear. Just like Lucky had always imagined someone would, because nobody in Lucky's life stayed.

That quickly, Scout saw with his heart, where it counted, why Lucky had been hurt so very much by Scout's blithe assumption that he would just hold some hands, use some power, and Walla-Walla-Washington, it was all going to be okay.

Lucky had seen too many people go out of his life—his parents, his grandparents—for that casual assumption that everybody would come back to hold much meaning.

But as Scout's feet touched down in grown-up land, where relationships were real and the promises lovers whispered at night held important ramifications for the morning, he also knew that he had to convince Lucky that *he* was the key to keeping Scout from disappearing into the great beyond.

"Frankly, no," Scout told him, keeping his voice gentle. "And now that I have, I can see why you got so mad. But I'm not trying to leave, here. I'm trying to find out how to free those trapped spirits, and I need your help."

"But why?" Lucky demanded. "Why is it so important! They're all dead. They've been dead for nearly two centuries! What does it matter that they had sadness in their lives? So does everybody else. Why do you have to risk your life to fix their sadness?"

Scout swallowed and wondered if he had enough grown-up skills to help Lucky understand this. "Because it wasn't only *their* sadness," he said softly. "It was all of our sadness. It was Kayleigh because she saw herself in the little girl who wasn't ever gonna be enough. It was me because I spent my entire life wanting to go beyond my boundaries, but I was so scared of what I'd be leaving behind that I had to wait until Alistair kicked me out to see what I could do." His throat grew thick with this next part, and his voice too, because this next bit was the worst. "And it's your sadness too, because you got left behind, and you spent so much of your life looking off in the distance, wondering if someone was going to come back to you, that you never looked for someone who was there waiting.

"You think Henry didn't have opportunities here, after Tom left?" he continued. "Because I'm betting he did. But he sat on that bench, staring off into the sunset, and he didn't give anybody a chance, just like you didn't give me or Kayleigh a chance. And Piers and his cousin are running away from exactly the sort of violence that killed those poor kids. Something about that clearing resonates in all of us, and that makes it our job."

"Why?" Lucky's voice had grown staticky and fractured, and Scout took a risk and took a few steps forward, taking Lucky's shaking hands in his own. "Why is it our job?"

"'Cause we're human beings, Justin," Scout said softly. "And human beings risk it all just by breathing. We risk love and loss. We risk having the person we care about most taken away from us. I-I *warped time and space* to keep Kayleigh with me. That's gotta mean something, right? That's gotta make me tough enough. Gotta make me someone you can trust. I won't leave you behind, baby. Not if I can help it."

Lucky swallowed, and it went down hard. "You said you'd never use that name," he said brokenly.

Scout took another step forward and wrapped his arms around Lucky's shoulders. Lucky held himself stiffly for a moment before allowing himself to be loved.

"Names are a big deal in magic," Scout said softly, holding on tight. "They bind us closer. They help us know a thing. You're Lucky, through and through, but the part of you that was a baby, that used to know how to trust—that part was Justin. That's the part I needed to hear me."

"Which part of you goes by Scotland?" Lucky asked against his shoulder, and Scout laughed softly, feeling so much stronger now that they were touching.

"The part that I left behind at Alistair's," Scout told him. "All that's left here is Scout, and he's the guy who'll move Wisps and haints and heaven and hell to get back to you."

Lucky tilted his head back to meet Scout's eyes. "That's a nice thing to say. It's not quite, 'Fine, Lucky, I'll leave it alone,' but you tried."

"Oh my God, you're a pessimist!"

"I'm a *realist*—"

Scout kissed him. Yes, sure, it was probably a chickenshit way to win an argument, but they were *kissing*, and that was *awesome*.

Lucky sighed and melted into him, and Scout pursued the kiss, his relief lending him an assertiveness he hadn't known he possessed. *Lucky would forgive him.* Not for taking over the kiss; Lucky seemed all aboard with that. But Lucky would forgive him for hauling them off into this adventure, this crazy, possibly dangerous, really appealing mix of magic and altruism.

Scout could see these people not only with his mind or his magic but with his *heart*. And that was the sort of community he keenly felt the lack of in his short life. He wanted to help them, but he didn't want to do it without Lucky by his side.

Lucky's fingers tangled in his hair, and Scout lifted Lucky up to his tiptoes so their groins were rubbing together, and Lord knows where that would have led if Helen hadn't taken that moment to tap on the inside of the doorway and say, "Ahem. Lucky, I told you we'd be by."

Scout had his back to the doorway, and Lucky—still standing on his toes—peered over Scout's shoulder. "Sorry, Helen," he said weakly.

Scout gave him a lascivious grin. "I'm not," he murmured, for Lucky's ears alone. "I was just going to shower," he called over his shoulder, and realized that Marcus was standing behind Helen, covering his mouth with his hand. "Kayleigh brought donuts. Grab one while Lucky catches you up."

"Coward," Lucky muttered, but Scout didn't feel like it was a retreat so much as it was a regroup. All he had to do now was convince Kayleigh, and with Lucky on his side, he could do anything!

Old Ghosts

HELEN AND Marcus walked into Lucky's studio bearing a bag full of sausage biscuits and, thank God, some cups of actual coffee with no dressings.

"It is like a parade of breakfast food running into my apartment this morning," Lucky muttered, taking the bag of food and flat of coffee with a nod of thanks. "What's next—a kid's chorus with breakfast burritos or something?"

"We didn't have one planned, but that would be rather charming, wouldn't it, Marcus?"

"I'd definitely fit it in my schedule, and I shall forever be disappointed that the Children's Burrito Choir has not yet made an appearance in Spinner's Drift, Helen. I don't see how we could have lived without it thus far."

Lucky regarded them both with a flat, unforgiving gaze. "You two should do standup," he decided before setting the food down on the little island in the middle of the kitchenette. "But if you can help Scout with the stupid thing he suggested we try next, I might forgive you."

Helen's eyebrows went up, and Marcus blinked a couple of times. "I was unaware we'd forged other plans," Marcus said.

Lucky sighed. Marcus had a way of making the simple sound much more complicated. "He came up with this one in the kitchen this morning," he said, scowling at the island counter as though the space alone was to blame. "I'm pretty sure it was Kayleigh's fault for trying to make coffee drinks. Can you believe she didn't even rinse out my blender?"

And with that he went to the sink to run water in it, aware that Helen had joined him, standing close enough to bump shoulders with him.

"So," she said, casting a glance at Marcus, who made shooing motions with his hands. Lucky might have rolled his eyes, but he was busy pretending he hadn't seen it.

"So what?" he asked, trying not to respond.

"So how was it, dear boy? Did you enjoy yourselves?"

"I hope so," Lucky muttered, feeling heat steal up his cheeks. "I just agreed to follow the guy into the great purple abyss. I hope we at least had fun."

She sighed. "Let's focus on the having fun for a moment, then move on to what you think Scout has committed you both to doing." Her voice softened, and Lucky had to stop running water to hear her. "Did you and Scout connect? You were both looking pretty cozy when we came in, and the bed looks… slept in."

Lucky grunted. "Are you momming me?" he asked suspiciously. "I don't remember Auntie Cree doing this, except for the first day of high school. This is what having a mother feels like, isn't it?"

"I certainly hope so, sweetie," Helen replied, chuckling. "I mean, I definitely failed the last time I was put in a situation like this. I'm hoping I've learned a thing or two since then. Are you ever going to give me an answer?"

What would it hurt? "It was great," he answered baldly. "I… it was everything I thought it would be, and I wish I'd done it sooner, except then I wouldn't have done it with Scout." He let out a big breath. "But I *did* do it with Scout, and I guess that means I need to stick with him and not bail on him when he scares me."

She gave him a half smile. "Okay, then. So, good on the sex, but you're scaring me on the pillow talk. What did he suggest?"

Lucky set the blender pieces in the dishrack, careful to turn the blade assembly upside down to keep people from grabbing them when it was put back together, and turned around to lean against the sink. Marcus was seated at the island, indulging in one of Kayleigh's donuts and waiting for him to go on.

"He wants to go to the clearing and hold mine and Kayleigh's hands while you guys do—" He waved his hands a little. "—hedge-witch protective things. He thinks that he can talk with one of the spirits to see if there's something we can do to put the people in the trap at rest. He… he really thinks that's important."

Helen sucked in a startled breath, and Marcus's eyes widened enough for Lucky to actually see their color.

Brown. The old man had very deep brown eyes.

"That's… that's—"

"Good idea, right?" Scout urged, breezing out of the shower in Lucky's pajamas and a T-shirt. Lucky realized he'd gone in to wash without his own clothes and had to give it to the guy—he could make an entrance as well as an exit. It must have been an occupational hazard of being a magician.

"It's terrifying," Helen snapped, scowling. "Why on earth would you even try to do that?"

For a moment, Lucky wanted to cheer. Hurray for having people on his side!

"Because, my dear," Marcus said softly, "he wants to help the spirits and protect the island as well."

"The way I see it," Scout said excitedly, seemingly oblivious to the look of hurt Helen was currently shooting Marcus, "is that something in this island wants to keep people safe. There's really no way Alistair wouldn't have found me by now, and Lucky's got mobsters hunting for him, for God's sake. This island wants to protect secrets. But that big… whatever. That big negative force hanging over it isn't protecting the soul trap. It's *trapping* them there, stuck in that limbo, reliving their losses day after day after day. I think if we could free them, give them a choice, give them a chance to rest… well, I think that would be a good thing, right? If we set their secrets free, I don't think that dark force will have any power over them." He smiled a little sadly. "Wouldn't it be great if Henry and Tom could meet again? I'd really love that, wouldn't you?"

Lucky groaned, loudly and with great irritation.

"Look at him," he told Marcus and Helen. "He's so cute! And he's so earnest. And he only wants the best and—gah! Why don't I have an answer to that?"

Helen sighed, regarding Scout with troubled eyes. "There isn't one," she said faintly. "When you see a great wrong, you should do whatever is in your power to right it. You, Scout, and Kayleigh are uniquely positioned to help do that. Scout's not wrong."

Scout tilted his head. "But…?"

Helen shook her head. "But Lucky's right to worry too. It's dangerous. And you're conveniently leaving out the fact that by saving these spirits, you may be releasing the thing that keeps secrets safe on the island. I would hate it if we went to all this trouble and suddenly Alistair and Lucky's mobster, Skaggs whoever—"

"Skaggs is dead," Lucky reminded her. "This could be Danny Ellis and the Kelly boys, or the Shanahans. I honestly didn't catch their names."

"Well, whoever they are, they could be the ones after you," Helen said shortly. "And they could suddenly find you if you take the spirit trap off the island. Have you ever thought of that?"

Scout shrugged. "I-I mean, Kayleigh and I were raised practically in captivity because Alistair thought it would make him a more powerful wizard. I wouldn't wish that, even on a spirit, in the name of my own safety and power. I think my emotional connection to Lucky and Kayleigh will keep me from getting lost, and I think this—this quest to free the people in the soul trap—might be the thing that saves our souls."

"It's a good thing you're not dramatic or anything," Marcus said unhappily. "I think you've found your calling on the stage."

Scout shot him a killing look and then stared at Lucky, looking worried. "But… but the thing about your mobsters," he said, chewing his lip. "It's all okay for me to get theoretically brave about Alistair finding us, but you did say it. Your guys are dangerous. I don't ever want you to get hurt because of me."

Lucky shrugged, remembering Scout's confidence—his *hope*—that if they could confront it, they could survive it. He realized that Scout may have seemed to have all the faith in the world, but he was the first to admit he'd never been hurt. He was afraid, just like everybody else on the planet, that the world might take the things he valued the most.

That included Lucky. "Here," he said, reaching into his pocket. "Let's ask at the source."

Scout, Marcus, and Helen blinked at him in surprise.

Well, yeah, sometimes he forgot he had a magic coin too. He pulled it out, the weight of it smooth and shiny in his hand, and flipped before he could think.

"Heads, helping the spirit trap puts us in more danger, tails it doesn't."

Everybody held their breath as he caught the coin in midair and slapped it down on the back of his arm.

The tails insignia blinked shinily at him, and he grinned.

"Yeah, I'm good for something. Whatever's gonna happen, it'll happen with or without whatever we're doin' here." He sobered. "But that doesn't mean it's not dangerous for Scout."

He got ready to flip again, but Scout put his hand up to stop him.

"Lucky, we can't rely on that too much. You know that, right?"

Lucky sucked air in through his teeth. "Yeah, I know. Sometimes knowing the future makes you change the future. I feel it in my stomach too."

"Then let's leave it as it is," Scout said, drawing nearer to fold Lucky's hand over his coin to stop the flip. His mouth flickered in a smile. "Just be by my side, okay?"

Lucky swallowed and nodded. "Yeah, fine, whatever." He tucked the coin in his pocket and sighed. "Sausage biscuits?" he said hopefully, and Helen and Marcus both nodded. They gathered around the island counter again, Scout and Lucky's shoulders touching as they leaned forward and started to eat.

"So," Scout said as they munched, "Kayleigh told me what *you* found. Want to hear what we found?"

And the next half hour was spent almost pleasantly as Scout and Lucky repeated their end of the story and discussed some of the implications.

Soon enough, Scout and Marcus went out the door so Scout could go to his apartment to get some clothes, and Lucky and Helen went up the stairs that led to the back stock room of the coffee-shop area so they could open the doors now that everything was prepped.

"You look worried," Helen said softly as she went to open the french doors to the gathering crowd.

"Well, you know," Lucky said with a shrug. "Getting attached here."

Helen laughed softly and dragged the doors open. "Aren't we all," she said, and before Lucky had time to ask her who she was getting attached *to*, because it seemed like she and Marcus were already a matched set, the crowd came in and things got busy.

It wasn't until Lucky was on his third customer that he realized Scout had simply gathered his clothes while Lucky had been doing dishes and then waved and left.

They hadn't had a goodbye kiss, and dammit, now Lucky knew that would be bothering him for the rest of the day!

About five minutes before Scout was due up on the little makeshift stage in front of the store, the coin in Lucky's pocket grew warm, hot enough to scorch the skin of his thigh, and Lucky had the sudden urge to run.

Rubber Bullets

KAYLEIGH HAD to work almost all afternoon, so apparently she'd asked Larissa and Piers to be his audience plants the night before. Scout didn't actually mind; Larissa was bright and enthusiastic, and Piers was canny and game. Together they seemed to be decent actors, and Scout figured he could call on them for help without too much damage to his act, right?

If nothing else, he could always call on Lucky.

The idea that Lucky would be watching him today like he'd watched every day since Scout had started taking over for Marcus warmed Scout to the soles of his feet—or the ends of his feet or the soles of his toes.

Whatever.

It made him super, super happy.

After working a fairly busy hour—apparently *everybody* wanted to order some of those chrome balls they'd heard so much about from the last show—Scout went to the little manager's room behind the cash register and put on his vest and cloak before running a little bit of oil through his hair to make the curls twirl in relief. He wasn't sure why Lucky hadn't noticed that his hair stuck out like a dark chestnut dandelion if it hadn't been combed and oiled, but it was true.

When he emerged, Piers and Larissa were waving from the store's entrance, both of them grinning happily, and Scout waved back, feeling bemused. It wasn't that he didn't like their company. He did, in fact, enjoy them both. They spoke the same language, much like Scout and Kayleigh, and once Piers got over his disappointment that Scout seemed to be taken, he was mostly friendly and helpful.

And Scout hadn't expected that after six weeks of wishing sadly for Lucky to pay attention to him, finding a friend would be this simple.

Lucky wasn't simple, and after seeing the world through books his entire life, he was starting to see that difference between friends and lovers the books were always talking about. Talking to Piers was uncomplicated. Even if Piers had something to add to the conversation, like asking if he should act skeptical when Scout was calling on him during the show, Scout felt free to disagree, to tweak, or generally banter with him.

But with Lucky things could turn suddenly intense when Scout was least expecting it.

Piers, for instance, wanted to be there when Scout, Kayleigh, and Lucky tried to make contact. He was excited about it, and so was Larissa.

Lucky had been terrified.

And while most of that fear had been on Scout's behalf, some of it had been… well, because *Lucky* was afraid of losing Scout. It wasn't just that Scout would be *lost*, it would be that Lucky wouldn't have him anymore.

And Scout was starting to realize exactly how real it was that somebody would care about Scout above all others. Scout knew he'd kill anybody—no hyperbole—for Kayleigh, but in a frighteningly short time, he realized he'd do the same thing for Lucky, and the thought scared him.

No amount of reading romance books had warned him that falling in love could be so *intense*, although heaven knows they tried.

And Scout had to clear his mind of all of that—which was really hard, because his skin felt all tingly after what he and Lucky had done in the dark of the night before—and focus on his act.

Even if it was only a cover for the fact that he really could do magic, he really *did* want the act to improve.

"So," he said, getting ready to do the juggling rings trick, "I need a volunteer from the audience. Who wants to come up and test these rings?"

He smiled, surveying the crowd. Some people were ignoring him and focusing on their ice cream or their fish and chips, but much of the crowd was right there with Piers and Larissa. Larissa had her hand in the air and was practically levitating like a feather in her desire to get picked. Piers had a bored expression and was simply holding his hand in the air as though he didn't expect much.

Scout allowed his eyes to wander, pleased with their entire demeanor—choosing either one would look organic and natural—when his eyes fell on two guys sitting at a table tucked between a giant planter full of nasturtiums and the stair rail leading to the upper walkway.

They weren't dressed right.

Scout and Kayleigh had learned a lot during those trips to Walmart as they'd traveled down the coast. They'd seen what people wore in upstate when it was cold, and they'd seen how the dress code seemed to relax a little as they drew near the South. It was still cool in the South, particularly as November neared, but there weren't many days during which a hooded sweatshirt and a pair of jeans didn't do the trick. Add some tennis shoes or, even better, some shoes that would plod happily across a beach and you had a perfectly average holiday uniform. The resort people tended to wear khaki a lot, often cargo shorts and some sort of trendy deck shoe, with brand-name hoodies, but the general color scheme was either average "dad blue" or the colors of local colleges or lighter khaki clothes with bright tropical sweatshirts in specialty fabrics.

Scout had seen tourist wear, including his own, so often he'd stopped analyzing which clothes looked natural and which didn't.

Until he saw the two guys in combat boots and frayed camouflage jackets and thought, *They don't belong here*.

Without thinking about it, he sought Lucky's eyes over the heads of the crowd.

Lucky was standing by the french doors, as he always was when Scout performed, even before he and Scout had spoken. Even from this distance, Scout could read the hesitation in his posture, could see his bitten lip, and his next thought was *He's going to run away*.

Oh no.

No no no no no.

Scout couldn't, absolutely *wouldn't*, allow that to happen.

"So," he said, looking straight at the two guys, both of them with long, unkempt hair and legs sprawled in front of them, tripping up the passersby. "Do you two gentlemen want to help me with my next trick?"

"Yeah, sure," one of them sneered. He had a scraggly sort of beard, and Scout had the feeling the man would snap his neck like a twig, with or without witnesses. "We'll be your best trick." He leered then, and Scout managed not to throw up in his mouth.

"Excellent. Come up here, then?"

The two of them looked at each other and chuckled, and Scout gave Larissa and Piers a meaningful look so they could overcome their surprise.

Then he caught Lucky's eye and looked at the two guys making their way up the stairs, their backs to Lucky, and gave a faint nod.

Lucky nodded back and then shook his head. Scout could read his lips as he mouthed, "Don't."

Well, Scout *would.* Would what, he wasn't sure yet, but he'd definitely do something.

"Since you two are coming up and we've got double the fun," he said, improvising as he went, "I need my friend up here to help me with this trick." He gestured to Piers. "Coming up is my cousin, Lightning Gestalt. He's going to stand across from me and catch this ring as I throw it and then throw it back. Can you do that, Lightning?"

"Sure can, Great Gestalt!" Piers said with aplomb, trotting up the stairs to the staging area in front of the store. He managed to beat the two guys in camo, both of whom were clunking up their set of stairs with grim purpose. As he reached Scout, he murmured, "What's doing?"

"Follow my lead," Scout whispered back before positioning Piers across from him, both of them with their profiles to the crowd. "Everybody see the rings?" he asked, showing them to the audience. He was gratified by the nods he got before he turned to Piers. "Test them out," he said, and this had been part of the practice, so Piers relaxed infinitesimally. "Nothing on the sides," he said, and Piers ran his hands along the rims.

"Nope," Piers said. "Nothing on the sides."

"You sure?" Scout asked him, winking.

"Positive," Piers said, and Scout turned toward the audience and, holding the three chrome-plated rings in one hand, neatly flipped one in the air, holding the second ring so they would clang in exactly the right place….

With a perfect tone, the two rings met and married, and he caught the top ring, allowing the second ring to dangle from the bottom.

"I'm not sure if we can trust him," Scout said to the audience, and he got a laugh and a smattering of applause. "Try it again," he said to Piers. "Anything in the center?" He held the last ring out for Piers to thrust his arm through, which he did, while the two gangsters lurked in the background, waiting for an invitation. This time, he turned the remaining ring toward them. "Anything in the center?" he asked, standing far enough away that they could only shake their heads.

"Only your ugly face," one of them said, trying to be funny.

Scout grinned at him. "Well, if that's what you see, they're obviously magic," he replied pertly, and the audience laughed along, ignoring the nastiness of the asshole on the stage with him. As the guy started to snarl, he turned so the audience could see the rings, as well as the two gangsters, and flipped the third ring in the air, catching it neatly on the other two as it came down.

"Ta-da!" he said brightly. "Like I said, magic!"

More laughter, more applause, and he kept the rhythm going. "Okay, Lightning, you stand there," he said. "No moving now! Keep your feet *glued* to the cement."

Piers's eyes widened, as they should have because Scout's magic, wild and angry at the thought of losing Lucky, was starting to thrum in his blood.

"Will do," he said, flashing the crowd a purposefully apprehensive smile. The crowd laughed appreciatively, and Scout thought maybe he'd have to ask Piers to help with the act more often, and then he welcomed the two men who had joined them. "You two," he said, "stand right there. Give room for us to throw the rings between us, but stand in the gap—" He ran behind them and positioned them so they faced the crowd. "—like so."

They smelled… metallic, he thought. Dangerous. Like metal and salt water. As much as he loved the smell of the ocean, this tang was altogether different. It rang of unwashed bodies and too much alcohol. Oh, if Scout hadn't known a thing about Lucky's past, he would still have wanted these two people off his island.

"Okay, Lightning," Scout said. "I'm going to throw this one, and you catch it." He tossed the first one in an eight-foot arc, and Piers reached up and caught it, bowing faintly to the crowd.

"Want it back?" he asked, throwing it in front of the two gangsters again.

"Sure! Have another!" Scout tossed the next ring to Piers, and he tossed it back. And again, and again, while he talked to the crowd, to Piers, to the men standing behind the passage of the tossed rings, watching intently, giving that path of spinning chrome through the air more and more credence, more and more belief, until Piers and Scout might as well have been carrying a big glass pane between them, as opposed to tossing shiny chrome rings.

"Thank you, sir!" Piers said to his last toss. "And have another!"

They had developed a rhythm such that one ring was always in the air, and Scout knew he was lucky—it usually took a lot of practice to get to this place, but Piers seemed to sense what he needed. Concentrating, with his magic dancing at its most intricate, he set that middle ring to spinning, alone in the center between them, hovering and spinning, so natural that it took a moment for the audience to catch its breath.

Scout grinned at them devilishly, keeping his magic in check, and turned to Piers. "Don't be shy," he said. "Throw me the next ring!"

Piers, eyes wide, did.

Scout caught it with his magic in midair, and it clanged with the other ring hovering, and the two of them began to spin together, whirling, the center of the spin the contact point of the rims.

"Well, that's awkward," he pronounced. "Here, let's see if this balances it out."

He threw the third ring, and they joined in a triskele, the space in the center of the three rings in contact acting as the fulcrum for their spin.

"What in the hell!" said one of the gangsters, obviously in awe.

"You guys ready to do your part?" Scout asked, sensing that same need he'd felt on the day he'd made the portal to rescue Kayleigh. This time, the need wasn't to rescue anybody, though, it was to send these guys far away. Far, *far* away, but there was only one place he knew that was far away.

"Whatever," the other gangster snapped, staring at the whirling rings as though afraid and trying to hide it.

"Really simple," Scout said, holding his hands out to the rings as though that was the force keeping them in check. "Do you see the gateway?"

The two of them nodded, and Scout drew a quiet breath of relief. The truth was, he *felt* the gateway created by the spinning rings, but he couldn't see it. The crowd could see it—they were gasping in appreciation. And the gangsters could see it, but they didn't believe what they were seeing.

But Scout was standing at a ninety-degree angle to it, and all he could do was have a little faith that this was going to work.

"Then walk right in!" Scout urged. "Don't be shy. Come see what's on the other side!"

"It's an illusion!" one of the men—the man with the beard—snarled. "I'll prove it to you! Come on!"

Three steps: one, two, three.

The two men disappeared, and the rings spun apart, giving Scout and Piers barely enough warning to catch them, two for Scout and one for Piers, as they came raining down.

In the gasp of silence that followed, Scout flipped one of the chrome rings in the air and let it come down and merge with the other. "Ta-da!" he said, wiping his brow with the back of his hand.

The crowd didn't stop applauding for nearly half an hour.

SCOUT HAD to work the counter with Marcus afterward, and his hands shook with the need to talk to Lucky.

"You're sure he's still there?" he asked Piers about forty-five minutes into his shift as Piers loitered back near the register and stayed out of the way.

"Yes," Piers said patiently for the twelfth time. "Larissa said they were slammed too. He's not going anywhere. Who were those guys?"

"I saw your act!" gushed the woman at the counter buying a deck of *Supernatural* Tarot cards. "Where did those guys go?"

"Only the magic knows!" Scout replied glibly, and it was damned near the truth. The magic had chosen the spot, but that didn't mean Scout hadn't gotten a glimpse of it as the rings had split up and gone whirling through the air. He finished her transaction and put the cards in a bag adorned with silver planets and stars, winking. "And maybe the cards if you ask them."

She laughed delightedly. "The cards are for my daughter, but maybe she'll get a straight answer!" she said as she walked away, her curly brown hair as fiercely dandelion-like as Scout's in the humidity. He felt a moment's fondness for her, and for the other plumpish, wifeish tourists who came into the shop looking for a bit of magic. They could often be the sweetest part of his day.

"Does the magic *know* where those guys are?" Piers asked, whispering fiercely as Scout turned away from the line for a second to get a drink of water.

"The magic's got a pretty good idea," Scout muttered back. "I need to call my brother to make sure."

"I mean, you didn't drop them in the middle of the ocean, did you?" Piers asked, looking worried.

"The Atlantic in October?" Scout retorted, horrified. "I'm not that kind of magician!"

Piers let out a relieved breath, and Scout turned toward the next customer, feeling panic in his chest. He really *did* need to call Josue, but first he needed to see Lucky!

Finally, finally, the last ferry left, and the long shadows stretched toward the east. Marcus gave him a grim look and said, "Meeting, your apartment. Helen and I will bring dinner!" and then nodded to him to leave.

Scout practically flew along the sidewalk to the book-and-coffee shop, finding Helen waiting on the last few customers of the day and Lucky bussing a full tub of glassware to the back for washing.

"Let me take that," he said, when he realized Lucky was about to drop it because he was staring so hungrily at Scout his hands had forgotten their jobs.

"And let me take that from you," Piers murmured, and Scout gave it to him almost reflexively, grateful for his friend—definitely a friend now, right?—as he hadn't known he could be.

Once Piers had gone to the back with the tub, Lucky grabbed Scout's hand and hauled him to the opposite end of the store, to the back of the bookshelves in a dark and quiet corner that only locals seemed to gravitate to, but they were all gone for the night.

"The hell was that?" Lucky asked Scout, but that was before Scout had his hands on Lucky's cheeks and was kissing him stupid. Lucky gave in immediately, all his fight obviously for show.

Ah! His taste, his smell! How could Scout keep going without it? How could magic exist if Lucky wasn't there in his world, *making* things magic in Scout's brain. Before, when it had been the mere dream of a Lucky, that had been enough to sustain him. But now? Scout needed him like fire needed fuel and fish needed wet.

He pulled away roughly, needing Lucky to answer him. "You're staying, right? They're gone. You can stay. You're not running, right?"

"Not running," Lucky panted. "Staying. Felt the coin burn. I was gonna talk to ya, I swear. Wasn't goin' nowhere." They leaned foreheads together while they both tried to master their breathing.

"Promise?" Scout begged. "You promise? You weren't gonna leave me?"

Lucky nodded and smoothed Scout's hair back from his forehead. "It's a mess," he muttered. "My God, you must have been sweating up a storm."

Scout grimaced. "It's the humidity," he said with as much dignity as he could muster. "Think I should put it in a queue?"

Lucky stared at him, seemingly at a loss. "A queue? That's what you're asking me now? You called those two bonobos up there and I almost shit my heart out my pants!"

Scout blinked. "Uhm, colorful?"

"*Terrified*! What were you thinking?" Lucky grabbed his shoulders and shook slightly for emphasis.

"That I, uhm, wanted you to stay," Scout said simply. "And if those guys were going to make you run, they needed to go away."

Lucky's eyes got really big. "Where did you send them? Scout, did you dump those assholes in the middle of the ocean?"

"Why does everybody keep asking me that?" Scout frowned. "But that reminds me, I really need to—"

His phone, that new appendage he'd been getting used to over the past two months, buzzed in his pocket, and he was pretty sure it wasn't Kayleigh.

"Uhm, excuse me." He took a step back and let out a breath when he saw the name on the front. "Sorry, Josue."

"Who even *are* these guys?" came his brother's exasperated voice. "Also, are you guys okay? You've been keeping in contact with Macklin's people, but I really miss you. You know that, right?"

Scout thought of all the isolation in the compound, and how he and Josue had shared a couple of smiles, maybe some eye contact, every day. It occurred to him that those moments were all that Josue had then too. And now Scout and Kayleigh were free and his brother was not.

"I do," he said gruffly. "We miss you too." He looked around the bookstore, thought about the island, and realized that if anybody needed to be there, khaki shorts, sunburnt nose, straw hat and all, it needed to be the brother who left the compound every day in a suit and came home every night to report to their father on things that Josue himself had never seemed to care about. "You should come here," he said simply. "You… where Kayleigh and I am now. I wish I could pull you out of there and let you run around here. I-I'd fight Alistair a thousand times so you could be free."

Josue gave a broken laugh. "That's never going to happen, little brother, but wherever you are, maybe someday I can visit." His voice firmed, as though remembering why he'd called. "Now about the two idiots who stumbled into the outer net of the compound, waving guns and bowie knives. Did you have anything to do with that?"

Scout sucked in a breath. "Well, it was… okay, not an accident. I needed them to be somewhere else. They were looking for a friend of mine the same way Alistair is looking for me and Kayleigh. It's not our fault Alistair's a dick and not my friend's fault these assholes want him either. You understand?"

"Yeah. I get it. But why here?"

"It's not like I've been around the world, Josue!" Scout said. "I thought of someplace I *didn't* want to be, and, well, there you go."

Josue let out a little cackle. "Well, the good news is, all they could talk about is some guy called Gestalt. Alistair thinks it's a rival wizard, and he's looking for that name in the family histories. The bad news is, they talked about an island…." Josue's voice trailed off. "Nobody can remember the name of it, though. It's weird. Not the yahoos who just left it, not Alistair, and not me. So wherever you are, you're protected somehow, which is great. But whoever this Gestalt is, you may want to warn him that he's on Alistair's radar now too, which might be not so great if he's the guy who sent them here!"

"I just told you *I* sent them there!" Scout protested. "*I'm* Gestalt! Why's that so hard to believe?"

Josue let out a little *oolf* of surprise. "You did. That's weird. It's like I've listened to Alistair tell me that you're not capable so many times I believe it, when I *know* it's not true." He made a sound like a man shivering. "Bwah. Scary."

"Man, Josue, you gotta get out of there. If Alistair is starting to fuck with your reality, you need to change your reality!"

For the first time, Josue seemed to take those words to heart. "You're right," he said, almost surprised. Then, "So was it you who broke Alistair's fireplace?"

Scout blinked, surprised at the change of subject. "Did what now?"

"Well, these three projectiles came out of nowhere, and you know Alistair's personal hearth—"

"The big brick phallus that he uses to intimidate people he locks in his little sanctuary to yell at?" Scout clarified sourly.

"Yes. That. Well, these projectiles—these round steel balls, I guess—came out of nowhere and broke the chimney. Just pelted it, one, two, three, and it crumbled. Alistair's starting to wonder who he pissed off."

Scout chuckled meanly. “Well, it’s not like I did it on purpose. I mean, everybody knows I can’t control my magic.”

Josue gave a derisive snort. “Oh, I think you can control your magic perfectly fine. It seems to be doing everything you need it to do exactly when you need it done.”

Scout gave another evil chuckle and then looked at Lucky’s anxious face as he tried to patiently endure the conversation. “Look, brother, I’ve got to go.” He hesitated. “Come look for me. Get out of the compound and try divination for where you should go next. If you don’t mean me any harm, I think you’ll end up here.” He thought of the endless blue of the ocean and the warmth of the sand. “If anybody deserves to be free, Josue, it’s you.”

It wasn’t his imagination; his brother’s voice had tears in it. “Thanks, little brother. You too. Take care. We’ll wipe these assholes’ memories and let them toddle home.”

“Good idea!” Scout said, suddenly excited again. “I know how to do that too. I’ll have to remember that next time!”

Josue’s laughter felt so real. “Take care of yourself, little brother.”

“You too.” The call ended, and Scout bit his lip, worried about Josue but needing to be okay with Lucky *now*.

“What?” Lucky prompted.

Scout smiled at him, suddenly exhausted. He’d sent two guys to upstate New York via portal, and it was like he didn’t remember how tired that could make a guy until right now.

“My brother, Josue, wants you to know that the two assholes with the guns and bowie knives have had their memories wiped of any time they spent here or in upstate, and they are now probably wandering around the tri-state area asking strangers if they know who they are.”

Lucky choked on a laugh. “Seriously?”

Scout shrugged. “I, uhm, wanted them somewhere you weren’t. The last place I ever want you to be is where I grew up, so, well, there they were. In the middle of the woods where I ended up after I got kicked out.” He gave a crooked smile. “’Cause, you know, I don’t want you to have to go anywhere.”

Lucky nodded, but he still looked worried. “But Scout, how’d they find me?”

Scout moved forward again and pulled Lucky into his embrace, grateful for his height and his reach, because he wanted Lucky to feel safe and this was the easiest way to do that.

"I don't know," he said, worried. "But you told me that the gang hunting for you had a witch—someone who was rolling the bones or whatever—tracking you. Josue said that the two guys didn't remember anything about the island, and even if they did, he and Alistair couldn't remember what they'd said. And seriously, it sounded like his own memory had gone wonky. I'm thinking that maybe the guys looking for you have someone innocent on their side. They're not having somebody's sister roll the bones so she can help her brother kill you. They're saying, 'Hey, sweetie, we need to find our friend.'"

"How do you know it's a sister?" Lucky asked suspiciously.

"I *don't*." Scout huffed out a breath. "I'm saying that whoever they've got tracking you must be totally innocent of *why* they want you. Because Alistair and Josue got nothing out of the guys I sent their way."

"Huh." Lucky glared at him, and Scout yawned.

"I'm sorry," he said behind his hand. "I'm sorry. I… that thing I did with the guys took it out of me. I'm sorry. I'm like, I totally want to spend the night with you, but first there's food, and then there's talking to people, and then there's—"

Lucky let out a breath and relented somewhat.

"Tell you what," he said. "You go nap. I'll finish up here. I'll meet you in your apartment when I'm done, and we'll figure out dinner then, okay?"

Scout smiled at him prettily. "Your apartment?" he asked. "Can we do yours? Kayleigh's like a herd of horses, which is weird because she doesn't *look* that big." He paused. "Wait—there's supposed to be a meeting at *our* apartment for dinner later."

"Yeah, sure, whatever." Lucky tried to grouse, but Scout could tell he was pleased. He dug in his pocket and came back with the keys. "You get some sleep in my apartment. We'll meet Marcus and Helen when you wake up. Just… you know. Take Piers to keep an eye on you as you sleep. Can you do that?"

"Wouldn't you rather have him here to help you finish early?" Scout offered helpfully, another yawn at the ready.

Lucky studied him, eyes narrowed to slits. "No."

Scout had no choice but to yawn again.

While You Were Sleeping

ONCE PIERS was in charge of half dragging an exhausted Scout down to the apartment through the back entrance, Lucky returned to help Helen clean up.

"Tomorrow's Monday—your day off, you know," she reminded him as he was busy washing glassware.

He glanced up. "I knew that," he said. "Why?" The island's tourist business was notoriously slow on Monday and Tuesday, picking up a little on Wednesday but getting super busy during the weekends.

"Because you and Scout both have the same day off," she said imperturbably. "But, you know, Marcus and I, we work."

They took turns taking entire days off, because their regular days were short-houred, although Lucky thought the shop was doing well enough that she could maybe get another helper or two.

"I know," he said. "Why? You gonna hire someone else so you can take two days off?"

"Perhaps," she said, nodding. "Wouldn't mind it. Marcus has Kayleigh and Scout. I could do with a couple of baristas, but that's not the point."

"What is?" he asked suspiciously.

"Well, you and Scout will have the day off, and you need everybody to perform the spell Scout's thinking about, and everybody won't be available. I'm just saying, I know your young man is driven, but tomorrow you will have him all to yourself. And while you may spend part of your time talking about magic, and hopefully part of that time making love, perhaps you could spend part of that time…."

"What?" Lucky asked suspiciously. "What would we spend the rest of the time together doing?"

"Well that," she said wisely, "is what you might want to find out. You've both had a lot of surprises that most young couples don't in the span of a few days. I think maybe tomorrow… well, it should simply be a day off."

Lucky thought briefly about things, such as Scout being carried away by a Wisp one night or randomly spotting gangsters in a crowd or even shaking hands with Lucky and being able to see the spirit trap.

"You know," he said, measuring his words, "I'm not sure if Scout's brain can ever really take a day off. I mean, Piers hits on him and bang. Piers has superpowers like me. Scout gets up to perform, and his father tries to take over his magic. I-I think maybe his magic always feels so out of control to him because he's just… I dunno. *Open* to it. He's *open* to the forces of the universe, to the things that nobody else knows but that he can see plain as the nose on someone else's face. He's never gonna be like anybody else. I mean, yeah, we may take tomorrow off and spend the day riding our bikes around the island or, you know, borrow Marcus's skiff and row out to John's Thumb and spend some cash on mai tais and a heated pool." John's Thumb was the unofficial island name for a swanky beach club owned by the Morgenstern Resort people. The resort provided transportation for its guests—for a price—but the island residents and employees were allowed access as long as they spent money at the bars and restaurants on the tiny spit of land. Locals eyed the Thumb with suspicion because, in spite of rising tide levels in the rest of the world, including the Spinner's Drift island chain, John's Thumb stayed exactly the same level, always.

"But it wouldn't matter," Lucky continued. "It wouldn't matter if we spent the day by a heated pool getting buzzed and making small talk. You can believe Scout's busy brain would get us into another adventure, or random attack droids from planet Sorcerous X would come for his scrawny ass, or killer bees would want to mate with his wild hair. A day with Scout is never gonna be normal." He smiled at that, thinking about Scout's wild hair that was much, much softer than it looked and about the way he never seemed flappable about outrageous things—like dropping two gangsters in upstate New York—but he got really passionate about making sure ghosts weren't lonely anymore.

"Would that be a problem?" Helen asked gently. "That Scout wouldn't have a normal sort of day?"

Lucky smiled a little. "No," he said. "Not even a teeny bit."

Helen put her hands on his shoulders, leaning over his back to kiss his cheek. "Then having a day off with him shouldn't be a hardship," she murmured. "And that's your last load of glassware for the sanitizer, and I've swept and mopped. By all means call us if something happens, but in the meantime, remember the sunblock, and definitely hydrate, but you two have a good day off, okay?"

Lucky smiled at her, feeling a contentment he couldn't remember since, well, since Auntie Cree had started getting sick, her heart, which had always been strong and steady, declining in a remarkably short number of days until it simply stopped working altogether.

"Helen?" he said, not wanting to get schlocky, but wanting to be grateful.

"Yes, dear boy?"

"I'm… I'm glad you gave me a job. And a place to stay. And, I mean, I know you're doing this as some sort of penance"—she'd never given him details, only that she'd deserted her post in some way—"but, well, you've been really kind to me."

"Oh, honey," she said with a sad sigh, "you're right that I've got penance to do. But you're not part of that. I gave you a job because I needed someone smart and hardworking, and I'm a nosy old broad about your personal life because, quite simply, I like you. You're not my penance. You're a perk."

He grinned at her, his eyes burning a little, but determined not to do sentiment, because they'd never been that way. "Well, you're definitely my boss, but you're a pretty good friend. Thanks for that."

She grinned, looking half her age, and she was sixty if she was a day in spite of the snarky T-shirts and the giant motorcycle she kept at Marcus's place, which she had reportedly driven into town last March dragging a small U-Haul with all her possessions behind it.

"Thank *you* for being a surly, irritable soft-touch who's worth my time. Now go chase down your boyfriend before giant birds swoop down out of the sky and try to nest in his hair. It really is remarkable, isn't it?"

Lucky nodded, flipping his own collar-length hair back with a simple twitch of his head. "He said something about a queue or a ponytail or whatever, but seriously, I'm like 'Buzz cut, my man. It's cute in your eyes and all, but we want you to live.'"

She cackled and sent him on his way.

WHEN HE got downstairs, he found Piers slouching against the outside entrance, arms folded, dealing with one-third of the Drift's small police/water force.

"I'm sorry, Officer…. What's your name again?" Piers asked suspiciously.

"Aldrun," he said. "Miller Aldrun." He was a relatively young man, maybe thirty, with regulation-cut brown hair, a square-jawed face with a divot on the chin, and thick-lashed brown eyes, which were currently focused on Piers with a mixture of sublime patience and irritation.

"So, Officer Aldrun, you wanted to talk to the Great Gestalt because… why?"

Aldrun grimaced. He had his helmet under his arm—his bike helmet—and was wearing the island uniform of khaki shorts with a utility belt featuring pepper spray and a taser. The resort had its own security, but the islanders counted on Aldrun and his two other counterparts to either monitor crime in the Drift or to call in big guns if anything more ferocious than a picked pocket or a bar fight erupted on their beat. He didn't exactly look tough or frightening, but he did look focused. Lucky emerged from the staircase, which came out right over the bathroom, and took in the scene—Piers in the outer doorway, keeping Aldrun at bay, and Scout, sleeping soundly in the bed, covers over his head, body curled into a protective little ball.

Abruptly he decided that Piers didn't suck and he could definitely stay.

"Yeah," Lucky said, putting on his best swagger to cross the apartment. "I'm sorry, what do you need to talk to Gestalt about?"

"Is his name really Gestalt?" Aldrun asked skeptically.

"Whatever his name is," Piers stated, that snooty rich tone in his voice that Lucky used to hate, "he is indisposed at the moment. What did you want to ask him?"

Aldrun let out a sigh. "We have reason to believe that two individuals disembarked from the ferry today armed with semiautomatic weapons," he said grimly. "Now, our last report was that these two individuals 'disappeared' during a stage performance with an individual we know only as the Great Gestalt and—" He gestured impatiently. "—he's sleeping right there! I just want to know what happened today and where those gun-toting gangsters went."

"Well, as far as Gestalt knows, they were hecklers from the audience that he used in the performance to give them a taste of their own medicine. He finished the trick, got them out of wherever they hid when they passed through the gate or whatever, and put them on the ferry out of town!"

Aldrun's jaw tightened, and Lucky tilted his head. Aldrun clearly didn't believe him, which was weird because it was the most obvious explanation.

"What do *you* think happened to them?" he prodded, exchanging glances with Piers.

Aldrun's eyes darted to the left. "I have no idea," he said. "I just need to make sure two armed individuals aren't running around the island and that your Gestalt didn't dump them in the middle of the Atlantic, either!"

"In October?" Piers said, mildly offended. "He's not that kind of magician!"

"And what kind of magician would that be?" Aldrun asked sourly.

"The kind who would drown two assholes in the middle of the ocean in hurricane season," Lucky shot back. "And yes, I know they were assholes because they were assholes to him during the show. But seriously, I'd look back on the mainland for them. As far as I know, they left after the final bow."

Aldrun took a step forward. "He's right there," he said, cajoling. "Why can't I ask him myself?"

"He's tired," Lucky said, not hating this guy but not wanting Scout to talk to him either. As unfocused as Scout seemed to get when he was tired, having him talk to any sort of authority seemed like a bad idea. "He works two jobs. Can't you wait until—" He heard the rustling in the bed behind him and the flapping of Scout's bare feet on the tile.

"It's fine," Scout said through a yawn. "No worries. Come on in, Officer." He yawned again, this one a doozy. Lucky thought he could probably count Scout's teeth.

"No he can't—" Lucky started, but Scout was a force of nature, as always.

"Don't worry," Scout said again, but this time his voice dropped tenderly, for Lucky alone, and he'd gotten close enough to put his hand in the small of Lucky's back, which Lucky had to admit did it for him big-time. "Come on in, Officer Aldrun. Piers, thanks so much for answering the door. I had no idea how tired I'd gotten!" With the manners of a marquis, Scout ushered the man in. "Lucky, do we have anything to offer to drink?"

"Coffee," Lucky said flatly. "Water."

"I brought some sodas," Piers said, smiling obsequiously. "They're in the fridge."

"That would be kind."

Lucky saw the way Piers was looking at Officer Aldrun with curiosity in his eyes, and something a little warmer.

Oh. Hey. Wow—it must be going around.

With an unhappy glance at Scout, he allowed himself to be steered toward his own kitchen so he could root the refrigerator for the pitcher of ice water he kept on hand and two of the sodas Piers had apparently moved into his icebox when he wasn't looking.

After serving everyone—Scout took the ice water—they all regarded each other over the island awkwardly, and then Scout broke the silence.

As only Scout could.

"So, you know the guys were armed, right? You could sense their weapons?"

Aldrun's wide brown eyes grew even wider, and Piers blew out a breath.

"Of course!" Piers looked around the island counter. "Duh! He's one of us."

Aldrun glared. "I am not. Who *are* you?"

Scout gave him one of those dreamy smiles and waved his hand in a circle, then turned it palm up. "Cupcake?" he asked, and Lucky looked in surprise at the confectioner's dream, big as a cabbage, that had appeared there.

On the top it had a big M.A. written in blue on the cloudlike frosting.

"Miller Aldrun," Scout said. "That's what you said, right?"

Aldrun took the cupcake warily, and then, to Lucky's surprise, took a bite out of it, closing his eyes blissfully.

"How'd you know?" he asked with a mouth full of sugar and frosting.

"This? Lucky guess." Scout winked. "But then, you're in good company for lucky guesses. Speaking of which, you sense weapons, right? That's why you knew those guys were armed?" he asked again. This time, disarmed by sugar frosting on a cupcake, Officer Aldrun nodded.

"Handy," Lucky said, not relaxing his scowl. "Small beat, you know who's armed—"

Aldrun swallowed. "Know who's crazy," he added. "Because lots of people have guns, but it's the crazy you need to be aware of. Anyway, I could feel armed and crazy get off the ferry. And then about the time I'd taken the skiff from the station on Kerry's Spit, it was just gone."

The station was on a small spit of land accessible to the mainland by car. In order to access the Spit, the tiny police force was outfitted with a number of watercraft and owned a small garage of scooters and bicycles that they transported by skiff. Lucky reflected, not for the first time, that being a cop for this little archipelago had some complications.

"Look," Aldrun said into the silence. "I asked around. Lots of people were really happy to tell me about the new magician and his fabulous act, and how the two jerks who couldn't keep their mouths shut got 'disappeared.'" He licked the corner of his mouth and eyed the rest of the cupcake with unfettered lust. "And you just made me a cupcake out of thin air. So I sort of need to make sure you're not… I dunno. Rasputin or Loki or someone who does bad things with magic, okay?"

"Well, those guys aren't dead," Scout told him. "Is that what you needed to know?"

"Are they being detained against their will?" Aldrun asked warily.

"No. My people are very catch and release. You'd approve." Scout waved his fingers. "Go on, take another bite. You know you want to."

Aldrun did, a slightly smaller one that did little to save his dignity. "Well, yeah, but they're crazy people with guns! Where did you release them!"

"Close to their home spawning point," Scout said, nodding "You know, where the other crazy people with guns reside so they can go be crazy people with guns together."

You," Aldrun said, looking a little hunted but still eyeballing the rest of the cupcake, "are making my head hurt. If they had guns and bad intentions, you are supposed to turn them over to the police!"

"No," Scout said, not even glancing in Lucky's direction. "No, because if they have guns and bad intentions, and *friends* with guns and bad intentions, then all I'm doing is making this peaceful little island a nexus for crazy people with weapons. But if I send them *back* to their friends, with no memories of how they got there or where they've been or anything about the Drift at all, well, they'll still be assholes with guns, but they will be where you expect to find assholes with guns, and cops with Kevlar and helmets can go take care of them."

"But—"

Scout waved his hands in the air. "We can't fix everything!" he said shortly. "I just got rid of bad guys without bloodshed. I'm calling it a win."

And then he yawned and sagged against Lucky a little. "I'm really tired," he said, and his irritation seemed to be entirely internal. "I'm tired, and now I'm cranky. You and Piers and Lucky talk about this. I'm going to nap."

Lucky gave a glare at Piers and Aldrun for good measure and helped Scout back to the rumpled bed.

"Well done," he said softly, pulling the blankets up to Scout's chin before kissing his forehead.

"Then why was he looking at me like I was crazy?" Scout asked, sounding plaintive.

"Your brain works a little faster than the rest of the world's, baby. You need to let the rest of us catch up."

"Upstate New York," Scout announced, and then he fell immediately asleep.

Lucky took a moment to look at him fondly before returning to the kitchen area to join the others.

"So," Miller Aldrun said thoughtfully, licking his fingers for the rest of the cupcake icing, "that was the Great Gestalt."

"Yup," Lucky told him. "Any other questions?"

"So, you and he…."

"Like this," Lucky replied, twining his fingers together. While they hadn't been like that *yet*, he figured he had plans for that night. "So you've got a… a mechanical magic thing too."

"A what?" Poor guy. He looked lost.

Leave it to Piers, with his innate pomposity or whatever to set him straight.

"Gestalt there figures there are three kinds of magic users," he said. "There are wizards who have *big* magic sort of baked in, and witches who learn how to pull the magic out of the world with spells and potions and whatnot, and, well, us. We have small, specialized skills—mechanics, like in a video game. So we're mechanics of luck, really."

Miller blinked, and Lucky got a five-second glimpse of somebody rearranging their world around new information.

"What… what mechanics do *you* two have?" He frowned, and Lucky noticed that one of his eyebrows seemed perpetually up, as though he was regarding the world with skepticism all the time. Given that Piers seemed to have *both* eyebrows up, as though continually surprised, he figured these two guys together might be a laugh riot, and he found himself rooting for Miller Aldrun and Piers whatever-his-last-name-was.

In answer, Piers raised both his eyebrows and the lights in the kitchen all went out.

And then came on again.

And then went out.

"Enough already," Miller grunted.

"We call him Lightning," Lucky said helpfully.

"And you?" Miller raised that eyebrow.

"Mine's secret," Lucky said, feeling smug. His coin was sitting in his pocket, cool and sleeping. Lucky knew enough about the thing to know that if this guy was a threat it would be burning a hole into his thigh.

Miller glanced at Piers, who shrugged. "We ask him important questions, he disappears and comes back with answers. That's all I know."

And now they both gazed calmly at Lucky, who stared back.

"I'm not gonna do it now. I'm not a circus pony. But I *can* tell you something about your crazy gun-toting bozos."

Miller tried a cop glare, but it was ruined by the fact that Lucky had just watched him make love to a cupcake and he still had icing on his upper lip.

"I'll take it," he said after a moment.

"They were from Philly," he said. "They were after me because of that thing I can do with the questions. I ran away because one gang was about to get wiped out, and I didn't want to be captured by another one—or shot—and here I am. So yeah, you see a gun-toting bozo on the ferry with a Philly accent, Scout and me would appreciate a heads-up. I'm thinking Scout can continue with the catch-and-release thing, but a little bit of warning would be appreciated."

Miller's mouth parted slightly, and Lucky wondered if he got a medal for a confession to a relative stranger. But trusting Scout had led to only good things, and so had trusting Helen. Maybe building a little community around luck mechanics wasn't the worst idea ever.

"Why are they chasing you again?" Aldrun asked, and Lucky had managed to get both of Miller's eyebrows to raise, so he figured that was his medal.

"'Cause the last guy figured out I could help him play the ponies. When the next guy wiped him out, I ran."

Aldrun swallowed, and for a second Lucky wondered if he'd seriously miscalculated based on Scout and a cupcake. Then he nodded.

"Okay." He pulled in a thoughtful breath. "I'll keep an eye out for bad guys from Philly if you—" He gestured in frustration at Scout, who had curled into a tiny ball like a pill bug, with the covers pulled over his head. "—don't let him drop bad guys in the Atlantic, okay?"

"He's not that kind of magician," Lucky and Piers said in the same breath, and Aldrun held out his hands.

"Okay! Okay! Fine." He let out a sigh. "But you guys will believe me, right? If I call you up and tell you there's trouble?"

Lucky and Piers both nodded, staring at him in surprise. "Well, yeah," Lucky said. "Why wouldn't we?"

A surprisingly bleak look crossed Aldrun's face, and Lucky had that sudden awareness that everybody had a story.

"It doesn't always happen," he murmured, voice harsh. "There's a reason for the Cassandra myth. Poor woman. It sucks to be telling people that there's something bad coming only to have people not believe you."

There was a strained silence, and right when Lucky was about to ask the obvious question—"What happened?"—Aldrun said, "Wait a minute. Are we the only people on the island who—?"

"No," Piers and Lucky both said in concert, and Lucky was starting to feel a serious kinship for the guy.

"But magic really isn't anyone else's secret to tell," Lucky added, relieved to see Piers nod. Behind them, Scout let out a light snore, and Lucky grimaced.

"Look, tomorrow's my day off, and seriously, me and him are goin' anywhere but here. But in the morning, if you want, meet us at Helen's place. You know where that is?"

"Books and coffee," Miller said dryly. "We all know where that is."

"Well, good. We're taking the first ferry out, but we can meet about an hour earlier. We can all have a conversation. It'll be cozy. But in the meantime…." He made shooing motions.

"He's sleeping," Aldrun acknowledged. He yawned. "Thanks for the sugar rush—man, I was so tired, I probably wouldn't have made it back to the Spit without it."

Piers gave Lucky an apologetic glance. "I think we can get you a place to nap if you need one," he said. "But let's you and I leave, and Scout can sleep."

With that, they both bid a courteous goodbye and slid out the front door, probably to go bother Marcus and Kayleigh and scare up the couch for their new friend.

Lucky cleaned up after their impromptu tea and then turned to see how Scout was doing.

Still sleeping.

Lucky moved restlessly around his apartment, wondering if he should try to read an e-book or maybe watch TV.

"Stop pacing," Scout murmured from the bed. "Sit next to me and read. I like you next to me."

Lucky gave a lopsided smile. That, as they say, was that.

As he propped himself up on the pillows and started listening to an audiobook, he kept one hand on Scout's hip and smiled.

KAYLEIGH CAME over about the time Lucky was thinking of getting up to make them dinner. She had big bowls of spaghetti with her and a long-suffering expression on her face.

"There is yet another strange man on my couch," she said disapprovingly. "But since everyone else is meeting at my place and Larissa is gonna sleep in Scout's bed again, and this guy swears he's going before nightfall so he can get back to the Spit, I may forgive you."

"Don't Larissa and Piers have, like, a suite at the resort?" Lucky asked, confused. He'd forgotten about the meeting at Scout's apartment, but apparently Marcus and Helen didn't need him and Scout to have a meeting. He set the bowls of spaghetti on the counter and *hmm*ed in appreciation. "Thanks for this, by the way. Your brother, apparently, can drop two assholes in upstate New York super easy, but he needs his nap time when he's done."

She gave a surprised laugh. "I should say so! Not even our father can portal people without some aftereffects. No, this is sleep well earned, my friend, which is why the two of you get dinner delivered."

"The two of us?" Lucky asked, curious.

"Well, yeah. You apparently protected him from the guy who's trying to wake up on my couch. By the way? I think Piers is eyeballing him like candy. You have nothing to worry about now."

Lucky gave a short laugh. "Well, not on that front. Your brother, though, he seems to be attracting luck mechanics like a flower attracts bees."

Kayleigh nodded, unsurprised. "But hey, knowing that people are armed and crazy is a pretty useful mechanic, you have to admit."

He held up his hands. "Not arguing. I'm just saying, I hadn't even *heard* this idea three days ago, and now there's me, Piers, this Miller Aldrun guy—"

"Larissa," Kayleigh said. "But her mechanic is really small."

Lucky made a "gimme more" gesture, and she laughed.

"Refillable drinks in the fridge."

"Oh my God," Scout said, remembering the convenient twelve-pack of sodas. "Let me guess, they're spilling out of your refrigerator—"

"We had to stack a couple of twelve-packs by the back door," Kayleigh told him, laughing a little. "I guess she's so excited to have people she can talk to or tell, it's kicking into overdrive. Maybe tomorrow we'll see if she can focus on coffee milkshakes and give the recycling can a break."

"But see?" Lucky told her. "That's what I'm talking about. I mean, it's like we're gathering here—"

"To help my brother," Kayleigh said, as though that was the most natural thing in the world.

"And you." Lucky waved his hands again. "Scout keeps saying you're a more talented wizard than he will ever be."

She let out a sigh. "Well, I could be, I guess. I mean, don't get me wrong. I could play the anything-you-can-do game like any other little sister. But Scout? What he lacked in power, or unadulterated rage, he made up for in wonder. In enjoyment. He *loves* magic. Make no mistake, he didn't think of being a stage magician as *ironic*, he thought of it as *exciting*. A chance to practice subtlety, finesse, and a little bit of hiding in plain sight all rolled into one. All these 'luck mechanics,' as you call them—this is one of the most exciting things he could possibly have dreamed of."

"What about you?" Scout asked curiously.

Kayleigh looked wistful. "I'll go on any adventure he wants," she said. "And not only because he rescued me once, pulling me through a portal he wasn't even supposed to be able to make. But because he rescued me every day. He snuck me out of the kitchen and into the woods and played with me, just because I enjoyed his company. Once, Alistair got so mad at me for defending Scout, he hit me with the power in his hand, which he claims he'd never done before. Knocked me through three layers of drywall."

"Oh my God!" Lucky gasped. "And you walked away?"

She shook her head. "Scout used magic to cushion me. It's the only reason I woke up in the sick room. I felt it wrapping around me like a blanket and keeping the worst of the force from caving my head in. He never once told me he'd done it, never once used it as leverage. Just was there when I opened my eyes. I told him I'd felt his protection, and he shrugged and said he wished it had been better. And that was it. So if all these luck mechanics are getting pulled to the island to help Scout on his quest, I'm one hundred percent behind that. He's always had my back, right? I'm fine if the whole world has his."

Lucky frowned. "He…. Was Alistair mean like that a lot?"

Kayleigh gave him a sympathetic glance. "You mean were we afraid for our lives? Well, I wasn't. Not until that moment, no. But Scout…. Scout had been, I guess, his victim a lot. I don't think he used physical force much, but if Scout messed up a potion, he had to drink it, even if it was lethal. That way, Alistair could be the one who saved him."

"Did that *happen*?" Lucky demanded, appalled.

She shook her head, a rueful smile taking the edge off what she was really saying. "Actually, no. But Alistair *thought* it had once. What Scout had done *should* have made it lethal, but, you know, Scout. He's such a sweetheart. It came out as soda—cola, I think. We didn't get a lot of junk food in the compound. He made a big show of oh God, he was going to die, and then he made sure I got some, because it was *delicious*."

Lucky made a hurt noise. "This is not…. How does someone like your brother *happen*?" he asked, wanting to crawl into bed and protect that weird, wonderful noggin on Scout's shoulders.

Kayleigh gave a sad little chuckle. "Magic. He's the reason for it. It's why I think he's insanely strong. He doesn't have a mean bone in his body. He's not going to take over the world because he can—he's going to fix the spirit trap on the island because he should."

"And we're gonna help him 'cause he's Scout," Lucky said, and it sounded simple and not thought-out at all, but looking at that softly breathing figure in the corner of the room, he got it now. He got why Kayleigh hadn't been so quick to forgive Lucky, either. Scout needed people in his life who were going to be kind and not going to desert him because of their own fears.

But then, Lucky had stayed that day. He'd felt the burning in his pocket, knew his enemies had almost caught up to him, and had stayed.

"Now you're getting it," Kayleigh told him. She yawned and stretched. "I work the magic shop tomorrow all day, which means it's Scout's day off. You guys do something fun, okay? I'll warn you, though, he's going to try to take you swimming on the east side of the island. It's cold as balls. I'm not even kidding."

Lucky snickered. "I know it is. Who goes swimming in the Atlantic in October!"

"My brother," she said softly. "And sometimes he needs someone to tell him something is a really bad idea."

In his head, he was already packing swim trunks and fleece. "And sometimes he needs someone who will do it anyway and then help him fix things when it goes wrong," he deduced.

"You really are getting it." She patted his cheek. "Enjoy the spaghetti!" And then she left.

Lucky had finished his dinner and cleaned up and then done some laundry in the industrial strength washer/dryer that Helen kept in the back of the kitchen for linens before Scout woke up. Lucky came downstairs hearing the comfortable sound of the dryer above him and found Scout sitting on one of the chairs in front of the television, eating steadily while watching *The Road to El Dorado* on Lucky's TV.

Lucky remembered what he and Kayleigh had talked about, how much rougher their home life had been than they ever let on, and how much the two of them adored cartoons.

He loved cartoons for the same reason.

He pulled up another stuffed chair and sat down next to Scout, quietly enjoying the movie. When it was over, he took Scout's bowl without a word and came back with a couple of cookies on napkins and a glass of milk to share. Next up was *The Emperor's New Groove*, and they watched that one appreciatively, laughing at the funny parts, giving commentary, and finally, when it was over, standing and stretching. Lucky switched off the lamp by the bed, which was the only light, then grabbed the remote from the arm of Scout's chair and clicked the TV off, leaving them in the ambient light from the window above the kitchen sink.

In the darkness, he helped Scout to his feet.

For a moment, they regarded each other silently. The air was so quiet they could hear the pounding of the ocean from beyond the breaker wall, and the moment grew heavy with promise.

"Scout?" Lucky said, not even caring that his voice cracked a little on the single syllable.

"What?" Scout asked huskily.

"When we go to bed tonight, I want to do serious stuff there. Serious stuff with you. And I don't want to worry about anybody else. Do you understand?"

"You mean, like, the boyfriend thing?"

"Yeah. It's real. Last night we were like, 'Until we can't stand it anymore,' and that's playing around. This is real. My biggest fear showed up on our doorstep, and I stayed, and then you got rid of it for me. I'm never gonna fuckin' leave you. You get that, right?"

Scout gave one of those dorky little smiles and ran his hand through his wild hair, making it part on the side a little.

"So, like, you're mine for life?" he said. "I can live with that."

Lucky wanted him so badly his stomach hurt with it. "You're gonna have to," he mumbled, taking Scout's face in his hands and pulling him forward. "I'm gonna make you mine tonight, and if I have to learn big magic to do it, you're never going to leave me."

"You're the magic," Scout said guilelessly. "I'll never want to leave."

He meant that too. Lucky squeezed his eyes shut, because they were burning and threatening to overflow, and pulled Scout in for a kiss.

For a moment their lips were briny, and the kiss was a little harsh, edgy and full with promises, uncomfortable conversations, and the ever-present threat of loss that both of them seemed to have lived through and embraced with their hearts.

But then, as with all things Scout, it softened and wonder crept in, and Lucky was transported to a place where the kiss was safe and Scout's arms were all the haven he'd ever need.

Scout's hands—wonderful, questing—ran up his back, under his shirt and sweatshirt, and Lucky ducked his head and allowed Scout to look at him. He was sturdy, he knew, stocky and muscular, and while not exactly a pinup, he wasn't bad. But Scout skated his lips along Lucky's shoulder like he was precious, too beautiful to touch, and Lucky threaded his fingers through Scout's hair and pulled him back for a harder kiss.

"Touch me," he ordered.

Scout grinned like those were words he'd been waiting for his entire life.

"I *love* touching you," he whispered, sliding his hands along Lucky's back, holding his fingertips out like the touch was sacred. "I've wanted to touch you since I first saw you." He shoved his hands in the waistband of Lucky's jeans and down along the backside, where he squeezed and kneaded. Lucky moaned and clutched Scout's shoulders harder, wanting so much, wanting *everything* in that moment.

He'd dreamed of having someone in his life, in his bed, but he wasn't like Scout. He hadn't read up on what they would do there. Their playful lovemaking the night before had delighted him, but he wanted something hotter, sweatier, more muscular right now. He wanted something irrevocable, that nobody could take away from him.

When Scout kept kissing hm, shoving his pants down, pushing him gently toward the bed, Lucky took his direction, wondering what Scout had in mind.

He ended up lying on the bed, naked, his legs spread as Scout made himself at home between Lucky's thighs. Scout's mouth on his cock was much more assured after their activity the night before, and his strokes were strong and firm.

Lucky moaned into the darkness around them, and Scout lifted his head. "Lubricant?" he asked. "I know you have some."

Lucky scrabbled around under his pillow where he'd put the bottle of slick he'd bought for his own pleasure. He handed it off to Scout, trying to find words for why this was different from what he expected.

Scout pulled off his cock, making sure to ply his tongue on the bell enough to drive Lucky mad, and said, "Wha?"

Lucky shook his head. "Keep… keep doing what you're—ah!"

Scout lowered his head again, and Lucky closed his eyes and lost himself in the moment, in the sensation, spreading his thighs and propping his feet on the bed, legs bent at the knees. He'd made a meal of himself, given himself over. Total abandonment and vulnerability, things he'd absolutely never shown another human being, were now Scout's to savor if he wished.

Lucky knew it was what *he* wanted, more than anything. He lost track of time for a moment, lost in the wonder of Scout's mouth, and then he felt Scout's fingers, cool with slick, push between his cheeks. A little wandering, a little exploration, and—

"Ah!" He lifted his hips in surprise, only to drive himself deeper into Scout's throat. He lowered his hips to avoid gagging Scout and found himself impaled more deeply on Scout's finger.

Scout's low chuckle told Lucky he found this situation *delightful*, and he used his tongue on Lucky's bell again. Lucky cried out and thrust forward; then Scout sucked a little harder and he rocked his hips back.

The burning in his asshole, the pressure there, was delirious, and Scout's mouth on his cock was sublime. After a moment he gave up on the surprise, on the order, and simply rocked forward and back, forward into Scout's mouth, back onto Scout's finger. He was enjoying the rhythm so much, only the extra pressure warned him that Scout had added another finger.

He groaned, finally admitting where this was going, and remembered his words.

"Yes," he whispered. "All of you, Scout. I'm ready. All of you."

Scout disappeared for a moment, leaving Lucky spread on the sheets and needing, and then Scout was back, his body covering Lucky's. In a moment, he placed the oiled head of his cock right at Lucky's entrance, and Lucky gazed up at Scout's cobalt eyes, almost completely black in the light from the window.

"Please?" he begged, fingers digging into Scout's biceps. "I need you so bad."

Scout nodded and slid forward, and for a moment, any doubts were driven out by the wonder of Scout's flesh in his body. A ring of fire appeared briefly behind his eyes, and then he breathed, pushing, accepting, and all that was left was pressure. And pleasure.

"Good?" Scout asked earnestly, and all Lucky could do was nod.

"Good," Scout replied, taking the nod for words. Slowly he withdrew, and Lucky whimpered in protest. Slowly he pushed forward, and Lucky moaned in delight.

"Very good," Scout said, almost to himself, chuckling gruffly. He pulled out and thrust again, and Lucky allowed himself to melt into the mattress, giving Scout permission to do whatever he needed to pleasure them both.

He was not disappointed.

Scout's thrusts became surer, more powerful, more *master*ful, and Lucky's arousal built higher and higher with every stroke.

Scout kept thrusting, kept *fucking*, and Lucky kept needing it, and more, and more, and harder, harder. "*Fuck me*!" he demanded, and Scout let out a cry of his own. Like Lucky's words had been a knife slicing through the restraints that had been holding Scout back, Scout's body became a purely sexual machine, moving inside Lucky like an earthquake, and Lucky was at his mercy, holding on for the ride.

Lucky's orgasm arrived like a freight train, taking him by surprise and throwing him right out of his own body, the sky opening up above his closed eyes, the brilliant light of pleasure searing his nerve endings, marking him forever, a creature solely possessed by Scout Quintero, never to belong to himself again.

He fell back to earth as Scout crested, and Lucky felt him spurting inside Lucky's body, hot and real, and Lucky shivered and came again, the aftershock rolling through him so slowly he thought he'd die in the release.

Scout moaned, burying his face in Lucky's neck as he came, and Lucky stroked the wild dandelion hair, whispering against his temple and telling him it would all be okay.

Their breathing stilled, and Scout captured his mouth in a gentle, searing kiss before sighing deeply and rolling to the side. Lucky was a mess, the come sticky, already starting to cool, but he was too boneless to get up.

"Wow," he breathed after a moment. Scout turned to him, stretching one arm up over his head and placing the other hand on Lucky's chest.

"Wow?"

Lucky managed to turn his head enough to see Scout's eyes dancing as his own breathing subsided.

"Yeah." Lucky captured the hand on his chest with his own and tugged it until it was over his left nipple—and his heart. "Wow."

"Holy wow," Scout said, completely serious. He scooted a little as the air cooled the sweat off their bodies and got close enough to kiss Scout's shoulder. "Definitely," he said. "Holy wow."

Lucky's eyes burned, but he couldn't look away from the amazing guy who had taken him to bed and done something "serious," as he'd said.

This was serious. Lucky had never been more serious. Was this why he'd run so hard? Had taken one look at Scout and done an about-face and tried not to engage? Because if he'd seen this coming, running from it hadn't worked. Surrendering to it and making light of it hadn't worked.

The only thing he thought might work was this, embracing it and begging for it and giving thanks every minute that this person had pretty much roped Lucky into his life.

"Holy wow," he repeated, smiling a little. His eyes spilled over, but Scout was curling into his body, pulling up the covers, cocooning them and protecting them and keeping them safe, so Scout didn't see.

Lucky closed his eyes, already drifting off, naked and messy and replete, when Scout murmured, "What were you going to say? Right when things got really intense? I-I was worried there that I'd done something wrong."

Lucky let out a chuckle. "I was gonna say I always thought I'd top." He chuckled some more, weakly. "Didn't realize I'd fallen in love with a hurricane."

"Mm…." Scout pushed up against him, snuggling aggressively, and Lucky raised his arm so Scout could put his head on Lucky's shoulder.

"You can top tomorrow," Scout mumbled. "Or later. Or in an hour. Or…."

He drifted off, and Lucky's shoulders shook with another chuckle that didn't touch his voice. Or never. He had the feeling it didn't matter who penetrated whom, Lucky was always going to be along for the ride.

Holy wow.

SOMETIME IN the night, Scout woke him up again, slowly, languorously, rubbing his stomach first, then his chest, then his thighs. By the time Scout's elegant, long-fingered hand had reached Lucky's cock, Lucky had rolled over and pulled his knees up to his chest, begging.

"Again. God, yes, again."

This time had been slower, dreamier, and when it was over, Scout's warmth disappeared for a moment as Lucky shuddered the last of his orgasm into the sheets. When Scout returned, he had a washcloth and a towel, and Lucky felt himself being gently cleaned off as though from a great distance. When he came back to himself, Scout had made him stand up so he could spread the towel down on the bed and neither of them had to sleep on the wet spot.

Shortly after, they were settled again, and Scout was spooning Lucky from behind, and Lucky heard his own voice from far away.

“This is nice. This is happy.”

“You know, I think you’re right.”

Scout nuzzled the nape of his neck, and Lucky settled more securely into his arms.

He slept deep and dreamlessly, trusting that Scout would be there in the morning.

Far Side of the World

"SCOUT," LUCKY said, frowning at him from their lean over the island counter in the kitchenette. "Are you sure that's what you want to do?"

"Well, yes," Scout said, smiling prettily. "Don't *you* want to get off the island?"

"Yes and no. I mean, yeah, 'cause it's an island, but no too. I haven't left since I got here in July. Why would I? The coin led me here—the island kept me safe. Why do *you* want to get off the island?"

Scout fidgeted. "Because Kayleigh and I drove straight through," he said apologetically. "When those two goons came at me, I couldn't think of one place to send them besides near the family compound. I mean, think of how much more poetic it would have been if I could have sent them to, I don't know, a police station in Charleston? And besides that," he said, biting his lip in thought, "I want to see what happened to Tom. Kayleigh said he died of cholera, and he worked for the Morgensterns, and I'm wondering if we could find his grave. I-I think it may be a key to easing some of the misery of the spirit trap."

Lucky blew out a frustrated breath. "But I thought this was going to be our day!" he said, and Scout grinned at him.

"It *is*. And we get to get off the island, and we get to see a city we don't know. I mean, looking for Tom is only part of it. I want to see the waterfront park and the old French quarter. And I understand there's a ghost tour we can take this evening. I already made reservations just in case you wanted to go!"

Lucky stared at him, nonplussed.

"You made reservations?"

"On my phone! Isn't that amazing?"

"Yeah, Scout. Those things are little miracles. I just… I mean, don't you want to go have fun?"

"Well, yeah! That's why I want to tour Charleston! It sounds like fun, and we can do some research, and that's fun too!" He stared at Lucky for a moment, his brow wrinkled with apprehension. Oh no. They'd said things the night before. They'd done things, things they couldn't take back. What if… what if in this one small, enormous thing, what to do on their day off, they were completely incompatible?

Scout's heart started to beat threadily, and for the first time since he'd found himself in the woods in New York, he felt vulnerable and stupid and small.

Then Lucky's expression relaxed, his square-jawed face growing handsome with his smile.

"No, I get it. I'm sorry. I just… you work so hard. And you really wiped yourself out last night. I worry, you know? That you'll spend all this time working for other people and not for you." He grimaced. "Us."

Scout nodded, seeing his point, and waved his hands wildly over his cereal bowl to see if he could explain. "I know this probably sounds nuts to you," he said, "but this mystery thing? This *is* fun. For my entire life, minus the last five to six weeks, my perfect day was spent slipping away from Alistair's lessons and all that grim disapproval, and being allowed to read books about the world and practice magic *I* wanted to practice and explore as much of the natural world as I could find. The entire *world* was a mystery to me. And getting to go on a tour of a town, particularly a bustling one like Charleston? And explore a bigger mystery than I ever imagined in *real* life? This is exciting! It's not even work!"

Lucky laughed then, and shook his head. "Yeah, but Scout, for you, work isn't work."

Scout felt his smile stretch his cheeks. "Well, no. It's not. It's a blast. I… the whole world can be so much fun. I just want you to come with me and see it. Is that so bad?"

"No," Lucky said softly. "We still have people after us, but, you know, I've got my coin, and you can make people disa-fuckin'-pear. You're right. A few tours of Charleston shouldn't be a bad thing." He grimaced. "But we've got to meet that Miller Aldrun guy in the coffeehouse before the first ferry leaves."

Scout chuckled. "Yeah, and we should probably shower and wash your sheets."

Lucky's eyes slid slyly to his phone. "We've got, uhm, a couple of hours before we have to meet everyone. You, uh, want to make sure those sheets are totally ready for the laundry?"

Scout practically danced where he sat. "I thought you'd never ask!"

THEY REACHED the coffeehouse a little before 10:00 a.m. and found Kayleigh pacing back and forth, muttering to herself, in their customary place in the back.

"What's wrong with her?" Scout asked Larissa, puzzled.

"Apparently she's not good at the magician thing," Larissa answered back.

Scout rolled his eyes. "She's great! She might need to practice a little—"

"Shut up, Scout," Kayleigh muttered, not stopping her pacing. "Go meet with your new luck mechanic and let me finish freaking out. It's part of my process."

"Ooh," Scout said, impressed. "You have a process! I need to find one or I'll never get any better."

"*Shut up, Scout*!" Kayleigh roared, and Scout hurried back to the furthest corner away from her.

"I forget how nervous she gets," he told Lucky sincerely, and Lucky nodded like he understood something Scout didn't.

They made their way to the tables and the couch and found Miller and Piers deep in what looked like earnest conversation. Scout smiled at them, feeling sunshiny to his bones, flipped one of the solid wooden chairs around, straddled the seat with his long legs, and leaned against the back.

"Hi," he said brightly. "So, uhm, what did you want to talk about?"

"Well, I don't know about you," Piers said dryly, "but I was telling him about Larissa's stalker so he knew what to look for in case he got one of his little feelings."

Scout's eyebrows went up. "You know, that's a really good idea. We should know about that—"

"We don't know what he looks like," Piers interrupted blandly. "But we assume he's sort of an average-looking white guy because our parents don't know many POC and they would stand out. He does creepy personal things—leaves flowers on her pillow while she's asleep. Drugs her cat so it won't wake her up in the morning."

"How did you know it was drugged?" Lucky asked, alarmed.

"It started puking," Larissa interjected. "We had to take it to the vet, and they said someone had given it an anesthetic that hadn't been measured correctly."

"What else?" Scout asked, staring from Piers to Larissa in horrified fascination.

"Steals my"—Larissa turned pink—"underwear. Only the pretty lacy ones. They just disappear."

All of the men wrinkled their noses.

"I'm so sorry," Scout told her. He'd grown up without any expectation of privacy. The idea that someone could have privacy and have it ripped away seemed horrifying.

"Thanks, Scout," Larissa said soberly. She was a pretty girl, maybe eighteen or so, with a long chestnut-colored braid, freckles across her cheeks, and large brown eyes. Scout felt a surge of protectiveness in his chest. Kayleigh had all that suppressed rage to keep her safe, but Larissa seemed so vulnerable.

"Did he do anything else?" Lucky asked.

"Killed all my plants," Larissa said sadly. "I don't know how he did it. It was weird. It was like, I'd walk into my parents' house and think, 'He's been here,' and then their plants would be sort of droopy, and by the time I got to my room, my plants would be *dead*. And my parents have a plant *service*. Nothing should have been dying at *all*."

"Not fabulous," Scout muttered, looking at Piers and Miller, who both nodded.

"Stalker with a mechanic power," Miller muttered. Then he brightened. "Which, you know, maybe now that I have people I can talk to about *my* power, I can figure out how to sniff this guy out."

"Oh please?" Larissa said, looking at Miller with begging eyes. "It would be *great* if I could feel safe again. I was supposed to start college this year. Piers was in his last year to get his law degree, and I was going to attend the same school for a year. We both had to put it off because of this, and I was *really* looking forward to it."

She smiled prettily, and Scout smiled back, enchanted. It was like being begged for help by a fairy princess. There was no sexual attraction involved; it was sheer charm.

"I can't make any promises," Scout said, looking at Miller, Piers, and Lucky, "but now that we all know what to look for, we can at least keep an eye out." He paused, chewing his lip. "And maybe the island is too. I mean, Lucky got a warning when his trouble was nearby. I'm thinking maybe running into Miller is a good thing. Miller can keep an eye on who gets on the ferries and such, and, you know, if his mechanic is knowing who's armed and crazy, maybe he really is our secret weapon."

"I do feel safer now," she said, inclining her head regally to the young peace officer, and he smiled, obviously as enchanted as Scout, and tipped his imaginary hat.

"So now that we're a secret club," Piers said, "do we do something? Invent a password? Meet once a week and have an agenda? What?"

Scout blinked at him. "Well, meeting once a week wouldn't suck," he said, "but that's just because Kayleigh and I aren't used to having a peer group we don't have to like because we live with them."

Kayleigh looked up from where she was obviously doing something complicated with her hands that would probably look a little better with the stage props and an audience.

"You all don't suck," she said shortly. "Dinner, mine and Scout's apartment, every Tuesday night. Club meetings may commence. It would be great if you brought extra food."

Scout laughed a little, and they all heard the ferry horn from the port outside. He stood and looked at Lucky, who smiled back.

"We're going to go check out Charleston for the day," he said. "We'll be back on the last ferry. Kayleigh, do you want me to pick up dinner to cook?"

She shook her head. "I have a thing I want to—"

"Wants me to make," Piers interjected smoothly. "I'll do the shopping."

They all looked at him in surprise, and he managed to look sheepish. "You all have been very hospitable. I'd like to return the favor."

Scout grinned. "Excellent. We'll see you back at the apartment." He stood. "Have a great day everyone!"

And then he turned and grabbed Lucky's hand, and together they ran for the ferry. They were both wearing jeans and hooded sweatshirts, and the wind whipped around their faces, tossing Scout's hair to a thousand different places and making Lucky look tousled and sexy. As they rushed up the on-ramp of the ferry and to the prow, where they could look out into the vast blue and anticipate their destination, he felt an absolutely glorious burst of joy.

Moments from their lovemaking that morning flitted through his mind—from the taste of salt on skin as Scout had skated his lips along Lucky's neck to the soft gasp Lucky had made as Scout had taken his cock into his mouth to the brightness of Lucky's muddy green eyes and the silk of his body as Scout had possessed him.

That had been *them*, brilliant bodies, unfettered spirits, and this was *them* now, under a dazzling October sky.

He closed his eyes and turned his face to the sun, keeping tight hold of Lucky's hand.

"Happy?" Lucky asked in his ear.

"So happy. You?"

Lucky let go of his hand and moved close enough for Scout to drape his arm over Lucky's shoulder.

"So happy," Lucky told him. "Let's go see the world."

Big Scary Things

IT WASN'T quite the world, but it was a cozy little metropolis, with a charming waterfront featuring a pineapple fountain and a picnic area where they ate a food-truck sandwich and some truly decadent rosemary Tater Tots while discussing their future.

"I mean," Lucky found himself stammering, "I *like* the island. I suppose we could go wandering when all is said and done, when everything is safe and all the guys in Philly are dead or in jail, but I don't want to go back to Philly, if that's what you mean."

Scout paused, looking thoughtful. "I-I know what you mean. It's like, I want to see the world, but I want a home base too. The good thing about the compound was that people would definitely miss us if we didn't show up for dinner, you know? I want to see so much, although I think coming up with a passport might take a bit of magic I don't know how to do yet. I don't even think we *have* birth certificates, Kayleigh and me, but we can figure it out."

Lucky started to chortle, his stomach muscles convulsing, the guffaws exploding out of his mouth, and Scout stared at him, hurt.

"What?" he said. "I mean, I know we're a little behind in the modern-world department, but—"

Lucky held up a hand to stop him and tried to get his breathing under control. After a minute, after he'd wiped his mouth off and sat up straight, he looked at this wonderful, beautiful man, his first and only lover, and shook his head.

"Baby," he said gently, "you can transport people from one place to another through holes in space and time. Why do you need a passport? There's no reason to get on a plane!"

Scout blinked and started to giggle. "I swear, it never occurred to me."

Lucky nodded, keeping his laughter at bay. "I mean, I'm sure there's logistics. You'd have to have your brother show you how to go places you've never seen before, but, you know, grab our luggage and step through a portal to our intended destination—or behind the hotel at our intended destination—and, you know, vacation has begun."

Scout grinned at him, a child's grin, as though Lucky's words had opened up the world for him.

"That's so odd. All this time I only ever thought about how much fun it would be when I got better at magic. I never really thought about what getting better at magic could do for me." He paused. "I mean, besides rescuing Kayleigh, that is."

"Are you sure she's the reason he's after you?" Lucky asked, not sure how this was possible.

"Well, I know he wanted to marry her off into something advantageous. Think Lucretia Borgia or someone like that. The women could have extraordinary value as commodities. I don't know why he'd want me back." Scout sighed. "I'm just not that important to him."

And a week ago, Lucky wouldn't have seen it, but they'd been close since then, had worn each other on their skin.

"That hurts you a little," he said, thinking he must be really dumb if he hadn't seen this before.

Scout shrugged. "I'm not sure why. The whole system was psychotic. I guess until the very end, I thought if I was good enough at magic, my father might love me." He shrugged. "Dumb, but you know. I guess the best part of that is what I couldn't summon for Alistair, I summoned for Kayleigh and for you. I mean, you're the people I'd rather have in my life, I guess."

Lucky grinned. "And I, for one, will never stop counting my blessings." He sobered. "Now we've got a couple of hours before the next ferry. Where to next?"

"I need to find out where Tom Marbury was buried, remember?" Scout said with a sigh.

"Well, I was hoping you'd forget," Lucky said sourly, "but since you haven't, c'mon." He stood and offered Scout his hand. "I'm not sure where you want to start."

Scout held out his phone. "Actually, Marcus and Kayleigh found it for me last night on the internet. See, Tom worked for the MorganStar company—it's the Morgansterns now, but back then they were trying to be fancy. They apparently had a *lot* of people die in the cholera epidemic in 1873. Their employees were living in sort of a shantytown, and the owners of the company refused to pave the streets or help with sewage. So, disease. There was such an uproar from the island—where the Morgansterns came from—that they offered to bury the dead with markers. There's a plot for island folks on the Morgenstern property, which is one of those big old mansions built post-Civil War. So we're doing two things, right?"

"We're touring a big old house and grounds and talking to a ghost," Lucky supplied dryly. "Yeah, Scout, I get it. An outing that's fun for the whole family."

Scout grinned. "Someday, yes."

Lucky's eyes narrowed as Scout grabbed his hand and hauled him through the waterpark to where they could catch a rideshare.

"What do you mean someday? Scout? Scout, what are you talking about?"

But Scout was on a roll now, and if Lucky wanted to guess about family and seeing Scout hold a tiny child and show it all the affection and fun that Scout had missed during *his* childhood, Lucky wasn't going to get in his way.

It was a good dream. Lucky was on board.

AN HOUR and a half later, after taking the walking tour of the MorganStar mansion grounds and ogling the beautiful landscaping with the graduated infinity pools that led up to the back of the mansion itself, complete with tilework and cabanas in which to dress, they were no longer laughing.

They'd split off from the main tour group and found the graveyard in the back, the nearly 250 graves sobering and tragic.

"There's whole families buried here," Lucky muttered. "This is the worst."

"Look," Scout told him, dragging him across a small plot of headstones to the plaque, where he began reading out loud.

> *Industrializing the South came with a terrible human cost. The MorganStar company, worried that taking care of its employees would cut into its profits, allowed them to live in squalor, to the great shame of the Morgenstern descendants. This graveyard is dedicated to the faithful employees who lost their lives in the cholera epidemic of 1873, and the Morgenstern family rededicates itself to serving the greater public good on this day, June 15, 2017 A.D.*

"Huh," Lucky said. "That's pretty recent. I wonder which descendant got that attack of conscience."

"I think Callan," Scout murmured, looking from his phone to the plaque. "He's the youngest, a little older than we are. Kayleigh says he's the one who keeps intervening for employee rights when she works the resorts. I'm betting he's the one who made sure the graveyard was kept up—it's apparently been restored—and made all the promises and stuff."

Lucky shrugged. "Go millennials."

Scout laughed and then sobered, looking around the graveyard.

Lucky seemed to catch his mood because he started looking around too. "What are you seeing?" he asked, eyes narrowed. The place was set in a two-acre clearing, and the graves were fairly close together. The clearing was bordered by trees, all of them fluttering with Spanish moss, so there must have been tributaries or irrigation ditches behind them. The yard itself was mostly sunny, but Lucky felt an abundance of… shadows.

Pale, insubstantial shadows that seemed to move, not with breeze or clouds or….

He shuddered and looked back at Scout. "Are we surrounded by ghosts?"

"Yup," Scout said, seemingly unfazed.

Lucky was very, very fazed. "Oh, the things I wish I didn't know."

"They're different than the ones in the spirit trap," Scout said analytically. "These ghosts are… they're like memories and dreams. There's an occasional dark one—" Scout grimaced and stepped aside while the sunny green strip to his left turned just the tiniest bit browner. "—but mostly, there's…." He smiled wistfully. "There's a lot of people remembering their best moments here. Families holding babies, young lovers, stolen kisses." He saw something else that caught his eye, and he looked even sadder. "And struggling against injustice." He gave Lucky a look that went many miles deeper than any pain Lucky had ever felt for himself, or even someone he loved, like Auntie Cree or Scout. "There's a lot of sorrow in the world, Lucky. We need to remember to hold on to the sunshine, okay? Remind me of this place if I ever start to forget."

While Lucky was still grappling with that, one hand to his chest while he sought for some means to comfort the man by his side, Scout's expression lightened.

"Oh, hey. What have we here? C'mon!" And with that he grabbed Lucky's hand and hauled him across the grounds. Lucky's view went from clouded with shadows to full-on theme park, and he could only be grateful Scout was bobbing and weaving like the spirits or ghosts or memories or whatever they were would feel solid upon impact.

"Scout," Lucky cried, mostly hoping to make him go a little slower, but Scout, hell-bent on his destination as always, kept going. Lucky was faced with either letting go and losing the experience of doing this with Scout, or holding on.

He held on.

Eventually their pell-mell dash ended at the corner of the estate, right before the manicured green of the yard faded into the darkness of trees and a wildlife preserve that Lucky hoped housed the happy, fluffy kind of wildlife and not the scaly, hungry kind.

For a moment, Lucky stood, panting, clutching Scout's hand and watching the movement of the shadows thrown by the Spanish moss as they danced across the lawn.

Then he held a little tighter to Scout's hand as he realized that the sun was behind clouds and there were no shadows.

"Look at them," he said in awe.

It was a little like a parade. People, old and young, caught between their best and worst memories, moved between the darkness of the trees and the brightness of the cemetery. Lucky watched a young man holding a little girl by the hand simply stroll into the light, pointing something out to the child as she skipped excitedly. The young man was wearing breeches with suspenders and a newsboy's cap. He could have been her older brother or even her father, and she looked at him adoringly. Their image flickered out, and Lucky watched the same young man, on his knees, doubled over and retching, crawl into the darkness of the trees.

He realized that the spirits he'd seen weren't static, stuck in one moment of their lives, but transitory, much like human experience itself, shifting from the best and the worst and the peaceful and the frantic, as easily as shifting from the shadows to the sun.

He stared helplessly at Scout, wanting a breath, a minute, to make sense of the great spectacle of the dead, but Scout was looking into the eyes of a handsome young man who seemed very familiar.

He was midsized by modern standards, about Lucky's height, which probably made him fairly tall by the standards of his day. Young—early twenties—in knee breeches, suspenders, and a striped shirt with a collar, he wore a battered newsboy cap and held a leather satchel slung around his shoulders.

Unlike the other specters floating between darkness and bright, this one seemed to remain stable. There were occasional flickers. He went from hale and healthy to peaked, with sunken eyes and starveled lips, and from smiling to grieving, but much of his life seem to have been spent with the quiet, steady-eyed gentleness he was currently regarding Scout and Lucky with.

"Hullo," Scout said, smiling warmly at the young man. "You must be Tom!"

Tom's face—and he was a good-looking lad, with a cleft in his chin and dimples in his cheeks—split into a smile.

"Islanders!" he said, the word aching with relief. "Oh please, tell me you're from the Drift!"

"We are," said Scout, that tender smile still in place. For a moment, Lucky was jealous of a man who'd died at least a hundred and fifty years ago. "Or we're new to the Drift, but we love it already."

"I can tell." Tom nodded soberly. "You've sort of a glow about you. I can tell those who love the islands."

"They're beautiful," Lucky managed, and his heart swelled a little. "I've… I grew up in the city, and I love being surrounded by the sea."

"Aye," Tom murmured, nodding. "Aye." He swallowed hard, and even though he was as transparent as the next ghost, Lucky could see his eyes brighten. "I've got… people on the island," he said, biting his lip. "A mum, a little sister, a-a friend. The best friend." He paused for a moment and took in the two of them, hands clasped. "A friend like you two," he said with a hesitant smile.

"A forever friend," Lucky said softly.

"Aye." Tom's chest rose and fell slowly, a being who hadn't breathed in a hundred and fifty years, fighting for the air to speak. "I've been away so long. I promised I'd return, and I'm afraid… afraid the world's fallen apart around their ears without me. Is that strange?"

Lucky brought his free hand up to rub his chest and thought of all the people on the island whose lives had been turned upside down in the best way because Scout had failed his father's magic test. Kayleigh, Marcus, Piers, Larissa—even that Miller Aldrun guy. Helen loved them. He fought brightness in his own eyes. *He* loved them. Loved Scout. Was terribly, fiercely in love with Scout.

"No," he said, while Scout seemed to be earnestly pondering the question. "No. It's not strange. Some people…. When they're gone, it punches a hole in the world. If you were loved, and loved fiercely, your world will miss you. Trust me." He fought not to look at the man by his side. "It's a real thing."

Tom gave a relieved smile. "That's good to hear," he said. "I want to get back so badly. I… it's like I can feel them, looking across the sea, looking for me, and I seem to have lost my way home."

Next to him, Scout made the most forlorn noise. "Well, then," he said, his voice gravelly. "Me and Lucky, we'll have to help you back, don't you think, Lucky?"

Lucky nodded. "Oh yes. We'll—"

"But wait!" Tom looked at them earnestly. "You won't know them! Here." And with that, he reached under the collar of his shirt and brought out a chain holding plain gold band, like a wedding band.

Almost identical to the wedding band that Scout had clenched in his fist when he'd followed the Wisp to the soul trap not even a week ago.

"A ring?" Scout said, taking it from Tom, holding it in his hand where it winked prettily in the cloud-filtered light from the sun.

"Yes," Tom said. "It's got an inscription in the center. You find the boy named Henry who has a ring like that, and he'll know it's me."

"Understood," Scout said roughly. "And in the meantime, we'll work to get you home."

A smile flickered across Tom's face, and then he was gone.

Together they looked inside the gold band. It read, *Henry's*.

"YOU'RE QUIET," Scout said later, as they stood on the prow of the ferry, headed for home.

"My heart hurts," Lucky said baldly, not sure how else to say it. "That's a long time, you know? To stare across the ocean and hope when…." This sounded stupid and romantic, but gah! He could still taste Scout's kisses! Still feel the void he'd left when he pulled out of Lucky's body. Still smell their come on his skin.

"When what?" Scout prompted gently, bumping Lucky's shoulder with his own. Lucky looked into his brilliant eyes and the hair that should have been ridiculous but was simply grander all the time.

"When you weren't sure the other half of your heart was staring back," Lucky said, lost, helpless, his throat dry. And that was it. The thing he'd feared, probably since he'd first set eyes on Scout six weeks ago.

That this brilliant, fascinating creature could fly away, leaving Lucky pining mournfully in his wake.

"He is," Scout said, turning to face him. "I am. I don't ever want to leave you, Justin."

Lucky swallowed, wondering what it was about the name he'd always hated as a kid that made him all melty now.

"I don't want to leave you either, Scotland Quintero," he said solemnly, expecting a smile from Scout.

What he got was Scout's widened eyes and a mild panic. "Uhm, maybe don't use that name off the island?"

Lucky widened his eyes in return. "Why? I thought, you know, you just didn't like it. It was like, sweet, like you called me Justin and I—"

"Well, yeah. But like I said, real names have power, and uhm…."

Scout gasped, and Lucky felt it—a pressure over them, like he couldn't breathe. He looked around frantically and saw a dark cloud coalescing over their heads.

"Scout?" he asked, frantically clutching Scout's hand in his.

Scout glared up at the cloud, squeezed Lucky's hand, and said, "I'll be at the clearing. Trust me, okay?" He gave Lucky his best, most brilliant smile, then let go of Lucky's hand and shouted, "C'mon, Alistair, you showy coward, come get me! It might not go how you want it to, I warn you!"

As if in answer, the cloud went vertical, much like the spinning discs that Scout had used to create the portal that had gotten rid of the two Philadelphia gangsters. Slowly enough to show some gravitas, the disc set itself down on the prow, giving the few passengers on the sparsely populated ferry a good eyeful of something they couldn't explain and showing Lucky and Scout a portal surrounded by an aura of fire. Standing on the rim, as though there were a dais there made for him, was a man a few inches shorter than Scout, but with cold indigo eyes and a salt-and-pepper-streaked gray beard.

"Scout," Lucky murmured, his heart in his throat. "No. Don't go. Don't…. We can…."

"Run?" Scout asked tenderly, skimming fingertips over Lucky's cheek. "You deserve better than that, Lucky. Don't worry." His goofy, dreamy grin popped out, and Lucky wanted to cry. "Have a little faith, right? I mean, I'm stronger than I look!"

And with that, he turned toward the man who must have been his father and said, "You'll never get her, you sonuvabitch."

And with that, he broke away from Lucky, and to Alistair Quintero's obvious surprise, he charged into the portal and leaped, tackling his father into the whirling magic gateway and disappearing.

The portal closed like the top of a drawstring purse, and one lone soul started screaming, leaving Lucky on the prow of the ferry, cold and alone and terrified for the goofy magician with the dandelion hair whom he loved with all his heart.

Alistair

SCOUT KNEW how to steer a portal. He'd done it once when he'd gone to get Kayleigh, and again when he'd flipped their friends from Philly back to the East Coast. He'd learned to control—albeit barely—the whooshing of his own blood in his ears and the sudden dip of magic when it was disbanded, zinging into the atmosphere like an electric charge.

He'd tackled Alistair to give himself a chance to take over the destination of the portal, and praise the saints, it worked.

Part of it was that the only place he wanted to be was home.

His real home. On the island with Lucky and Kayleigh and the kindly Marcus, who didn't seem to expect anything from him but that he tried his best. With Helen, who was so fiercely protective of Lucky that she lost her temper when he knew she didn't mean to. Where the waves and the sun and the sand all met and frolicked and quarreled and danced like old friends.

He'd felt strong on the island, comfortable. His whole life, Alistair had simply pulled magic out of the air and expected Scout and the other boys to follow. Alistair had always dictated what came next and always had the advantage.

Scout wanted Alistair on his own turf. He had that now, a place he understood, small and sure, where he was familiar with the market on the corner and the times the ferries ran. He felt when the sun would hit his apartment bed and when the air got sticky and cold with the evening wind in the autumn.

This was his place. He knew the ghosts here by their first names, and where the library was, and he could plant his feet where the sea met the sand and show Alistair the way home.

The portal dispersed, and Alistair and Scout were flung along the beach, rolling down the sand, and Scout pulled himself to his feet and took a quick look around.

Yes! There was the clearing, and there was Tom's bench, and there were the spirits Scout had visited, the ones trapped in the saddest, most destructive pattern of their days and not allowed to flow from the good to the bad to the peaceful until their hearts were full and ready to rest.

He felt the presence of the Wisp, breathless and quivering on the edge of the clearing, and the dark and terrible presence of the thing that had tried to drown him twice, once in the ocean and once in the layers of memories that wrapped around the trap itself.

They were both there, the good and the bad of this place, coiled to face an intruder. Well, Scout wasn't an intruder. He lived here. Scout and Lucky had spent the day planning to be here. Travel? Yes. But their hearts were already tangled up in the island's history, in its tides, and Scout wouldn't leave. Those were his mysteries, his and Lucky's to solve, and he wouldn't let Alistair push him or Lucky or Kayleigh off their own island.

And he'd never leave them.

He'd had his fill with lovers and sisters and brothers pining to be with one another across sea and sand. He was all for putting an end to that crap right now.

"What are you doing?" Alistair screamed, pulling himself up on the edge of the surf. He was wearing his big important wizard's robes, velvet and trimmed in gold fur and mystical symbols, and he'd landed in about three feet of water. The weight of the robes dragging him down must have been exhausting and ridiculous,

"I'm having this out," Scout said, thinking it was obvious. "My God, Alistair—it's been nearly two months. You're still trying to chase us down? You know the people keeping you busy have lives and jobs and such. They've been trying to keep Kayleigh and me safe, but I've got to tell you, they can't do it forever."

"Safe? What do you *mean* safe?" Alistair, the man who had plucked Scout from thin air and tried to coerce him to give over his sister, sounded surprised. "Kayleigh's duty is to come home—"

"Kayleigh's a fucking *adult*!" Scout snarled. "She's got no duty to you. You've been chasing us because she's been given away in marriage to someone she's never met. Not because you love us. Not because you want to apologize for being an insufferable fascist autocrat—no. Because your possession told you to fuck off, and you want it back."

"You *stole* your sister from the family's demesne," Alistair retorted, sounding legitimately hurt. "Kidnapping—"

"She came willingly!" Scout wondered if there was some sort of magical wake-up potion he could give his father but then decided that a woke Alistair might be a deadly Alistair, because that asshole did nothing in moderation. "She leaped into my arms, and I portaled us out of the damned compound. And she grabbed my hand, and we've traveled together since. Not because she owes me or because I feel duty toward her, but because we *love* each other, and that's what you do."

"That's sentimental crap, Scotland!" Alistair snapped. "That girl is a commodity that was meant to keep our family safe and provided for over the span of a generation. Do you not understand? I made a *deal* with Callan Morgenstern's father, to provide his son with a wife of good stock and wizarding grandchildren. I signed that deal in *blood*."

"Well, pay for it with your own blood," Scout snapped back. "Your daughter is *not property*!" He felt his body fill with anger then, swirling and crackling like an electric wind.

Alistair licked his lips, and Scout regarded him quizzically. Scout's father had always been larger than life, stern, commanding, contemptuous of any weakness, but here, on this beach….

He was overdressed, bedraggled, and well, desperate. His wizard's robes, which looked great when he was conducting a ceremony in his oak-paneled study, or even outside on the grounds during a Samhain bonfire, were swampy and ridiculous now. Scout had gone rolling in the sand, and he was used to being dusty and unkempt, and his hair had never listened, but Alistair's dignity, his presence, had taken an amazing hit in the same landing that had left Scout feeling empowered and substantial.

Alistair was smaller.

"You will stop this madness now," Alistair commanded, his voice shaking. "The entire future of our family is at stake."

"But should it be?" Scout asked, because this had been bugging him. "Shouldn't everybody there be allowed to make their own way? I mean, think about it—if Josue ever decided to do a Macklin and bail, you people would be *fucked*. And he stayed, 'cause he's a standup guy. But how fair is that, to tell him he's got to go work this big financial job and he can't have a life of his own?"

"He's got a wife and children," Alistair said, looking bewildered.

"That *you* picked out for him. As far as I know, they never speak!" Privately, Scout had always wondered if Josue hadn't been like Scout himself—gay as an Easter parade but too honorable, too entrenched in family duty, to say something.

"Josue is important to the family!" Alistair argued. "He helps us sustain our wealth, our home, our—"

"You know," Scout told him, hands on hips, "Kayleigh and I have paid our own rent for the past six weeks, earned our own wages, bought our own food. I mean, we don't have much, but you know what we do have? Free choice. We pay taxes, which sucks, but it also means we help other people who might have a tougher time, and roads, and that's fine too. It's not a bad life, Alistair. You should let your children live it. Because I'm telling you, that thing you're doing with the barracks and the military upbringing and the 'my way or the highway'—that shit *blows.* I mean, if Kayleigh and I had known what we could accomplish with some fake IDs and a car, we would have been out of there way earlier."

And apparently that was Alistair's breaking point. His lofty tone, his attempts at intimidation, all of them fled.

"We didn't even want you! You're not valuable to us. It's Kayleigh we want! And I don't care if you're happy. That wasn't my function as a parent!"

Scout's jaw clenched. Oh. Well. Now he knew. "Which explains why you sucked at it," he retorted. "And you know what? Kayleigh and I *did* need that from you. If you'd shown her even the smallest bit of kindness, she might have married this guy out of pity, although it would have been a mistake. But you threw her through a wall, Alistair. You're not getting within a mile of her."

"And you're going to stop me?" Some of Alistair's power came back with his derision.

"Where are we, Alistair?" Scout asked. "Are we by the compound? Because that's where your portal was going. Is that where we ended up?"

Alistair shivered almost convulsively, some of the coldness of the seawater and briskness of the wind probably seeping in through his senses. "I have no idea where we are," he said, and for a moment, he sounded lost. He took a deep breath, and Scout watched him consciously square his shoulders. "But it won't matter, because we won't be here for long."

Scout knew what magic felt like, had known since he was very small. *His* magic felt like a delicious tickle, like a twitch of the feet when a dancer hears a melody or the seduction of vanilla to a pastry chef. It had always been a summons, a promise, a much-anticipated invitation to the delight of play.

But he'd also known, again since he was very small, that Alistair's magic felt different. Alistair's magic was a sledgehammer, a freight train, a vast and terrifying presence, much like the darkness that lurked over the clearing itself.

And suddenly he knew why he'd brought them here.

Alistair's magic was charging, like the force between a great meteor and the atmosphere of a planetary titan, and Scout's feet were beginning to tap. He tilted his head and smiled a little, thinking about Kayleigh and how happy he'd been when she'd wrapped her arms around his neck and urged them far, far away.

It had been one of the best moments of his life, surpassed only by the night before when Lucky, prickly, surly Lucky, had given himself over to Scout's wide-eyed amazement. Their lovemaking had taken him to a place like magic but better, *beyond* magic, where the sounds Lucky made, his touch, the way he seemed to need Scout and only Scout was the greatest sorcery Scout could have ever conceived.

But those moments came with promises. Promises to keep Kayleigh safe. Promises to not leave Lucky alone, and in that moment, he realized that these two promises might be mutually exclusive. Lucky had begged him to stay on the island that day, but Scout had urged them to leave. Scout still believed it had been the right move, but Lucky had been right too. Scout had made himself vulnerable to Alistair. Lucky's reverent murmuring of Scout's name had obviously summoned the beast, and now Scout was needed for the reckoning.

He was pretty sure he could do this, but he wasn't sure if he could walk away.

Still, he was *absolutely* certain that he had no choice.

He looked at Alistair, who was moving his hands with definitive, sweeping motions, shaping the world, the forces of wonder, the forces of *magic*, to his specifications. Scout's worst trait as a magician had been that he had no patience for that sort of showmanship. The magic was there; it didn't need to be petted—or assaulted—into submission.

He moved his hands absentmindedly, all of the island seeping into his senses. The cold of the spray, the heat of the sun-warmed sand, the roar of the surf and whisper of the wind, the taste of salt and the grit blown between his lips, and the smell of the greenery, of the tide, of the sky—all of it permeated his muscles, his core, his very breath.

He felt the presence at his back, the one so afraid of change it had almost killed Scout in that first evening of how-do-you-do, and the tension from it was growing.

It was furious, but not at Scout.

And still, Alistair's movements were growing grander and grander, the freight train of his magic gaining speed.

Scout's own movements were growing too, but with dance, with the grace imbued by years of practice, of natural inclination, with joy.

Scout was so taken with the delight of wielding naked magic that dance was a simple extension of himself, and he waited patiently, lost in movement, as Alistair gathered enough force to make Scout's hair crackle around his head with suppressed electricity.

Scout didn't need to watch Alistair do this. It was all in the taste of the air.

"Scout, pay attention!" Alistair's voice cracked like a whip, but Scout had years to ignore it. "This is your last chance to simply give in."

Alistair wasn't giving him a chance—not really. Scout had fallen for this "last chance" bid too many times. There was always punishment at the end of Alistair's rainbow. Scout ignored him, continuing to build his own spell in the static crackle of Alistair's sudden stillness.

Alistair bunched his muscles for the throw, and right when he was about to release, far too committed to turn back, there was a commotion across the sand.

"*Scout, no*!"

Scout didn't need to turn toward the voice to know Lucky was there. Kayleigh too, and Marcus and Helen and even Piers and Miller Aldrun.

How did they get here so fast, he wondered, just as Alistair's power came charging for his chest.

Gracefully he stepped aside, using a deft gesture to deflect the ball of malice up over the clearing, to the dark and dreadful presence that had so threatened him not three nights before.

Alistair gasped, as entangled in his own magic as a wizard ever was, and as Scout watched, his father sailed up, over the stretch of beach they stood on, heading straight for the darkness above the clearing, the thing that blocked out the stars.

His own magic was starting to blow a mighty wind through the beach, starting at the clearing and pulsing out. The force of darkness opened its great gaping maw and pulled Alistair inside.

Alistair reached out with a tendril of power, and as Scout made sure the darkness would slam shut, trapping Alistair inside, he felt an unbreakable cord wrap around his waist and haul him into the darkness as well.

He'd known this would happen. Alistair wasn't stupid.

But Scout could keep them both trapped inside the thing until Alistair wasn't a threat anymore. Scout could set Kayleigh free.

"I'm sorry, Lucky," he called, hating that it should come down to this, to this terrible choice, just as the magic rope between him and his father tightened and he hurtled toward the void over the clearing, the one so black there were no stars to be seen.

Holy Wow

LUCKY STARED into the empty place on the ferry deck where Scout had stood not moments before.

Gone?

He was… gone?

I'll be at the clearing.

Desperately, Lucky whirled to lean over the prow, searching the waters beyond. For a moment, he could see nothing but a vague smudge in the distance, where his island sat—no, *their* island, the center of their world, the place that had held both of them as they'd built a world of safety together.

Lucky took a deep breath, and in that stillness, he felt his coin burn in his pocket.

It was trying to tell him something.

"Yeah, well, where the hell were you when Scout's father descended on us like the fury of angels, huh?" Lucky asked sourly, but he was reaching into his pocket at the same time.

It was both hot and cold in his hand, and he rubbed it between his palms, trying to get his brain in a place where he could ask questions.

What…? Heads they're on the island, tails they're somewhere else?

No sooner had he thought it than the coin leaped out of his palm like a jumping bean and landed heads up.

"You are being very helpful," he said on a sigh of relief. "And I forgive you. Now, if only I could figure out how to get there, like, *now*."

The coin jumped again.

Lucky stared at it. "But if I ask you an open-ended question," he explained patiently, realizing that he'd begun to regard the thing as an old friend, "you just hover there in front of me looking creepy."

The coin jumped again—and landed heads up.

"O… kay…." Lucky stared at it one more time. "How do I get to Scout right now?" and with that he flipped it in the air.

And it started whirling, looking surprisingly like the rings Scout had flipped about the day before, spinning them until they formed a great big—

"Oh my God," Lucky breathed. "I am seriously the luckiest sonuvabitch on the planet. You've been just hanging out able to do that?" he asked his old friend, the coin that had saved his life.

In answer, the coin spun faster, whirling, its field expanding until Lucky could see the beach in front of their clearing with Scout and Alistair standing upon it, apparently yelling at each other, if Lucky could read a single nuance of their body language. Above them, looming like a black umbrella, was an incredibly foreboding cloud of… of what? Of anger? Of evil? Of unresolved parental issues, because Lucky had plenty of *them.*

But whatever it was, Lucky realized, it was way above his paygrade.

"A little to the left?" he asked his spinning coin friend, and the image shifted a bit until it would deposit him right *there*. Right in front of Helen's shop. Well, maybe a little lower. There. His apartment, where a newly made bed sat in the corner, with fresh sheets in preparation for the night to come.

Oh God. Lucky had to get him back.

"There," he said gruffly. "I can come up and get everybody from the back. Nobody has to see me arrive."

He took a deep breath, not sure how he was going to get his coin back after this.

"Thanks, little friend," he said, some of his emotion, his desperation, swelling his throat. "I really can't stand to lose him."

And with that, he ignored the wondering gasps of the people on the ferry prow and stepped through the portal.

He landed on the tile of his front room, stumbling to his knees a little, and he turned around in time to see the portal turn back into a coin again, flipping more and more slowly until he caught it in his hand.

"Thanks, little friend," he murmured again, and then he turned toward the stairs that led up to the store and hauled ass.

He hit the back room at Helen's at full speed, arriving with a clatter right when Larissa got there with a big load of dishes for Piers, who was up to his elbows in suds.

"What're you doing here?" he asked in surprise.

"Helping," Larissa said. "Also, earning money. But helping. The hell?"

"Scout's in trouble," he panted. "Larissa, you go next door and get Kayleigh. Piers, you and me need to run to the beach. He's gonna need all of us by the clearing—"

"I'm coming too!" Helen said, bustling in from the front.

"Fair," Lucky told her, not sure he knew how to argue. In a second, he and Piers were hurtling out of the store at full speed while Helen told everybody in the coffee shop that she'd be back in fifteen minutes and they could wait for their coffees or come back for refunds as needed.

Lucky didn't hang around to see how that worked for her.

He was barely cognizant of reaching the stairs down to the beach, but he did curse the sand that slowed him down. Behind him, he could hear Kayleigh calling his name, probably asking for details, but dammit, he didn't have *time*. Scout and Alistair were on the beach, alone, and Scout didn't think he was as strong as Alistair, and Alistair didn't think much of Scout at all!

As he drew near enough to see them, hear their words hurled at each other, he could also see Alistair, standing by the water's edge, gathering nothing short of a storm behind him. A terrible, crackling, ominously dark ball of magic had built up, and Scout? Well, Scout looked like he was doing tai chi.

As Lucky got close enough to call his name, Alistair cut loose with the ball of magic, and Scout, graceful as the dancer he was, simply deflected that surge of power over his shoulder.

Lucky stumbled to a halt to see where it had gone, and in a heartbeat, he saw the presence Scout had talked about—the giant void of stars and the absence of light, the thing that had swallowed Scout and barely spit him up, choking on sea water and so, so cold.

With a cry, Alistair went flying over the sand as though pulled by a rope wrapped around his waist. Whatever he'd thrown into that dark void, it was dragging him with it, and for a moment Lucky had hope. Alistair would get caught in that terrible black oceanic void, and he and Scout would be left there, and they'd be fine, and—

And Scout was getting dragged into that void too.

"*Scout*!" Lucky cried, and behind him, the others screamed his name too. Without thinking, Lucky turned toward the clearing and ran like he had wings on his feet.

THE PLUNGE into the protective darkness was as suffocating and icy as Scout expected, but it was also, somehow, fleetingly familiar.

The last time, he'd been stunned, shocked that something in the world would be so cold and yet so lulling at the same time.

This time, he thought he recognized this feeling. He knew what this was. He'd just… *just* felt it. It had only a moment ago smothered him, but he'd been standing on the sand, and he'd heard….

He'd heard Lucky's voice, calling his name. And Scout had known he still had to risk plunging into this darkness.

And he'd grieved.

Oh. Grief. *That's* what this was!

The cord around his waist tightened, and he looked up to see Alistair using his hands to carve out a portal in the icy depths of the supernatural grief, and Scout stared at him.

He was simply *portaling* out? Using magical means to escape this terrible, terrible loss?

Alistair gestured impatiently for Scout to swim closer so he could use the portal, and for a moment, Scout thought about it. Escape with Alistair, then escape Alistair, then return to fight another day.

He'd reached up a hand, his lungs burning, to swim toward the light when he felt a tug on his ankle. He glanced behind him and sputtered, because he saw not only Lucky, both hands around Scout's ankle, but Kayleigh, her arms around Lucky's waist, and Marcus, his arms wrapped around Kayleigh's thighs. Marcus was partially out of the dark presence of grief, but even through the undulating, warbling surface of the dark pool, Scout could make out Helen with her arms around Marcus, and shadowy figures beyond Helen, their arms wrapped around her to ground her.

All these people, braving the terrible cold, the chilly depths of bottomless sorrow, all to keep Scout right there on the island, where he belonged.

Scout turned away from Alistair and reached down to grasp the rope of magic wrapped around his waist. He thought about all the times he'd needed love, craved attention, adulation, from Alistair, and all the times Alistair had coldly rebuffed him, had ignored him and been cruel to Kayleigh—to all of the children in the compound, actually.

That was how, he realized.

That was how you cut the cords that bound you to someone who didn't deserve your care.

With indifference.

He parted the rope without thinking about it, just like Alistair had for years and years and years.

Alistair stared at him for a moment, and then, Scout assumed, took his own portal out.

Scout's lungs were bursting, his eyes—stinging with the salt water he was submerged in—were starting to only see gray. He made his body limp and allowed himself to be towed backward and backward and backward, until he lay gasping on the beach, Lucky sobbing on top of him, Kayleigh by his side.

"Where'd Alistair go," Kayleigh managed, after choking up seawater for several minutes.

"Who cares," Scout rasped. "We'll never grieve his absence," and with that, he laughed softly and hysterically to himself while the others hauled him to his feet, dragged him to Lucky's apartment, and practically poured him into Lucky's bed.

HELEN, MARCUS, and Kayleigh helped Lucky strip Scout down and put him into warm, clean sweats before tucking him into bed. Then to Lucky's surprise, while those three went to change—and to tend their businesses—Piers and Larissa stayed to help *Lucky* dry off and put on sweats, because he was *exhausted.* Once Scout hit the mattress, Lucky was so tired he might have collapsed in a wet heap on the floor without their help, and he was stammeringly grateful as Piers dropped his clothes on the bathroom floor.

The metallic clink of something heavy in the pocket of his jeans caught his attention, and he managed to mumble enough to Piers that Piers put his lucky coin on the bedstand before Lucky rolled next to Scout's shivering body and fell fast asleep.

When they woke up again, it was night.

Kayleigh was asleep on Lucky's recliner, curled up like a child, and the smell of stew—something hearty with potatoes—filled Lucky's apartment.

Lucky grunted and tried to sit up, and Kayleigh told him to hush. "You and Scout need to eat," she explained with a yawn. "A lot. You both did lots of big magic and used lots of energy, and you get to eat and sleep for a day before you go back to work." She pretended to scowl. "You lucky jerks."

"Next time you can drown in… in whatever," Lucky finished weakly. He'd recognized the emotion immediately when he'd entered the darkness that lurked over the soul trap of the clearing.

Kayleigh's eyes narrowed speculatively as she dished up two big bowls of stew. One she set on the bedstand by Scout, kissing his forehead gently when he didn't even stir, but the other she brought over to Lucky. She handed it to him, wrapped in a towel because the bowl was hot, and he looked at the spot on the bed next to him.

With a smile, she made herself comfortable and patted his thigh through the covers.

"We're sort of like family now, aren't we?" she said.

Lucky shrugged. "Not that I have any, but yeah."

She nodded and regarded him thoughtfully. "What was it?" she asked after a moment. "What was the great darkness? Scout didn't know the first time, but he… he kept mumbling something as we were dragging him back. Do you know what it was?"

Lucky nodded, swallowing hard past the lump in his throat. "It was…." He took a breath. "It's the feeling I had when I realized Auntie Cree wasn't going to breathe again—she died in her bed, and it had been just her and me. It's that thing in the pit of my stomach when I realized I was going to have to leave my home, my Auntie Cree's house, and the city I grew up in with only the cash in my pocket, because otherwise I'd be dead." He thought, but didn't say, it was the feeling he'd had when Auntie Cree had come to fetch him when he'd been mostly a baby and his grandmother had saved him from a life of poverty and want. Instead he focused on the most immediate moment, the moment he'd known exactly what the darkness was, the briny, bone-chilling suffocation that had threatened to take away his boy and his breath at the same time.

"It's the feeling I had when he disappeared off the deck of the ferry," he said gruffly. "And I thought for a moment I'd never see him again. I get why he wasn't afraid of it, you know. He'd never experienced it before."

Kayleigh's hand tightened on his knee. "Grief," she said roughly. "It was grief. All those people, grieving over Tom. It must have collected over the clearing, trapping them all, making their spirits sick with it." She let out a breath. "How do you think we get rid of it?"

Lucky took a bite of his stew and shook his head. "I don't know, but if I know anything, I know your brother has a couple of ideas."

She nodded and kissed his cheek. "Just set that down when you're done," she murmured. "I'll come in tomorrow and clear it up. You made a portal, Lucky. You shouldn't have even been close to being able to do that. You get some sleep. You're gonna need your rest." She stood, yawning. "I'm gonna go to bed in my own room. Larissa and Piers are there again. It's not even weird anymore."

"Like family?" Lucky hazarded.

"They could be," she agreed. "Night, Lucky. Take care of my brother. We'll talk again tomorrow night, okay?"

"Deal," he said, taking another bite of the savory, hearty meat-and-potato concoction in the bowl. "Thanks, Kayleigh."

"Any time."

Lucky finished his dinner in another couple of bites and then did as Kayleigh bid him and set the bowl down on the bedstand. Then he curled against Scout's body again, reassured by his steady breaths that when he woke up in the morning, he wouldn't be alone.

He knew he'd be warm and loved, and his lover would be in his arms.

SCOUT COULD hear Lucky's faint snoring before he realized that Lucky's strong arm was wrapped around Scout's middle, holding him almost breathlessly tight.

Scout struggled against Lucky's heavy arm for a moment before whispering, "Baby, I've got to pee."

That seemed to be the magic password, because Lucky uncurled enough for Scout to pour himself out of the bed and make his way to the bathroom, pausing to splash his face and brush his teeth.

He was getting back into bed before he realized Lucky was awake and looking at him, his eyes wide and fathomless.

"Hey," Scout murmured, sliding close enough to tangle their legs.

"Hey yourself." Lucky reached out to skate his fingertips along Scout's cheekbone, and Scout closed his eyes and smiled.

"Thanks," Scout said, getting close enough to rub his lips along Lucky's chin.

"For what?"

"Bailing me out. Getting reinforcements." He frowned, and it occurred to him for the first time that he and Lucky had been an hour away from home when Alistair had come to get him. "How did you do that, by the way? How did you get to the beach so fast?"

He pulled back to see Lucky's expression and was surprised to see him grin.

"What?" Lucky asked, and his voice was all swagger. "Did you think all I had was the coin in my pocket?"

Scout stared, delighted. "Are you saying that you used the coin somehow?"

Lucky shrugged, terrifically full of himself. "It started burning against my leg, right? So I pulled it out and flipped it, and all I could think of, man, was how to get to you. And… and it's like you were talking about getting Kayleigh. Suddenly, I could see the beach through the portal the coin was making, and…." He shrugged. "I couldn't do it by myself, though. I knew that as soon as I saw you guys squaring off. So I had it drop me in my apartment so I could get to the coffee shop." He chuckled. "I got no idea what the customers thought because I sprinted through there screaming that you needed help, and, you know. Our guys. Fuckin' cavalry. It was great."

Scout swallowed. "Wow. We've got a cavalry. And you can fly. Imagine what we'll do tomorrow."

To his dismay, Lucky's eyes went overbright, and he made an obvious effort to control his breathing. "Not that," he rasped. "Scout, you may not know what that darkness over the clearing is, but I do."

Scout put two fingers over his mouth. "I know now," he said, his own eyes burning. "I felt it. Alistair had hold of me, had power wrapped around me so tight I couldn't breathe, but that was okay, right? That was, well, my entire childhood, I guess. Familiar. But I went flying through the air after him, and I…." His turn to control *his* breathing. "I heard you call my name. And I thought 'I might never see Lucky again,' and…." Dammit. His voice would *not* break. "And it overwhelmed me. The grief, the absolute, soul-crushing knowledge that I might not see you again. And then I was in the darkness, and I went, 'Aha. Now I know.'"

"Is that why you didn't fight back?" Lucky asked, his voice worried. "Until I grabbed you?"

"It just hit me," Scout murmured, wanting to hug him like this forever and ever and ever, "that if I went through the portal Alistair was opening, I might be able to breathe, but I'd feel like that, suffocated and cold, forever. But if I followed you, I could have…." A tear broke free, and his voice with it. "I could have mornings like this."

Lucky gathered him in, comforting him when Scout had wanted to do the comforting, whispering into his ear, his hair, that it was okay, they were having their morning, and it was glorious.

Oh, it was. It was everything Scout had ever dreamed about real life, about a family, a lover, except it was better, now that Scout had imagined life without it.

He needed Lucky so badly.

He pushed up, capturing Lucky's mouth in a hot, briny kiss that Lucky returned, and suddenly holding each other wasn't enough. Their fingers grew frantic as they pushed at clothes and kicked at covers, and for a moment life was sheer frustration as Scout wrestled with his sweat bottoms when *all he wanted was to touch Lucky's skin*!

And then they were naked, mouths voracious as they took turns kissing, licking, stroking every bit of tender skin available.

Scout wanted to devour Lucky, and apparently Lucky wanted the same thing. They ended up on their sides, faces to groins, and for a moment Lucky's cock bobbed maddeningly away from Scout's mouth right as Lucky closed his mouth on Scout's cock. Scout's vision went white with pleasure, Lucky's hand on his hip immobilizing him so he couldn't use Lucky's mouth in a flurry of lust.

He shuddered as he contained the need to come without tasting Lucky first and locked his fist around Lucky's cock, pulling it into his mouth slow and hard, plying his tongue wildly on the underside as Lucky used the same trick on him.

Lucky gasped, dropping Scout's cock from his mouth, and Scout took over eagerly, scooting some more so that he was between Lucky's legs, looking up into his face as his head lolled back on the pillows and his lips parted when he made tiny sounds of pleasure.

Scout took him all the way into the back of his mouth, wanting to hear those some more.

A few more of those and Lucky bent his knees and splayed his thighs, the invitation so open, naked, and erotic, that Scout absolutely had to take him up on it.

"Lube," he gasped between sucks, holding his hand out for the pass. He took the bottle Lucky fumbled into his hand and snicked the lid open, squeezed slick onto his fingers before testing Lucky's entrance, stretching gently. Lucky's sex noises got louder, and Scout wiggled against the bed, his erection hard and hot and swollen. He wanted so badly, but first….

He added another finger, and Lucky managed words.

"Just… just do it, Scout," he panted. "Please. I need you."

And Scout left finesse and slow lovemaking for another moment. He pushed up the bed and positioned himself at Lucky's entrance, pausing for a moment to enjoy the feel of their bare flesh pressed together and to look into Lucky's eyes.

"I need this," he murmured huskily. "Every day, I need you."

"Me too."

Scout took his mouth then before thrusting slowly in.

Lucky groaned, greedy, and spread his legs even farther, pulling them up so Scout had the perfect angle. Scout slid inside all the way, and they both groaned, because it was like coming home.

"Now," Lucky ordered. "Now."

Ah! When would Scout get tired of this? At ninety? A hundred? When did the waves get tired of rocking and receding against the shore? Every thrust was wonder, and every withdrawal was need, and he did it again and again and again and again….

"Touch me," Lucky begged, arching his cock against Scout's abdomen, and Scout reached down between them and stroked in time to his thrusts.

Lucky seemed to hold his breath, and then he gasped, his mouth opened as if to cry out, although he made no sound.

"Ahhhhh…," he breathed, and his back arched, his chest pulled up by the sheer force of his orgasm. His body gripped Scout in a clench of iron, and Scout's eyes rolled back in his head, all of the business reduced to the roar of the ocean as he came.

He collapsed against Lucky, hips still thrusting, and Lucky made a soft, happy moan of completion.

"Someday I want to top," he mumbled.

"Sure," Scout agreed. "But you gotta speak up. I want you all the time. That was… that was…."

"Magic."

"Well, we oughta know," Scout agreed, pushing up on his elbows to kiss Lucky's forehead.

"Trust me," Lucky said. "I know."

TRUE TO Kayleigh's prediction, they both slept some more, but eventually they rolled out of bed and showered and made coffee and then talked some more about the day before.

"So how do we fix it?" Lucky asked broodingly over his coffee. He'd taken it hot that morning, with lots of cream and sugar but definitely hot. "We know that the big presence is grief, and we know that Tom and Henry need to be brought together, but there's a couple more mysteries in that soul trap."

"True," Scout agreed. He'd showered and put some of Lucky's product on his hair so it didn't look so much like a wavy brown dandelion, but even with it slicked back to his shoulders, he looked sleepy and tousled and well sexed.

Lucky had done that. He'd made Scout well sexed. It was something of an accomplishment. Lucky was gonna enjoy it.

"We still don't know what will happen to the island's equilibrium once we do fix it," Lucky said, worried. "I mean, I *like* it as a haven now. I *like* the fact that it's the tourist trap that keeps its secrets. I don't want to wreck that."

"Hey," Scout murmured. "Have a little faith, all right? Remember—nothing good ever happens by letting spirits fester in pain."

Lucky let out a breath. They'd covered this before, and Scout's point was no less valid now. "You're right. Just… I don't know. Where do we start?"

Scout yawned. "Well, we start by having breakfast. And then going back to bed because I'm beat."

"God, right? That whole… magic thing. I'm getting why you had to sleep so much the last time!"

Scout gave him a sweet smile. "It's so awesome that you know that now. We're gonna have to practice! We're gonna have to see how good you can get! Maybe there's other coin-connected magic—"

Lucky held up his hands. "Whoa. First things first. Have you contacted your brother's friends to let them know what happened with Alistair? Maybe they can relax a little, you know?"

Scout nodded. "Yeah. I'm doing that when we're done here."

"But what about—"

Scout gave him his best goofy/dreamy grin. "Is this how we're gonna be?" he asked winsomely. "You always taking care of the details, me with the big ideas?"

Lucky smiled stupidly back. "God, I hope so. Your big ideas are the best, Scout. I can follow you anywhere if you keep having those." He sounded like an idiot, but he didn't care. His past had been, if not vanquished, at least rendered far less deadly. Scout's past had come back with a vengeance, and they'd beaten that too. They may have to keep whacking at the demons that haunted them, but by heaven, they were both ready and waiting to keep each other safe as those demons reared their ugly heads.

Scout's grin grew. "Good. Good. You keep trusting me with the big ideas, and I'll keep having them. Because I've got a big idea that's a doozy. Let me call my brother and his friends, and then we can have lunch or dinner with everyone else and I'll explain it to you. But first?" He yawned.

"A nap?" Lucky hazarded.

"Yeah." Scout's grin grew *evil* now. "And then?"

Lucky stepped into his space, welcoming the brush of his lips. "We make love?" he guessed.

"Yup," Scout agreed. "'Cause that's what makes the rest of the fight worth having."

"Works for me." Lucky kissed him back a little harder. "With maybe one little tweak…."

Their kiss grew, and Scout walked him backward to the bed. "I like the way you think," he murmured.

"This time I top."

"Sure."

Well, maybe next time. But there would definitely be a next time. Their adventures were *far* from over.

Epilogue

"MR. MORGENSTERN, your ten o'clock is here."

Callan Morgenstern looked up from the report he'd been typing for his father, butterflies starting in his stomach. He'd been anticipating this meeting for reasons he couldn't quite put a finger on. There wasn't anything new about the names: Marcus Canby was a well-known businessman on the island, and so was Helen Verde. They ran stores in close proximity to each other, and tourists from Callan's family resorts were frequently their customers. The odds of them coming to him with anything from complaints to new ideas to synergize their businesses weren't long. Callan's *job* was to work with the island residents to keep the Morgenstern name sparkly and pristine in the business world. No price gouging or driving the little guy out of business on *his* watch.

But something… was it the names? Was it the "and associates" attached to them? Or was it the "Regarding Island History" tag that piqued his curiosity. He'd tried his little trick of "listening" to the wind, but as often as he'd ventured to his fourth-floor balcony to feel the breeze from the windward side of the island touch his face, he wasn't getting much. Or rather he was getting *too* much. Too many voices, some of them quite archaic, and too many words. He heard the word "scout" a lot, as well as "lucky," but they didn't mean much to him.

Sometimes too much information was even worse than not enough, and all Callan had was the butterflies in his stomach to tell him this meeting was going to be more than he could even anticipate.

"Send them in, DeeDee," he said, smiling. Deirdre Hollister was old enough to be his mother. Pure island native, with skin tanned to leather and hair that had been bleached by sun and wind, she still enjoyed dressing professionally for his office—within reason. During the hot summer months, she wore shorts and sandals, and when the humidity of the winter months got too much for even the staunchest hair product, she insisted on a double braid down her back. Both looks made her appear younger and far more carefree than she acted as his assistant, but she was such a good assistant, he wouldn't have cared if she'd worn jeans and sneakers.

"Of course," she said, and then she paused. "Callan? Just to warn you. This is an… interesting bunch."

Callan grinned. "Can't wait! Send them in."

She disappeared and, in a moment, returned, leading in a surprising procession of people.

Marcus and Helen were as he'd pictured—older, a little weathered, but sharp and interested in their surroundings. Once they were in his spacious office, they took their seats on the outer edge of the room, and he looked at the other people who had followed them, raising his eyebrows when he recognized Piers Constantine and his cousin Larissa. Piers and Larissa's parents were friends of Callan's father, and he knew they'd come to the island looking for safety after Larissa had been stalked by someone who seemed quite dangerous. They gave him a little nod and a wave, saying they remembered him from various functions they'd attended with their parents, and then they took seats on the outside with Helen and Marcus, along with, if Callan was not mistaken, one of the members of the local constabulary.

The last three people into the room were young, and they stood front and center, a stocky young man with sandy hair over his collar on one side and an absolutely stunning young woman with long dark hair and penetrating brown eyes on the other.

In the middle stood a tall, gangly young man with hair that threatened to break out of its product at any moment and a goofy, disarming smile.

Callan stood and shook their hands, looking around to perhaps get a clue as to why the rest of the room seemed to be deferring to these three.

"Uhm, Callan Morgenstern," he said, genuinely perplexed. "What can I do for you?"

The young man in the middle grinned. "Uhm, I'm Scout Quintero, and this is my boyfriend, Lucky, and my sister, Kayleigh." He cocked his head as if inviting a confidence. "You may be familiar with the name?"

Callan's jaw dropped with dawning horror. "Oh God," he said, looking at Kayleigh with absolute contrition. "I'm so sorry. I mean, *so* sorry. Has my father been at you to commit? That's my fault. I don't want this marriage. I keep telling him I'm *gay*, but I swear to God, he's not listening."

Kayleigh's face, intense, with high cheekbones and those razor-sharp eyes, relaxed, and she gave him a relieved smile. "No worries," she told him, as though this were the understatement of the year. "If you could give *our* father a call, he could maybe stop threatening Scout's *life* to give me back."

Callan sank into his seat. "Oh Lord. Really? Your *life*?" he looked at Scout as though begging him to refute her, but the young man nodded solemnly.

"Yes," he said, sober and grave. "And it's been a colossal pain in the ass, but it's only one of our concerns."

Oh wow. This meeting was both better and worse than he could have anticipated. "One?" he asked, surprised. "But first…." He looked at Kayleigh meaningfully. "I've seen you before. Are you perhaps the reason one of the biggest coalitions of polluters in the Southeast all went home after a meeting and changed their ways?"

Kayleigh's grin turned cagey. "I don't know. Was that a bad thing?"

Callan laughed, bemused. "Not at all. It does make me wish I swung your way, though, but no. I was so relieved. Those toads were a wart on my conscience. Well done."

She inclined her head. "My pleasure. But you do need to listen to Scout. It's quite important."

Scout grinned at her. "Told you," he said, and she wrinkled her nose at him.

"Well," Callan said, blinking. "You have my interest. What can I do for you?"

Scout's own expression went far away. "You can move the remains of one of the people buried in the estate in Charleston to a clearing on the windward side of the island."

Callan gaped. It took him a minute to recover himself. "I can what? For why?"

Scout put his hand in the pocket of his jeans and pulled out two objects that he set very carefully on Callan's desk. Callan picked them up and looked at them, raising his eyes at their apparent age and their simplicity.

Then he saw the inscriptions. *Tom's* and *Henry's*.

"Whose are these?" he asked, as they seemed to hum in his palms, telling him of old loves—and old griefs.

Scout nodded approvingly, as though gauging his reaction and finding it to his liking. With a graceful movement, he pulled up a chair so he could lean over the desk and command Callan's complete attention.

"Let me tell you a story," Scout said slowly, "about two boys in love, and how one went away to make his fortune and the other gazed forever after to the sea."

Callan's heart softened, and he leaned forward too. "It sounds sad," he said quietly.

"It gets sadder," Scout replied. "But we—you—can do something to fix it, if only you believe."

And with that, Scout Quintero, a wizard much like Callan himself, began to spin the most fantastic tale.

By the time he was done spinning, Callan was spun neatly into the thread, ready to change the story forever.

Keep Reading for an Excerpt from

Shortbread and Shadows

Hedge Witches Lonely Hearts Club Book #1

by Amy Lane

Shortbread and Shadows

BARTHOLOMEW AND his two best friends moved about his giant refurbished kitchen seamlessly, even though their minds were racing. The thing they'd just done had seemed so harmless—their coven cast spells all the time, right? Small spells, big spells, and yeah, they'd seen one backfire, but that had been a special case, right? The guy had asked them, and then he'd intervened, and it turned out he'd been asking for a super-vindictive reason, and it hadn't been the coven's fault the guy's theater had been mobbed by crapping turkeys that had ruined his roof and driven him out of town.

But most of the time, the magic was good—helped them find jobs, helped them find their glasses, helped them not make stupid decisions about their love lives, and generally helped them.

Until this time, when it had knocked the entire seven-person coven on their asses, and the carefully constructed spells everybody had been planning to recite had burned to ash as they watched, and each member of the coven had blurted the one desire they'd tried to hide the hardest.

Bartholomew had no idea what his friends had blurted—although they all seemed to know and be embarrassed—but he knew what *he'd* shouted into their magic cone of power and it was….

Oh God, so embarrassing.

Six foot, three inches of auburn-haired, luminous hazel-eyed, broad-chested, joke-cracking, gregarious, kind, clever embarrassment, and Bartholomew was too embarrassed to even finish a conversation.

He swallowed against his want for Lachlan Stephens and tried to concentrate on his business, but Jordan, their default leader and the friend who'd brought them all together, was at his elbow.

"Don't worry too much about it, Barty," he said softly. "We all screwed up the spell."

Bartholomew just shook his head, unable to even voice what he was thinking to Jordan, not now, not in the heat of the moment.

"Barty," Alex murmured, walking into the kitchen with flour from the storage shelves in the garage, "you've got to snap out of it, man. This product list is huge. We're going to be up until God knows when!"

"On it," Bartholomew said smartly, but Jordan stopped him.

"Barty, I know it's not easy for you to talk to people—I mean, besides us. But… but what would it hurt? Just to say hi to him? Ask him to coffee?" Jordan grimaced. "I mean, if nothing else, the magic was trying to tell us something about lying to ourselves."

"You know me," Bartholomew said briskly. "The only lie I tell myself is that Lachlan Stephens could be so much as interested. But Alex is right. I know the others are still cleaning up the mess, but we need to get a move on."

Jordan sighed. "Magic isn't the only thing that solves things for us, Barty. Sometimes it's just stepping up a little."

"I'll step up after we're done baking," Bartholomew said, forcing a smile. "Sometime around 3:00 a.m."

Jordan gave a groan, and the others from the coven got there, filling Alex and Bartholomew's house with willing helpers—none of whom wanted to talk about the spell gone wrong.

Which was fine with Bartholomew. He could spend his time mooning over Lachlan Stephens, knowing he was out of reach.

The truth was, Lachlan Stephens was a giant broad-shouldered unrequited ache in Bartholomew's heart, and in spite of the spectacular moment of failed spellcasting, Bartholomew didn't have the slightest idea of what to do about it.

He would just have to keep this burning need to talk to Lachlan, see his smile, hear his deep voice, stroke those beautiful wooden creations of his, sanded to a sheen…

Brush Lachlan's hand with his own.

Get close enough to smell the combination of cedar and sweat and kindness.

Oh God. All of that. He was going to have to keep *all* of that in his heart, and not bother the rest of the world with it at all.

As Bartholomew broke out his recipes and his supplies and directed everybody to a different section of the kitchen and gave them their own duties, he managed to keep them all in his heart.

But as he was moving from station to station, adding a hint of vanilla here, a dash of cinnamon there, some chocolate, some white chocolate, some brown sugar everywhere, that yearning, that desire for Lachlan to *love him* wept from his fingers in every recipe.

It must have.

That was the only way to explain what happened next.

Heart of Living Wood

"MORTY?" LACHLAN stage-whispered. "Are you sure you put him in the right place?"

Morty Chambers, Lachlan's second cousin, looked up from his computer at the registration desk of the Sacramento Convention Center and rolled his eyes. "You say that like we haven't done this dance for over a year and a half," Morty said dryly. "Yes—see? Here's the floor plan."

"But he's not here yet!" Lachlan was starting to get worried. Everybody else on the vendors' floor was already set up.

"Look, Lock—same as I always do, at your request. His booth is right next to you, where he will continue to ignore you because he isn't that excited about you, no matter what you think."

Lachlan let out a grunt. "No, no, that's not it."

"Face it, Lachlan. He's just not that into you or he would have said more than boo to a mouse over the last two years!"

Lachlan let out a *sigh* of frustration. Morty did have a point, but then, Morty wasn't on the receiving end of a big pair of gray eyes and a mouth full enough to promise all the delights of Sodom.

Or maybe shortbread, since that was the guy's specialty.

"No," Lachlan said, confidence in his voice that he was far from feeling. "I really don't think that's it." Lachlan didn't elicit that response from people, dammit. He… he was cute! He knew it! He was smart, he was funny—he'd worked hard at that! Taken improv classes, taken drama, done college standup. He'd been shy as a kid. Who wasn't? But people *liked* Lachlan. He could usually walk into a place and gauge which girl or guy, as in this case, would be his for the taking.

He'd *gotten* that vibe from Bartholomew Baker; dammit, he *knew* he had. But a year and a half of dedicated pursuit, and nada.

"Then what?" Morty demanded. "This kid—I've seen him. You talk to him, and he gets all cow-eyed and quiet. You think that means he *likes* you?"

"Well, yeah," Lachlan said. "He's shy." It had been a while, but Lachlan recognized the signs. Bartholomew Baker, who didn't even laugh at the pun that was his last name, was perhaps the quietest man Lachlan had ever met. But Lachlan, who actually worked on his funny stories with his sister at home, had seen Bartholomew cast sly glances and small smiles his way when Lachlan had been engaged with his own customers, and whenever they were both quiet, he'd seen, and appreciated, Bartholomew's wide-eyed silences as Lachlan tried to entertain him.

He'd also seen Bartholomew get into the conversation, grow somewhat animated, and then stop himself, as though hearing an unkind voice.

Those were the times he bolted for the bathroom, leaving Lachlan in charge of his bakery booth, as Lachlan was obviously not to be trusted with his words.

Whatever voice Bartholomew heard that made him do that weird bathroom thing, Lachlan would like to give it a good talking-to. For a while he'd been able to do his own thing, date around, sleep with the occasional offer, but rarely twice. Lately, though, there'd been nobody. Lately, he'd been dreaming about that kid—big gray eyes, sand-colored eyebrows arching expressively. At first glance Bartholomew appeared pale with just the slightest tan on his face and wrists, with perfect skin.

A little closer and Lachlan could make out freckles on his nose and a teeny brown mole in the corner of his mouth.

And his smile was crooked—almost physically so, because he bit his lower lip on the right side every time he let his lips quirk up too far.

Lachlan pulled his attention back to Morty with an *actual groan* of frustration. "Morty, I swear by all that's holy and unholy, Bartholomew Baker is crushing on me as bad as I'm crushing on him. He's just too shy to so much as have a conversation."

Morty scraped back his thinning hair from his shiny scalp and blinked at Lachlan through little teeny rodent eyes. Lachlan wasn't sure which branch of the family Morty was really from, but his mother had always told Lachlan to be nice to Cousin Morty because he was blood.

Lachlan had sometimes suspected she meant "He *gave* blood," but that was immaterial.

"Well, that's a laugh riot in a relationship," Morty muttered. "The actual hell, Lock! How are you supposed to have a good time with someone who looks panicked and bolts every time you say 'Good morning'!"

Breathe. In through the nose, out through the mouth. Meditation. And Morty might live to set Lachlan's schedule for yet another week.

"Haven't you ever looked out across a calm lake? It's beautiful at first. Everything's reflected in the surface—the sky, the mountains, the trees." *Like Bartholomew's eyes,* he mooned, but he wasn't going to say that to Morty. "But underneath that pretty surface, there are some *really* awesome things going on. Fish are fighting the good fight, downed airplanes, hidden treasures, and the pureness of water itself. Don't you want to dive right in?"

"To where some mutant fish just swam out of a skeleton to nibble on my toes? No!"

"Oh my God, you're missing the point!" No wonder the guy had two ex-wives.

"Yeah, probably," Morty admitted, rolling his eyes. "But that doesn't change the fact that the floor is open in fifteen minutes, and you need to finish setting up, and Mr. Wonderful still isn't here!"

Lachlan had to check the vendors' floor again to be sure, because Bartholomew was always at least half an hour early. He *had* to be. He had too much to do, including set up luscious draperies in teal green and turquoise blue with his logo in the center that he used as tablecloths, and a wooden rack that was somewhat substandard in workmanship but very clever in design in that it showcased row upon row of tidy loaves of different kinds of sweet bread without ever once allowing the soft little bricks to squash each other. He also had a rack—again, the workmanship was substandard, but the purpose was perfect—for row upon row of large wrapped cookies and blocks of shortbread, all with a sticker showcasing his business logo and a website and phone number for *Shortbread and Shadows* baked goods and catering.

And that alone would be a complex setup, but Bartholomew wasn't a one-man show.

He had a smaller rack that advertised soaps and essential oils that his friends made—*Jordan's Oils* and *Kate's Boudoir*—and another rack that sold bright pot holders and hanging kitchen towels made by another friend—*Pincushion Products*. And of course, he needed to bring in his back stock, because nobody could bake like Bartholomew, and it didn't matter how shy he was, those tiny loaves sold big.

In one of his rare moments of volubility, Bartholomew had professed that he'd thought of selling those giant jelly jars with the dry ingredients of a recipe mixed inside and the list of wet ingredients that needed to be added on the lid.

"Why don't you?" Lachlan had asked, enchanted. When he *did* speak, Bartholomew's gray eyes grew wide and luminous, and his cheeks got this excited little crescent of pink along the cheekbone.

And his voice was so much deeper than anyone expected, every single time he talked.

"Because I don't know if it will turn out the same," he confessed, his face going blotchy and scarlet. "When I bake, it feels like magic, right? And sometimes I throw in ingredients that I never would have thought of and call it my Magic Cookie or Magic Loaf for the day, and make that part of my recipe. I wouldn't really have a chance to… you know, touch my work, if I didn't see it through to the end."

"It's a calling," Lachlan replied, looking at his own shelves full of cunningly made little toys, plant racks, walking sticks, bookends, and wall plaques. "It's like, when you're doing your thing, that craft understands you. Your fingers, your hands, your heart—they all take you to the right place."

"Yeah," Bartholomew had said, and Lachlan realized they were gazing stupidly into each other's eyes. At that exact moment he'd thought, *Yes! Bartholomew is going to kiss me! Or ask me out! Or say "Marry me and let's adopt!"* and Bartholomew had leaned forward on his little stool and his eyes had fluttered, and Lachlan had leaned forward in return and….

Bartholomew zoomed up from his chair and bolted for the booth's exit in the back, calling, "'Scuse me, I've gotta pee!"

Lachlan had almost cried.

And he didn't feel so great right now, looking at the empty booth where Bartholomew was supposed to be.

Fretting, he started to put the finishing touches on his own booth, with his bold, plain logo in black and white. Since it was an alternative-universe fiction con of some sort, he made sure his wooden swords with the intricately carved handles as well as the magic wands with *their* intricately carved handles were all prominently on display. He also made sure his cashbox and Square were exactly where they were supposed to be, and his business cards—designed by his sister, so they looked better than his tablecloth—were easy to spot.

He saw the first few customers wander onto the floor and had a shock. What convention was this again? He pulled out his program and raised his eyebrows.

Para-Fantasma-Con.

Oh. So paranormal, science fiction, urban fantasy, and probably epic fantasy as well. That would explain what the cosplayers in *Lord of the Rings* regalia were doing side by side with the entire complement of *Voltron.*

And trailing behind them was practically all of Hogwarts.

Wow. Just… wow.

That was some eclectic fanbase. He summoned a grin, because he really did love seeing everybody all dressed up and in character, and then his eyes drifted to Bartholomew's booth and the grin fell away a little.

He should have been there by now.

All of a sudden there was a kerfuffle by the entrance, and Lachlan looked up in time to see Bartholomew and four other people Lachlan vaguely recognized, loaded with boxes and hauling ass through the beginning throngs.

"Bartholomew?" Lachlan asked, surprised.

"Sorry," Bartholomew muttered, dodging around half of Hogwarts. "So sorry." He smiled greenly at Lance from *Voltron*, his gaze so faraway he didn't even notice the guy was decked, hot, and appreciative of Bartholomew's gray-eyed beauty. "So sorry." He hustled to the booth and looked around with a little moan.

"Oh, guys. I… I'm seriously… I don't know where to…."

"Here," said the wide-shouldered, no-necked guy that Lachlan recognized as Josh Hernandez. "Kate'll stay here and help you set up, and we'll go get the rest of your stock, deal?"

Bartholomew nodded, eyes losing some of their glaze. "Yeah. Thanks, Josh. Guys. I don't even know…."

Alex Kennedy was a compact person with rusty hair and the scalpel-sharp gaze of an analyst. Any kind of analyst—Lachlan wasn't picky.

And today he looked like he got dressed in a hurricane.

"None of us could have anticipated…." Alex threw his hands in the air.

"God," Kate said. "Seriously. None of us." She was a voluptuous girl with brown-blond hair, green eyes, and the most adorably pointed chin Lachlan had ever seen.

But she wasn't looking adorable now—she was looking scared, as all of Bartholomew's friends shuddered at Alex's words, including Jordan Bryne, who even Lachlan had to admit was the most beautiful man he'd ever seen. Taller than the others, with striking cheekbones and shock-blond hair, he looked like Alexander Skarsgård's younger brother.

"One thing at a time," Jordan said. "We'll go back and get the rest of the stock. Barty, you and Kate start setting up. Kate, maybe make sure you use the smoky quartz, brown jasper, and amethyst weights to hold down the drape. You brought them, right?"

"*So* on it," Kate said, nodding. "And I've got the sage and lavender in the diffuser." She grimaced. "You, uh, wouldn't want to run a protection circle, would you?"

Jordan shook his head. "All I brought were the gold and orange for success. I didn't bring black, brown, or white. Sorry."

Kate shrugged. "No, no. We were all…." They shared a look and let out a breath.

"Okay. Let's get moving."

Jordan, Josh, and Alex took off, and Bartholomew and Kate started the sort of ritual dance they'd practiced often to set up. Bartholomew's friends didn't always stay for the whole event, but Lachlan had to admit they were great at setup and takedown.

Except in this case they both kept stopping and looking around, seeming to breathe a sigh of relief whenever things appeared perfectly normal.

"Can I help?" Lachlan asked after a moment when their shaky hands were making him twitchy.

"Sure," Kate said at the same time Bartholomew said, "That's kind, but we've got it."

Kate leveled a killing look at Bartholomew. "Isn't that how we all ended up in this mess in the first place?" she demanded.

Bartholomew looked at her unhappily and swallowed, then looked at Lachlan and smiled shyly. "I'm sorry," he said. "Thank you, Lachlan. That would be nice."

Lachlan had to refrain from holding his hand up to his heart, because it fluttered badly. "What do you need me to do?"

"If you could shake the tablecloth out and set up the racks," Kate said quickly. "I'll set the stones up in formation." She sighed. "I wish we had some damned thread."

"I can get you some yarn," Lachlan offered. "Here, let me set up the racks and I'll go ask Ellen. She does spinning and weaving demonstrations. I'm sure I can get the colors you need."

He took the tablecloth from the plastic bin Bartholomew kept for setup without needing to be shown. He'd watched Bartholomew countless times, Bartholomew so completely immersed in his task, sticking his tongue out of the corner of his mouth while muttering to himself, that Lachlan could have set the booth up in his sleep.

Which reminded him.... "You guys know, I've seen your booth setup a thousand times. I've never seen the stones *or* the string. What are you using them for?" Particularly when everybody seemed so stressed and out of time.

"Nothing," Bartholomew said at the same time Kate said, "Protection."

Lachlan's hands stilled as he settled the tablecloth, the pentagram with the cookie in the center logo facing out toward the gathering crowd.

"Protection?" he asked. "From what?"

Bartholomew licked his lips and gave Kate a pleading look. "Kate, do we really have to—"

"Barty, there was a flock of starlings. And I know the damned things are always spinning around in the fall, but they were flying *upside down*."

Bartholomew's face—already sort of pale and hard to tan—went downright mashed-potato pasty. "But here… there's no magic here," he practically wailed. And then his eyes, gray and shiny and luminous, met Lachlan's. "Almost no magic here," he whispered apologetically.

Lachlan grinned, both trying to get him to snap out of whatever funk he seemed to be spiraling into and charmed.

Almost no magic. Like Lachlan *was* magic. Lachlan's instincts had been right on point. Bartholomew *was* that into him!

"We don't know that for certain," Kate snapped. "And after those starlings…."

They both shuddered, and even Lachlan, who knew nothing about magic or omens, could tell that a giant flock of birds flying upside down was bad on both points.

"What makes you think it's you guys?" he asked.

"We cast a spell," Bartholomew said, surprising him. In spite of the rather whimsical name of the booth, *Shortbread and Shadows*, Lachlan never would have expected someone as… well, grounded, to be mixed up in something like witchcraft. Dress up for the conventions, yes. Bartholomew had a rather handsome set of bardic leathers, done in green, that he wore sometimes when he knew for certain the theme was Renaissance or sword and sorcery. But actually casting a spell?

Lachlan shifted uneasily. "Who's you?"

"Never mind," Bartholomew whispered. "Here, give me the racks—"

"No, no. I'll set up the racks. You stock them."

Lachlan got to work on the wooden racks, attempting to find some purchase. "I just never knew real witches before," he said, smiling like it wasn't a bad thing. "My grandmother used to leave out beer for brownies, though."

Bartholomew and Kate met eyes. "I'll tell Jordan," she said, like they'd actually said something. "He'll probably try it."

"Try what?" Lachlan worked very hard not to break the wooden rack he was fiddling with. "And please don't take this the wrong way, but this thing is a cheap piece of shit, and I'd love to make you another one that might actually set up without threatening to snap into kindling."

"I…." Bartholomew cleared his throat. "Your work's too good," he said. "I'm afraid to even price them out with someone who knows what he's doing."

"Our friend Dante made these," Kate said. "During his woodworking phase. He, uh, didn't stick with it long."

"For you, I'd do it at cost," Lachlan said, only because "free" would sound too much like a come-on, and for heaven's sake, he had Bartholomew talking! The surest way to shut him up would be to make him feel like there was something more at stake than shelves.

Bartholomew looked at the shelves and then looked at Lachlan. "Oh, I couldn't—"

"Sure you could," Lachlan said, deciding that wasn't a no. "I'll bring you the first one next week. There's nothing wrong with the design here. It's just the craftsmanship is a little—" He searched for a word. "—inexperienced." To his amusement, Bartholomew's cheeks went bright red.

"Not everyone is… uh… experienced," he said weakly, and a thick silence fell, interrupted only by the clicking sounds of the shelving.

"There," Lachlan said, organizing the shelves where they usually went, in an even, three-point presentation across the table, with a gap on either side for taking money. "Kate, is this fine for where you want your stones?"

"Yes," she said. "Thank you." She shot a glare at Bartholomew. "Barty, do you want to help him round up the yarn? I'll set up the stock."

Bartholomew sent Lachlan a hunted look. "Sure," he said. Then he seemed to pull fortitude from his feet. "Lachlan, I can go talk to Ellen. You have your own booth to look to."

Lachlan looked behind him and almost groaned. A troop of four high-school-aged attendees were gathered around the wands, each one of them wearing a scarf of one of the four schools of Hogwarts that had obviously been knitted by hand—possibly by one of the wearers.

"I'll be right back," he said. "Bartholomew, you keep stocking. I want to talk to you."

He wasn't sure if he imagined Bartholomew's "meep" or if he'd actually made the sound, but either way, he appreciated the sentiment. Lachlan finally had an excuse to butt into Bartholomew Baker's life, and he wasn't going to waste a second of it.

Award winning author AMY LANE lives in a crumbling crapmansion with a couple of teenagers, a passel of furbabies, and a bemused spouse. She has too damned much yarn, a penchant for action-adventure movies, and a need to know that somewhere in all the pain is a story of Wuv, Twu Wuv, which she continues to believe in to this day! She writes contemporary romance, paranormal romance, urban fantasy, and romantic suspense, teaches the occasional writing class, and likes to pretend her very simple life is as exciting as the lives of the people who live in her head. She'll also tell you that sacrifices, large and small, are worth the urge to write.

Website: www.greenshill.com

Blog: www.writerslane.blogspot.com

Email: amylane@greenshill.com

Facebook: www.facebook.com/amy.lane.167

Twitter: @amymaclane

Follow me on BookBub

Hedge Witches Lonely Hearts Club

Book One

SHORTBREAD AND SHADOWS

Amy Lane

The recipe was supposed to be for cookies—he got disaster instead.

Hedge Witches Lonely Hearts Club: Book One

When a coven of hedge witches casts a spell for their hearts' desires, the world turns upside down.

Bartholomew Baker is afraid to hope for his heart's true desire—the gregarious woodworker who sells his wares next to Bartholomew at the local craft fairs—so he writes the spell for his baking business to thrive and allow him to quit his office job. He'd rather pour his energy into emotionally gratifying pastry! But the magic won't allow him to lie, even to himself, and the spellcasting has unexpected consequences.

For two years Lachlan has been flirting with Bartholomew, but the shy baker with the beautiful gray eyes runs away whenever their conversation turns personal. He's about to give up hope… and then Bartholomew rushes into a convention in the midst of a spellcasting disaster of epic proportions.

Suddenly everybody wants a taste of Bartholomew's baked goods—and Bartholomew himself. Lachlan gladly jumps on for the ride, enduring rioting crowds and supernatural birds for a chance with Bartholomew. Can Bartholomew overcome the shyness that has kept him from giving his heart to Lachlan?

Hedge Witches Lonely Hearts Club

Book Two

PORTALS AND PUPPY DOGS

Amy Lane

Witchcraft they know—their own hearts, not so much.

Hedge Witches Lonely Hearts Club: Book Two

Sometimes love is flashier than magic.

On the surface, Alex Kennedy is unremarkable: average looks, boring accounting job, predictable crush on his handsome playboy boss, Simon Reddick.

But he's also a witch.

Business powerhouse Simon goes for flash and glamour… most of the time. But something about Alex makes Simon wonder what's underneath that sweet, gentle exterior.

Alex could probably dance around their attraction forever… if not for the spell gone wrong tearing apart his haunted cul-de-sac. When a portal through time and space swallows the dog he's petsitting, only for the pampered pooch to appear in the next instant on Simon's doorstep, Alex and Simon must confront not only the rogue magic trying to take over Alex's coven, but the long-buried passion they've been harboring for each other.

Hedge Witches Lonely Hearts Club

Book Three

PENTACLES AND PELTING PLANTS

Amy Lane

He'll do anything to fix his coven—even confront his own demons.

Hedge Witches Lonely Hearts Club: Book Three

A month ago, Jordan Bryne and his coven of hedge witches cast a spell that went hideously wrong and captured two of their number in a pocket of space and time. The magic is beyond their capabilities to unravel so, in desperation, they send up a beacon for supernatural aid.

They don't mean to yank someone to their doorstep from hundreds of miles away.

Once Macklin Quintero gets past his irritation, he accepts the challenge. The tiny coven in the Sierra foothills is a group of the sweetest people he's ever met, and he's worried—the forces they've awakened won't go back in their bottle without a fight.

But he also wants to get closer to Jordan. Mack's been playing the field for years, but he's never before encountered somebody so intense and dedicated.

Jordan might quietly yearn for love, but right now he's got other priorities. The magic in the cul-de-sac doesn't care about Jordan's priorities, though. Apparently the only way for the hedge witches to fix what they broke is to confront their hearts' desires head-on.

Hedge Witches Lonely Hearts Club

Book Four

HEARTBEATS IN A HAUNTED HOUSE

Amy Lane

Never lie to magic about affairs of the heart.

Hedge Witches Lonely Hearts Club: Book Four

Dante Vianelli and Cully Cromwell have been in love since college, when Dante saved Cully from the world's worst roommate and introduced him to his friends. Seven years later, they're still roommates and they're still in love… but they've never become lovers.

Now a catastrophic spell gone wrong has cut them off from their coven. Wandering their suburban prison alone, separated by the walls of their own minds and gaps in the space-time continuum, Cully and Dante are as stuck as they have been for the past seven years.

And they'll remain lost in their memories—unless they confront the truths that kept them from taking the step from friends to lovers and trust their friends and coven to get them out. But it's easier said than done. Those walls didn't build themselves. Dante's great at denial, and Cully's short on trust. Can they do the work it will take to get into each other's arms and back to the sunlight where they belong?

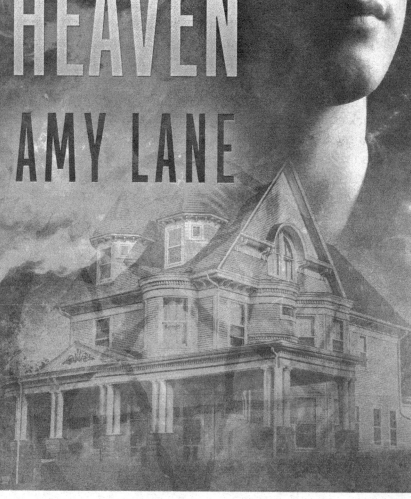

ALL THE RULES OF HEAVEN

AMY LANE

All That Heaven Will Allow: Book One

When Tucker Henderson inherits Daisy Place, he's pretty sure it's not a windfall—everything in his life has come with strings attached. He's prepared to do his bit to satisfy the supernatural forces in the old house, but he refuses to be all sweetness and light about it.

Angel was sort of hoping for sweetness and light.

Trapped at Daisy Place for over fifty years, Angel hasn't always been kind to the humans who have helped him in his duty of guiding spirits to the beyond. When Tucker shows up, Angel vows to be more accommodating, but Tucker's layers of cynicism and apparent selfishness don't make it easy.

Can Tucker work with a gender-bending, shape-shifting irritant, and can Angel retain his divine intentions when his heart proves all too human?